The Dolan Girls

S.R. MALLERY

The Dolan Girls
By S. R. Mallery
Copyright © 2015 by S. R. Mallery
All rights reserved.

No part of this book may be used or reproduced by any means, graphic, electronic, or mechanical, including photocopying, recording, taping or by any information storage retrieval system without the written permission of the author, except in the case of brief quotations embodied in critical articles and reviews.

This is a work of fiction. Names, characters, places, and incidents either are the product of the author's imagination or are used fictitiously, and any resemblance to actual persons, living or dead, business establishments, events or locales is entirely coincidental.

Contact: www.srmallery.com

ISBN: 1519695241
ISBN-13: 13:978-1519695246

DEDICATION

To my family and all those who made up the Wild West

TABLE OF CONTENTS

DEDICATION iii
OTHER BOOKS BY S.R. MALLERY vi
ACKNOWLEDGMENTS i
CHAPTER ONE - 1861: Young Kisses 1
CHAPTER TWO - The start of it all – 1856 Nebraska 18
CHAPTER THREE - 1861 – 1871: harsh realities 33
CHAPTER FOUR - Returning Home: 1883 46
CHAPTER FIVE - Taming All Devils: 1883 59
CHAPTER SIX - 1883: Different Encounters 71
CHAPTER SEVEN - Buffalo Bill and Beyond 86
CHAPTER EIGHT - Shifting Winds 102
CHAPTER NINE - All Manner of Changes 107
CHAPTER TEN - "We Never Sleep" 119
CHAPTER ELEVEN - Full Circles 133
CHAPTER TWELVE - Temptations 152
CHAPTER THIRTEEN - When Chickens Come Home To Roost 168
CHAPTER FOURTEEN - Tightening Up the Reins 183
THANK YOU 201
ABOUT THE AUTHOR 202

OTHER BOOKS BY S.R. MALLERY

Unexpected Gifts: A TRUE AMERICAN FAMILY SAGA: Can we learn from our ancestors? Do our relatives' behaviors help shape our own? In *Unexpected Gifts* that is precisely what happens to Sonia, a confused college student, heading for addictions and forever choosing the wrong man. Searching for answers, she begins to read her family's diaries and journals from America's past: the Vietnam War, Woodstock, and Timothy Leary era; Tupperware parties, McCarthyism, and Black Power; the Great Depression, dance marathons, and Eleanor Roosevelt; the immigrant experience and the Suffragists. Back and forth the book journeys, linking yesteryear with modern life until finally, by understanding her ancestors' hardships and faults, she gains enough clarity to make some right choices.

Sewing Can Be Dangerous And Other Small Threads: WHEN HISTORY, MYSTERY, ACTION, and ROMANCE ARE ALL ROLLED INTO ONE! These eleven short stories range from drug traffickers using hand-woven wallets, to a U.S. slave sewing freedom codes into her quilts; from a cruise ship murder mystery with a quilt instructor and a NYPD police detective, to a couple hiding Christian passports into a comforter in Nazi Germany; from an old Salem Witchcraft wedding quilt curse to a young seamstress in the infamous Triangle Shirtwaist Factory fire; from a 1980's Romeo and Juliet romance between a Wall Street financial 'star' and an eclectic fiber artist, to a Haight-Ashbury love affair between a professor and a macramé artist gone horribly wrong, just to name a few.

Tales To Count On: Curl up and enter the eclectic world of S. R. Mallery, where sad meets bizarre and deception meets humor; where history meets revenge and magic meets gothic. Whether it's 500 words or 5,000, these TALES TO COUNT ON, which include a battered women's shelter, childhood memories, Venetian love, magic photographs, PTDS fallout, sisters' tricks, WWII spies, the French Revolution, evil vaudevillians, and celebrity woes, will remind you that in the end, nothing is ever what it seems.

ACKNOWLEDGMENTS

Books are usually collaborative efforts and *The Dolan Girls* is certainly no exception. To my astute beta readers: Donalie Beltran, Sharon Cox, Judith Kilcullen, Judith Lucci, Elaine Marshall, Amy Metz, Graydon Miller, and Steven Ramirez, all of your input/insights were truly invaluable. Thanks as well to Vivek Rajan Vivek, for steering me into this genre in the first place, and last, but by no means least, to Patricia Zick, for all her fine editing, formatting, and endless support.

CHAPTER ONE
1861: Young Kisses

Cora Dolan refused to talk about what had happened six years earlier, ten miles above town. Sealed up as tight as a snail in the cold she was, even to her sister Minnie, who was there with her the whole time; even with Thomas, who held her heart.

Yet one star-flushed night, as the wind's edges were chilling and the shortening days were trumpeting the around-the-corner autumn, the two sweethearts pressed against a neighbor's barn door, and Cora opened her mouth to share her past, then paused.

"What is it, Cora?" Thomas whispered, his steady arm around her sixteen-year-old waist, his mouth brushed against her ear. "Tell me what gets you sad sometimes. Let me help you."

She forced a smile. "I'm all right, truly I am," she said, placing her right hand gently over her heart for a couple of seconds. With her arms then draped over his broad shoulders, she uplifted her face for a kiss.

"Oh, Cora," he said softly, his lips heading toward hers, "I love it when you put your hand over your heart. It's so sweet. So trusting."

Suddenly, a horse's sudden *clop-clop* broke their embrace, sending them scurrying off to Cora's residence. Several blocks away, still running, laughing, holding hands, they slowed their pace down to a stroll as they passed the livery stable, the local blacksmith, the church shut tight for the night, the brand new post office, and the local saloon with its strong bouquet of whiskey and beer wafting into the air. Finally they stopped in front of the red-curtained Madam Ana's, South Benton's second watering hole, the place for pleasuring most any man.

And home to the Dolan girls.

"I guess it's good-night, then," her young suitor murmured, angling for another kiss.

A male snicker rang out. "Well, well, well. What do we have here?"

Out from behind the southeast porch post stepped a slightly older young man, his black hat cocked forty-five degrees, his leather jacket opened, his six-shooter holstered just below his waist. He moved in close.

"Cora, sweet thing, why in the world do you waste your time with such a greenhorn, huh?" he sneered. "Be like the gals you live with and try a real man for once!"

Thomas stepped in front of Cora. "Wes, that's no way to treat a lady. Let her *be!*"

The stepbrothers faced each other. "Don't you threaten me!" Wes spat back, splaying his tall, wiry legs and fingering his new grown mustache, as if to further prove his manhood.

"That's rich—me threatening *you*. Now, leave us alone!"

As Wes half walked, half hitched away, chortling, Cora clutched her protector. "He's always so scary," she whispered.

"Ever since we were little, he's been a sick sonafa bitch. Sorry, Cora. Why, he didn't even shed a tear when his pa and my ma both died, never said a thanks to old man Preston when he took us on as ranch hands. Enough said." One cheek muscle twitched.

Thomas pulled her around in front of him and gripped her shoulders. "Rest assured, I'll *never* let him harm you, Cora. *Never.* Besides, ever since I whipped him good during last year's hog wrasslin' contest, when he was thrashin' a hog with no need to, he knows better than to take *me* on!" He laughed. "You should have seen his face when we were finished!"

"Why does he sometimes have that strange walk?" She bit her lip on its lower right side.

"Years ago, Wes was throw'd off of a horse, bit the dust, so to speak. The doctor said he'd probably always have leg trouble, especially if he was tired or if it was raining or cold."

"That must have been hard for him."

"I suppose it was. It also didn't help when my stepfather told him straight out, 'Serves you right!' Anyway, after that, sure enough, if he's tired or the weather's wet or cold, he walks like that."

"I see." They continued drifting back toward her home, arm-in-arm in silence, until they reached her front porch. "Thomas?" She half-whispered.

"Yes?"

"About what Wes said. Do you mind that Minnie and I live with those women inside?"

"The doves? Of course, not! They're just people like anyone else, no better, no worse. " He drew her close. "But you, I think you're beautiful, Cora. In fact, you're perfect."

Concentrating on his piercing blue eyes, she leaned in for a kiss. All of a sudden, they heard Madam Ana inside, laughing with one of her customers while an out-of-tune piano clunked loudly in the parlor. Although the kiss ended up much shorter than he would have liked, he said nothing when Cora turned and swung the front door open to head toward the back of the house where she shared a bedroom with her sister Minnie.

Just inside, Cora walked into the parlor, with its red velvet wallpaper and red carpeting, stretching out onto the large, winding staircase that led upstairs. She continued on, past the central eye-catchers of the room: a large maroon settee, piled high with plump, satin pillows, and a glittering chandelier hovering overhead that word had it, cost a small fortune. Nothing was too good for the ambitious Madam Ana Prozinski from Russia, she was always being told.

"Cora!" called out Becky, a voluptuous blonde squeezed into a purple, gusset-enhanced corset, high-heeled boots, and her famous black velvet choker. "While we've been workin' here a month of Sundays, *you* get to make a night of it! For two cents, I'd love to know what you've been doin'!"

"Yup, I reckon she just got a lick and a promise!" added a red-petticoated Julie to a chorus of shrieks and laughter.

Amy, in a rose colored shimmy and fishnet stockings, chimed in. "Look at her red face! Did you ever see anything so perty? It's just like…"

"She's always pretty!" Julie interrupted. "Talks fine, too. Must be all those speakin' lessons from Pete she's always taking."

"Yeah," Becky said, chuckling. "She talks like one of them refined ladies, but she's also so pretty she could be one of us. I'll bet she could bring in those cowboys by the wagonloads! She's…"

Madam Ana strode into the room "Girls, *enough!*" You know I take no stock in dis kinda talk. Leave Cora be. Now go back to verk!" She looked around at her employees and clapped twice. *"Now!"* she barked.

The doves instantly went about their business, chatting with a few stray cowboys and Cora's tutor, a well-dressed, poetry-reciting gentleman named Pete.

Madam Ana turned to her young charge. "Cora, *kotik,* where you been so late? With Thomas?"

Cora nodded.

With a knowing grin, Madam Ana cradled the girl's elbow and gently pushed her through the parlor and down the hall toward the Dolan girls' bedroom. As Cora got undressed and climbed into bed next to her sister, she smiled in the dark, knowing someday she was going to marry her Thomas, and thinking that perhaps she was the luckiest girl in the world, after all.

* *

A week later, on a cold blustery day, she was called into Madam Ana's office.

"Cora, I need you to run errand for me. You go to Mr. Mahoney's, yes?"

"Of course, I'd be happy to," she replied, excited at the prospect of being able to indulge in her favorite past time: reading dime novels.

Walking over to the store, she hummed, still shrouded in the love of her kind, handsome Thomas and buoyed by the freedom from house chores that day.

"Miss Cora! And how are we this fine, cold day, hmm?" Mr. Mahoney, the shop owner, was always courteous to her even if several of the 'good' women in town weren't.

"I'm fine, thank you, Mr. Mahoney. Mrs. Ana sent me here to buy…"

"Yes, I know what she needs this time of the week, the same as always. I'll go get the items and be back in a minute. Meantime, help yourself to some butterscotch candy, child. The missus made it up special."

"Thanks, Mr. Mahoney. That's very kind of you," Cora replied absentmindedly, as she headed for the dime novel rack.

She picked one out entitled, *Buffalo Bill in the Land of the Spirits,* and opening it up, eagerly started reading. Three minutes in, an eerie, gravitational pull lifted her head up from the book to glance out the window toward the street. Across the lane, stood Wes, leaning against the saloon's hitching post, watching her carefully. No smirking, no hat tipping, no movement, except to suddenly kick viciously at a stray dog trotting by and laugh at its pitiful whimpers. Then back to watching her.

She looked down at the book again, her hands shaking, her heart rattling, but by the time she ventured another peek, he was nowhere in sight.

"Here we are, young lady, everything that Mrs. Ana asked for." Mr. Mahoney handed a large parcel over to the teen. "Child, are you all right?"

"Yes, yes, I'm fine!" she answered quickly, and with a slight nod, hurried out the door, glancing both ways before darting off to Madam Ana's.

Her first instinct was to tell Thomas, then thought better of it. After all, she reasoned, his brotherly relationship with Wes was bad enough, why make it any worse? So she kept quiet, and after a day or so, her pulse returned to normal.

* *

All too soon, December was closing in on the town. Flannel petticoats replaced cotton ones, fortified boots and wool muffs became commonplace, and Madam Ana's was growing more and more festive by the hour. In order to satisfy her sensibilities, and of course, those of her customers, there was much to do—extra candles to be lit, punch bowls filled, and a frequent march down to Mr. Mahoney's shop was without question.

"Minnie, Cora, these new tablecloths need extra lace. Please go to Mr. Mahoney's shop and bring me back supplies for next veek. But don't take too long; I vill need you both here to help me with cooking."

"I never take long. Why in the world would you say that, Mrs. Ana?" Minnie retorted.

Ana stared at Cora. "No Buffalo Bill dime novels today, right, Cora?"

Cora gulped. "How did you know?"

Ana chuckled. "I know *everytink* in this town!" She placed an arm around the girl's shoulders. "Now scoot, both of you!"

They could still hear her laughter as they stepped down onto the street and instinctively lifted up their skirts and petticoats to avoid the all-pervasive mud. Mud that softened the ruts left by an occasional team of wagon wheels flicked against buildings as horses paced by, and tracked into the foyer of the town's only saloon on a nightly basis.

Behind the main street, the pungent smell of fresh cut wood was powerful. Buildings in various stages of construction were being put up: houses, barns, stores, another livery stable, another saloon of a lower order, a new school a quarter mile off, a second church for those Baptists escaping the country's East Coast's political storm. Hammering filled the air like a rhythmic choir—heavy handed, tight-fisted, syncopated, and steady, as Minnie and Cora strolled arm and arm down the street. Humming, giggling, and remembering old times in Ireland, they marveled at the fact that they had somehow survived it all.

At the shop, Mr. Mahoney was friendly as ever, handing out a generous portion of candy. Cora hurried past the dime novels.

"That is dreadfully big of you, Cora!" Minnie said, giggling.

They decided to hasten their return to Ana's by taking a couple of abandoned alleyways back, singing Irish songs and having a grand old time.

"Remember the time we all..." Minnie started as Wes stepped out from behind a crate and blocked their path.

"Well, well, well. If it ain't the Dolan gals!" He sniffed, then released a wad of spit on the ground in front of them.

"Wes! What is it you want?" Cora's voice thinned to a squeak.

"What is it I want? Why, ain't you always the high-toned one! Guess those lessons have paid off!" He sneered at her and leaned in closer. "You, Cora, I want *you*, but I'll take your older sister as well, even if she talks as rough as the rest of us."

Cora could feel Minnie bristling beside her.

"If you know what's good for you, Wes Garrett, you'll leave us alone!" Minnie barked as he snickered gleefully.

Grabbing Cora's trembling hand, the older Dolan marched them both forward, elbowing his shoulder as she passed him, then sparking a run all the way back to Ana's, his cackles echoing behind them.

"He's the devil incarnate!" Cora said once they reached their front porch.

"Oh, pfft! I think he's all bluff. All he needs is a good goin'-over. Don't be scared, Cora. I honestly don't think he will ever...Oh, honey, please don't worry," Minnie finished, folding her tearful sister into her arms.

* *

After that, Cora's days were filled with sideway glances—purposeful glances up and down Main Street, studied glances in Mr. Mahoney's shop, furtive glances when she was out with Thomas.

"Cora, you seem so nervous. What's wrong?" he would ask.

Her answer was always the same: "I'm all right, truly I am."

Finally, one evening when they were cozying up next to one another, holed up in the stables with the gently nuzzling horses and the scent of new, mounded hay, Thomas questioned her once again.

"I've noticed you still seem so nervous. Is it about Wes and that time? When push comes to shove, his bark is far worse than his bite, you know."

Nodding, she held her tongue. Perhaps Minnie and Thomas were right. Perhaps Wes was bluffing after all.

Two days later, the young couple was sitting on a wooden bench outside of the church talking in low tones and looking up at the light gray sky readying itself for a soft snow. Suddenly, a couple of cavalry soldiers four-beat gaited into town, straight-faced, shoulders back, and stopping in front of the new post office. Mr. Johnson, the postmaster, came out looking officious, his chest puffed out a good inch.

"Where do you want to set up, fellers?" he asked.

One of the soldiers got down from his horse. "How's about right in front of your place? You prepared what we requested?"

"Yes, indeedy. Here they are." The postmaster unrolled two recruitment posters for the Union Army of the Potomac.

A small crowd gathered, muttering a collage of comments: "This ain't our war, let the rest of the country fight it, not us!" and "We're actually going to war? Oh dear, oh dear," and "Lordy, Lordy, save us from President Lincoln and Jefferson Davis! We just want some peace!"

Cora and Thomas wandered over, Cora, still lost in her thoughts. A tall cowboy, with what appeared to be a brand new Stetson and red scarf, tossed out the first question.

"How long you men here in town?" His tone wasn't particularly friendly or curious, simply flat, like one of those new telegraph machines ticking out a telegram.

One of the soldiers answered, "As long as it takes."

Thomas pulled Cora aside. "I have to tell you something," he said.

She turned to him, smiling, expectant, one hand over her heart.

"It seems I have to go away to pick up some supplies for my boss. He has monstrous need of it, and it's only sold in Omaha."

"Oh?"

"Yes, I'll be gone a couple, maybe three days, that's all."

"When is this happening?" She was already missing him as she watched him cradle her hand in his.

"In a week. And when I return, there's something I want to tell you," he muttered.

What did he mean by that? Her heartbeat picked up speed. Marriage? A family? She wished she had the courage to ask him, but knew she didn't.

Instead, that evening, standing on Ana's porch with him, she made sure her goodnight kiss was particularly long, bringing on the closest to passion they had ever reached. Melting into his body, she tasted his lips, felt his strokes. But when new, inexplicable sensations started budding in her, she pulled back, a little scared.

Opening the front door, she could hear his deep sigh behind her, and she almost turned around to face him again, but the doves were already calling out their hellos, so she continued her retreat.

Yet inside, she loved how she could still feel his lips on hers, still remember his touch on her back, her arms, and her waist. Trying to recall the exact words he had whispered to her before they kissed was more difficult, what with the piano banging, and Pete, drunk as a fiddler, was spouting Shakespeare. So she dashed upstairs, and finding an empty room toward the front of the house, pulled the lace curtain back to watch him ride away over the hill and into the darkness.

Downstairs in the parlor, things were unusually jovial. As she walked down the steps, Cora could hear Madam Ana announce to Minnie and the leftover crowd that Shakespeare was being performed in a neighboring town the following week and wouldn't they all like to go?

She wasn't really surprised by Pete's enthusiasm or the cheers erupting from the doves. After all, he lived and breathed Shakespeare, and the ladies were always up for any side trips. But when Minnie performed a little Irish jig, she grinned. Maybe a little excursion would be good for them all.

* *

It couldn't have been a better day for Shakespeare. December crisp, and the first streak of light bringing with it a sunny lull to the otherwise dreary sleet and snow. Thomas had left for Omaha, and Ana's household was all a bustle.

"Come on, Cora, get a move-on!" Minnie called out from the parlor, high-keyed.

Cora heard her but didn't respond until Minnie poked her head into their room.

"What's wrong?"

"I don't think I'll be coming." A pale, flushed Cora wheezed, sitting on their four-poster bed, still in her chemise.

"What do you mean? I never heard of such a thing!" Minnie planted her hands on both hips.

"I feel a bit under the weather, is all. You should go on without me."

"I know you, Cora Dolan. You're just feelin' blue about your Thomas gone for a few days. Well, this trip will do you good. Take your mind off of him."

"It's *not* because of him, Minnie, I swear! I just don't feel well, that's all."

Shrugging, Minnie left, muttering, "Suit yourself."

Five minutes later, Ana paid a visit to feel Cora's forehead. "No fever. Still, you shouldn't be here alone. Pete is going to stay vit you."

"*No!* He shouldn't have to do that! I'm a grown woman, you know."

Ana laughed. "Says he can perform better than any Shakespeare actor and besides, I tell him he could have glass or two of free likker because he stay here." She rubbed her hands together. "It's all settled, then. Rest up, *kotik*, and vee'll see you this evening."

Ten minutes later, Cora made it over to the window in time to watch them all exit in a cloud of female chatter, generously sprinkled with laughter and bonhomie. Two horse and buggy teams had been readied and as was her custom, Minnie, armed with a borrowed muzzle-loader rifle, was all set to draw up the rear. As the group trotted off, Cora staggered back to bed, expelled an expansive breath, closed her eyes, and slept for several hours.

Fully rested and feeling better, she woke to the sound of Pete in the parlor, rummaging around, the clinking of glasses prominent, the popping of a bottle uncorked barely audible. With her energy somewhat returned, she put on an old, simple gingham dress and wandered into the main room to investigate.

There he was, searching through the liquor cabinet, his gray, bushy beard sticking out sideways like two flying carpets. As soon as he heard her enter, he swiveled around.

"Well, my girl," he said, "here we are together. Alone. But as Percy Shelly would say:

...The pale purple even
Melts around thy flight;
Like a start of heaven
In the broad daylight
Thou art unseen, but yet I hear thy shrill delight..."

Cora smiled. The very best part of Pete had always been his recitations, certainly a rarity in this barren land, and the main reason why she treasured his elocution lessons, even though Minnie called her an 'odd stick'. Then she frowned.

"Pete," she said, watching him swill down three full shot glasses, one after another. "What time is it? Mrs. Ana told me you were only going to drink a little."

"What's a few more going to hurt, eh?" He patted his right pants pocket. "Fact is, everything is in apple pie order, seeing as I brought my trusty protection. You are safe with me, my girl, mark my words." Pulling out his small Colt pocket revolver, Cora got nervous.

"What's *that* for?" she cried.

"Mrs. Ana said you shouldn't stay alone. *Fair is foul and foul is fair. We hover through the fog and filthy air.* Macbeth, don't you know."

She tried to nod, but as she watched her 'protector' guzzle four more whiskey-filled shot glasses, she burst out, "Pete! I think you've had enough liquor, no matter *what* Shakespeare would say!"

He laughed. "I do believe Mr. Shakespeare would most definitely approve of my drinking. Indeed, it is my understanding he tossed back quite a bit of alcohol himself in his day."

Standing up, he straightened his tie and let forth a litany of Wordsworth, Shelley, Shakespeare and the newer bard, Walt Whitman.

With a hefty sigh, Cora returned to her room to first make the bed, then lift up their mattress, where she had stashed her latest Buffalo Bill dime novel.

* *

Wes had also spent part of his day drinking, holed up over at his favorite haunt, the local hurdy-gurdy dance hall saloon, where, for just a fifty-cent piece, the girls sure knew how to give a cowboy a rousing romp, while lady singers belted out the likes of *Old Dan Tucker* and *Buffalo Gals*.

Dressed in far flashier outfits than Madam Ana's doves, they seemed to pay no heed to a fellow getting corked up and carrying on. While Ana's establishment maintained a certain decorum in their parlor, here, unbridled debauchery was the norm.

Ruffled skirts, petticoats more colorful than a rainbow, and boots covered in tassels were as common as toys on a Christmas morn. While Ana employed at least one bouncer to maintain order between the girls and her customers, the saloon gals carried pistols or daggers in their boots, and truth be told, at that close range, they had never missed a target yet.

Low-cut bodices, breasts spilling out like soft pillows, and bared, rounded shoulders mimicked some of the nearby hillocks covered with soft mounds of snow. Bright-colored silks and chiffon ruffles bombarded the senses as fancy garters adorned tempting female legs to such a degree that men didn't know if they were coming or going, until it was too late, until their week's pay was gone, or they'd lost every penny in a card game fueled by card sharks.

Wes' favorite gal was Inez, and whenever he entered, customers knew better than to come in between the two of them. But a dreadful head cold had incapacitated her, and she was missing from the scene that day.

"Where's Inez?" he demanded, his voice slurred by alcohol.

The bartender chuckled, then stopped when Wes stood up and wobbled over.

"Where's Inez?" he repeated.

"Wes, she's sick as a dog today. There are many other lovely gals here today. Take your pick!"

Wes spat into a nearby spittoon. "They ain't worth a mouthful of cow chips! I want *Inez!*"

A portly man in a pinstripe shirt and tattered old vest spoke up. "Hey, you, come on over. I know'd gist what you're goin' through! Have some 'coffin varnish' with me! Don't worry, I'm payin'."

"You know what I'm goin' through, huh?" Wes plopped down and grabbed a swig of whiskey straight from the bottle. His voice cleared a bit, although his face dribbled sweat.

"Yup. I had a hankering for some, well, you know. Had skedaddled over to Madam Ana's, but when I got there it was all closed up. Closed up dead as a bone orchard, it was. There was a note on the front door. Said they'd all gone to see a Shakespeare play in Braintree, or some such stuff."

"Closed up like a cemetery? No one was there?" Wes took another quick swig.

"Pretty much, but I ain't no coffee boiler. I got spunk, I tell you. I took action."

"Yeah? What'd you do?" Wes asked, a wicked grin crossing his face.

"I went around back and noticed some movement inside. Someone was home—no one regular, mind, just a young girl reading a book."

Wes leaned in, intense. "A young girl reading a book?"

"Yup, a young girl. Hey! Where ya goin'?" he called out as Wes banged open the swinging doors.

* *

Cora couldn't get over the escapades of Buffalo Bill. Did he really do everything that was mentioned in these novels? It couldn't be. Why if he did, he must have been superhuman! *Wouldn't I just love to meet him, if only to ask him some questions,* she mused, blocking out Pete's increasingly half-seas-over state of mind.

Did he really save one settler wagon train after another from certain death at the hands of the Indians? And once he saved the day, did he really scalp all those Indians, and then hold them up for audiences to see as he toured the country?

Suddenly, the house seemed so silent, so still. More quiet than it had ever been.

"Pete?" she called out, placing the dime novel down beside her. There was no answer. She shook her head. Probably out cold, like always.

She leaned back against the pillows and picked up the book again. Concentrating on Buffalo Bill, she soon forgot all about Pete's drinking.

Then she heard it, just outside her door. *Step-slide-step.*

"Alone at last," said Wes, half growling, half gloating.

She jumped up off the bed and ran into the farthest corner, her breath coming in sharp waves, her shoulders hunched forward.

"Pete's here, Wes. Please g-g-go."

"G-g-go?" he said, moving toward her, as he made fun of her stutter. "I don't think so, Cora. As for Pete, I tied him up tight as a hog. Face it, girl, it's time for you to know what it's like, what it's *really* like to be had. By a *man!*"

He removed his gun belt and carefully pulled out his six-shooter—the one with several notches carved into its handle. Each notch, according to

Thomas, a reminder of an animal maimed or killed. Carefully, he rested it on the side table and fingering his mustache, took a step forward as he started unbuttoning his vest.

"Guess I can put another notch on my gun after this, huh?" He moved toward her.

Instantly, she angled past him to race out the door and through the house, screaming at the top of her lungs, her hair flying behind her, eyes bulging out of their sockets. She could hear him behind her, always behind her, not by his heavy breath, but by his snorts, grunts, and a faster and faster *step-slide-step*. Every time she managed to escape his reach, she knew full well he was letting her escape. That was his true pleasure—a slow, steady, perverse hunt.

As she reached the kitchen, she could hear Pete's muffled cries off in the distance, but she had no time to worry about him. Her only thought was about finding some kind of weapon.

Suddenly, Wes had caught up with her, and as he shoved up against her body, his hands closed around her neck. His glazed eyes focused on her face, his strength, even in such a roostered state, strong as an ox. But he was sloppy. He took one hand off her neck to stroke her virgin cheek, and she seized the moment. Reaching to the right, she grabbed a large knife, the one she had used just the other day to help Mrs. Ana chop up some turnips.

With all her might she tried to stab him but missed, and as they tussled for the knife, she felt his rancid breath on her face, heavy and liquor-soaked. He was beyond control, beyond anything but his animal instincts. Flinging away the knife, he drew back and smacked her face so hard she flew across the room and landed on the floor in a crumpled heap. Stunned, she tried to raise her head, but he hit her again and again, using words she'd never heard before.

"P-p-p-p-lease, I..." she tried, but he knelt over her like a wild bull, victorious as he pressed his knees against her arms.

Head throbbing, senses dulled, she started drifting off as if in a dream, with only the haziest awareness of Wes as he unbuttoned his pants.

* *

The trip to Braintree seemed a tad longer than the return to South Benton. Mentally drained from the high-toned Shakespearean language, all the women sat in silence for the better part of the ride home. According to

Minnie, it was ever so fine, but for the rest of them, including Madam Ana, they were simply looking forward to getting a good night's sleep.

Approaching the back of Madam Ana's, Minnie looked over toward the kitchen and back quarters. "That's strange," she noted.

"Vat's that, Minnie?"

"The kitchen's lit, but the rest of the downstairs ain't. I wonder…"

From inside, a man's voice rang out. "Serves you right, Cora Dolan!"

Like a shot, Minnie pulled the muzzle-loader out of its saddle sheath, charged over to the back door, and entered. Inside, it was quite dark, but off toward the parlor she thought she heard something. Someone was trying to call out a few words, but they sounded eerie, stifled somehow. Step by cautious step, she headed toward the kitchen, shouldering her loaded rifle and straining to hear anything.

All of a sudden, she heard a man grunt with satisfaction. "Well, you ain't so special anymore. Not for Thomas, not for *anybody!*"

Minnie wasted no time. Running into the kitchen, ready to do battle, she stopped, horrified. There was Wes, his pants down around his ankles, standing over an unconscious Cora, the top of her gingham dress in shreds, with a thin trickle of blood seeping from between her legs. Catching sight of Minnie, he instantly yanked his pants on.

"You son…of…a…*bitch!*" Minnie straddled the floor with both feet and aimed her rifle. Just as she clicked the trigger, Wes ducked, his right shoulder taking a slight graze.

Dropping the useless one-shot weapon, she leapt over to him and tried to claw at his fleeing body, swearing revenge, but he was too quick. He ran out of the house, panting, and using the dark night as cover, disappeared from sight.

* *

By midnight, the sheriff appeared. "Now ladies, calm down, calm down!" he said. "I *promise* you, we're gonna search high and low for that bastard!"

Madam Ana let out a loud snort. "Since ven do you ever help us, Sheriff?"

Sheriff Inwood sighed. Dealing with Wes' crime was one thing, tackling the overwhelming hostility in the room was quite another. *There goes my Saturday night lovin,'* he thought as he assessed his next move. *Better be good to these ladies.*

"Would anyone happen to know Wes' hideout?" he finally asked. Nothing.

Becky cleared her throat. "What about his stepbrother, Thomas?"

"Becky!" the madam exclaimed. "You know Thomas is innocent. He's nothing like his stepbrother."

"Yes, that's true, but what *about* Thomas?" The sheriff asked, coming over to the voluptuous Becky and practically falling into her ample cleavage. "Where was he earlier tonight?"

"Right now, he's out of town and don't you *dare* blame him!" Minnie snarled from the doorway.

Everyone swiveled around. The sheriff shifted his stance.

"Where you been, Minnie?" he asked, noticing the girl's blazing eyes and right hand stained with several drops of blood.

"Taking care of my sister, of course!"

Nodding absently, he faced the crowd again.

"We're gonna have justice in this town one way or the other," he said. "People are demanding it, and if Thomas knows anything about Wes' whereabouts, I'm sure as *hell* gonna find out. Frankly, I have no choice. I heard tell, through my deputy, that there's a vigilante forming right now as we speak, and they're out for blood. Wes or anyone in his family, it's all the same to them!"

Madam Ann stared at him for a moment. "Ven did this happen?"

Sheriff Inwood sighed. "Seems some of the menfolk can't abide a girl getting hurt, no matter what house she lives in."

"Interesting. Vell, that's all vee have tonight, Sheriff. You should go now so we can help our Cora."

As soon as the law officer left, she stood up and quickly turned to Becky. "Now go to Pete like da vind. Tell him I need to see him right avay. Go, *GO!*"

One look at her employer's face, and Becky knew better than to disobey; and within minutes a distraught Pete was holed up with Ana and Minnie behind closed doors. Heads together, the three of them stayed deep in conversation, all through the girls' chatter and the angry crowd gathering over at the Sheriff's.

"According to Cora, Thomas went for some supplies for Mr. Preston," Minnie said.

The madam nodded. "Go, then, Pete, ask that old man Preston vhere he is. Do it for Thomas. He cannot come back here, it's not safe."

"Madam Ana, Minnie, I feel so terrible," he sobbed. "If only I hadn't been drinking."

"No time for that, Pete. Vhat's done is done. Now, go to Thomas. Do it for him."

"And do it for Cora. She mustn't see Thomas maybe gettin' himself killed!" an exhausted Minnie added, no longer able to fight back her tears.

* *

The next day, outside the Omaha Inn, Thomas was saddling up his horse when Pete appeared from out of nowhere and tapped him on the shoulder.

"Thomas, we need to talk," was all he said.

"*Pete!* What in the world? What's wrong? *Tell* me!"

"Not here, not now. Let's ride out of town a ways first."

"Tell me this instant!" Thomas demanded as he leaned forward, one neck vein throbbing.

"Outside of town first," Pete replied, his usual literary 'pearls of wisdom' conspicuously absent.

Two miles out, beneath an old oak tree, Pete was trying to control a distraught Thomas. "I know, son. I know it's hard, but it wouldn't do any good to get yourself killed, now would it?"

"But I have to see her, I *have* to!" An odd expression washed over his face. "How is she? Did he...?"

"Yes, Thomas, he did," Pete replied, his eyes welling up. "That poor girl's had enough bad luck to fill a lifetime. I doubt if there's room for any more."

"I should be *there* for her! Look, I'm *not* Wes."

Pulling out his handkerchief, Pete blew his nose. "Of course, you aren't, but the townspeople are looking for justice and revenge. Believe me, they're in no mood to quibble about which brother did it! Besides, she's just too shaken, too fragile to see *anyone* right now. Trust me, Thomas, you just can't go back there."

Thomas stood firm, his mouth in a flat line, his jaw clenched. "Nothing you can say will convince me, Pete. I'm goin' to see her."

"No, no, you mustn't do that!"

"Pete, why do you look so scared?"

"I'm not. It's just that..."

"What? What?"

Envisioning the already assembled lynching party, the older man gulped. "I didn't want to tell you this, but she told me she just didn't want to see you, my boy."

"I don't believe you!"

"*Trust* me, she was very emphatic. 'I don't ever want to see him or any other Garrett ever again!' she told me," he said, the guilt of his lies washing over him. But the boy's safety was uppermost in his mind.

Thomas slammed his fist against the tree. "That *damned* Wes! My whole life, he's always tried to get me in trouble. Always tried to get our pa to blame me for what *he* did."

Suddenly his face contorted with anguish. "Oh, Pete, what should I do? Where would I go?" A single tear had edged down his right cheek.

For a long time, they were shrouded in silence. Finally, Pete spoke. "You ask where you should go? Here's an option. Get away from here. Go fight for your country, my lad, that's what you should do. Maybe it'll help to forget Cora. There are recruiters everywhere, you know."

Although he slowly nodded, Thomas' face hardened. "Pete, I'm not leaving 'til you at least give me some real answers."

Pete cocked his head to one side. "Answers?"

"Yes, it's time someone told me what happened to Cora when she was a little girl, before I met her. I reckon I deserve that, at least."

There was a brief pause. "Yes, I reckon you do, dear boy. I was there as well, of course, but a while ago Minnie told me the details of what happened to them. All I can say is, it was quite something."

CHAPTER TWO
The start of it all – 1856 Nebraska

The settlers had come from all over. Fueled by the 1854 Kansas-Nebraska Act opening up these two territories for new settlements, they didn't care whether or not they were suddenly allowed to choose between a slavery or free area, they were simply hungry for a fresh start, either away from the choking drudgery of urban cities, or their impoverished homelands.

Now, as the sun gently headed toward the horizon and the evening breeze kicked in, the hum of homesteaders, farmers, children, pioneer women, cowboys, and immigrants hovered over the Indian-confiscated lands like mosquitoes just itching to land.

The Dolans had arrived after escaping from potato-famined Ireland and were weighed down by two mule team-drawn prairie schooners. Gillian Dolan drove the first wagon, his ten-year-old daughter Cora sitting by his side. Mattie, his wife, guided the second, nervous yet proud of her first handling of such a heavy load. Minnie, fiercely independent, trailed the pack, defiantly clicking at her horse and relishing her important position in the traveling order. It had been an exhausting two-week journey for the family, but finally here they were, buzzing with exhilaration and high hopes.

On the outskirts of the race, they were met by several U.S. cavalrymen, demanding the family show their acceptance letter before the official land rush rules could be handed out. Gillian handed his wrinkled, official document over with shaky fingers while Minnie stood back and scoffed.

THE DOLAN GIRLS

Authority did not sit well with her, even as a fourteen-year-old.

"Now, Mr. Dolan, you and your family arrived a little later than some of the others, so you'll just have to find a spot anywhere you can. First come, first served."

Two tough soldiers from the 21st Cavalry stood nearby, rigid, unyielding. For all the grandeur of their Colt army pistols, cavalry sabers, cream-colored 'wrist-breaker' gloves, and dark blue uniforms laced with shiny brass buttons, no smiles ever crossed their chiseled faces.

Behind them, the last of the wagons were approaching—jostling, wood shifting, wheels clicking, leather underbelly straps squeaking, and horses snorting as they weathered the terrain, like determined ships swaying over small, endless waves.

Maneuvering through the crowd, the Dolans managed to snag a space to call home for the night; nowhere near the starting line, but not as far back as all the newcomers would undoubtedly end up. Once there, Gillian insisted on checking all the straps on their side barrels and heavy furniture. Mattie fiddled with her coffee grinder, traveling mirror, kitchen chest, and brass oil lamps. Cora hugged her new gingham-dressed doll, a present for the occasion.

"Mattie, why you be insisting on bringing this heavy dresser is a puzzle to me. I can make you one as soon as we're on our new homestead," Gillian complained, shaking his head.

"*What?* Take away me dresser? 'Tis as much a treasure for me as me mam's brass lamps, for goodness sake. No, no more sacrifices like back home. In America, I will have whatever things *I* be wanting around me, I will!"

Recognizing 'the look,' her husband quickly retreated. "All right, Love, all right."

Cora grinned, while Minnie watched the exchange with a jaundiced eye. She never got what *she* wanted, it seemed.

Once fires were lit and dinner plates unpacked, Minnie could sense the mood of the entire camp changing. Everyone was turning jovial, their 'great adventure' within sight, their need to release some energy, palpable.

After supper, Mam finished cleaning up and rubbed her hands. "Let's look around together, all right Gillian? I'd like to get to know me new neighbors."

Nodding, he cupped Cora's hand and led Minnie and Mattie through a maze of wagons, carts, horses, mules, and dogs, greeting people cordially, expecting a similar treatment in return. But it was not to be. Stopping by an elegant carriage, where a well-dressed family had actually brought along two servants, they endured a disdainful scowl from the wife before moving on. Minnie was about to turn back around to shoot off one of her infamous 'evil' faces toward them, but shrugged instead. Not worth the effort.

A small group of women quilters were next—buttoned-up gingham dresses, high-topped boots, tight-bunned hair slicked to a sheen—all busily weaving needles in and out of various quilts, as if the next morning might bring an end to the world.

Mattie approached them. "My, what lovely work you all do," she exclaimed, eyeing the vibrant coverlets with their intricate stitching.

The reception was chilly. You'd think Mam had uttered the most foul, inappropriate words ever, like she had not an ounce of gentility at all. As she walked by them, Minnie harrumphed as loudly as she could at the unfriendly ladies.

A simple black, box-like wagon displaying the words, *PETE'S CELEBRATED MEDICINE* brought an "Ach, we have a doctor here!" from Mam. From a passerby, Minnie heard, "Oh, no! A snake oil salesman in our midst, a real four-flusher!"

On one side of the wagon stood Pete, a brocade-vested friendly sort, handing out candies to children stopping by. Then he held up a dark glass bottle.

"Step right up, ladies and gentlemen, and learn all about my ace-high elixir! Not only for the liver, it also purifies the blood, to help you get through them hard days! None like it!" he announced to anyone who would listen. "To quote the great poet Henry Wadsworth Longfellow,

> *Listen, my children, and you shall hear*
> *Of the midnight ride of Paul Revere,*
> *On the eighteenth of April, in Seventy-five;*
> *Hardly a man is now alive*
> *Who remembers that famous day and year…"*

When that fell short, he began reciting Shakespeare, well aware of its effect. More and more people gathered as he deepened his voice: *To be or not to be, that is the question…"*

Minnie became an instant fan. She sucked on his candies and nodded knowingly at his theatrical sales pitch, but Gillian heeded the passerby's warning, and after a few minutes, steered her away as the salesman broke off his soliloquy to call after them, "This ain't no Kicka-boo medicine like you're likely to see further down the wagon row. This here medicine is of the first water!"

"But Da, he was so nice and he helps people!" Minnie cried.

"Ach, Minnie, you're young still. Trust me, when I say you need to be staying away from the likes of him."

"But, Da…"

"No more But's, me girl! Come."

NEBRASKA HERE WE COME decorated a small cart close by, and as they walked passed it, they noticed a black man and two white companions in the process of tightening up their fiddle strings. Twisting and plucking, they paused to look at the Dolans, then grinned. Minnie smiled. Heaven have mercy, some friendly folk!

"You fellas fiddle players?" Gillian asked.

"We surely are, mister. We surely are." And with that, the black fellow rested his violin on his left shoulder, nestled it close to his ear and played several bars of *Turkey In the Straw*.

"Oh, that's *grand*, that is!" Mattie exclaimed. "Reminds me of Ireland and our jigs."

"Perhaps later, we can swing on by and visit, to play to the gallery," one of the white musicians said.

"The gallery?" Mattie looked puzzled.

"Audience, Missus, an audience!" The lead musician dipped his head in a short salute. "By the way, my name is Everett, and these here two deadbeats are Charlie and William.

"Deadbeat?" Minnie asked this time.

"Everett's just joshin', he meant no harm. It's just his way," Charlie laughed, carefully putting his instrument away in its case.

"I'm Gillian Dolan, and this here is me family—me wife, Mattie, me daughters, Minnie and Cora."

"Proud to know you all. Perhaps we *will* pay you a visit later on," Everett tossed out as the family moved on.

Mattie swiveled around and nodded enthusiastically. "Oh, yes, that'd be lovely. And be sure to bring your fiddles!"

Watching her da looking down at his wife with such love, Minnie melted. What a pleasure it was to finally see her mam happy. What a rarity these days. Perhaps things would work out after all, in this new, wide-open territory.

Next they came across a strange looking family, all dressed in solid black. Each member more subdued than the next, they nodded cordially, and one of them even managed a "Good evening to thee."

Minnie suddenly noticed a young man standing off to one side holding a camera and tripod. He stepped toward them.

"They're Amish," he explained softly. "From Pennsylvania." He stretched out his hand. "My name's Bradford Jones, photographer for *The Cincinnati Daily Gazette*."

"Ach, a newspaper man," Gillian sounded impressed. "Why are you here, might I ask?"

"You might, indeed! I've been sent here to help record the Land Rush tomorrow. After all, this is big news!"

"It certainly is for us!" Gillian beamed, flashing a smile as broad as all of Ireland, as Mattie looked on.

All of a sudden, Bradford waxed philosophical. "As Alexander Pope said, *Hope springs eternal in the human breast!*" When the family showed signs of shuffling away, he added, "Remember, folks, tomorrow brings new beginnings. I tell you what. I'll come on by and take a photograph of your family for posterity!"

Mam nodded. "That'd be a grand honor. Thank you kindly, Mr. Jones."

"Bradford, dear lady. Bradford," rung out clear as a bell, but his "See you tomorrow," faded fast as the Dolans continued on their way.

At least eight wagons over, they learned some good news from a settler. "Did you know that the Land Committee is offering extra canteens of water for tomorrow? Now, ain't that fine as cream gravy!" an older man commented, puffing on his pipe and discharging a fast wink.

Minnie had no idea what cream gravy was, but she sure could follow the man's finger pointed in a southeasterly direction. Nodding their heads and chorusing more "Thank you, kindly," they made a quick detour over to the right spot, then waited in the long line to load up.

They stood behind a cluster of female foreigners, and as time passed, listened to their unintelligible chatter. Finally, one of the women turned to Mattie. "We are from Norway. Where you from?"

"We be coming from Ireland," Mam said, smiling. Hugging her skirt was

Cora and just behind her, stood Minnie. Gillian produced a smile as well.

It was as if a curtain had suddenly dropped down over the woman's face. "Ah…" was all she uttered before turning back to her companions. Bewildered, the Dolans looked at each other, searching for some kind of answer. How much of Nebraska was going to be like this?

"Why would they say that, Da? We were just tryin' to be friendly." Minnie always asked the questions that nobody wanted to answer.

Mattie glanced over at Gillian, before studying her shoes. "Later, Minnie. I'll tell you later," Gillian answered.

Minnie produced the thunderous look she always did when she was stifled.

"Now, Papa! Tell me now!" she yelled, but it fell on deaf ears until later in their wagon, with the flaps down and the sun fully set.

"Minnie, this is something that happens in America, don't you know," her da started. "We're not as welcomed here as I had hoped," he continued, telling her about the *No Irish Need Apply Here* signs he saw posted in shops when they first landed in New York. "But that's in the past. Tomorrow we be getting our land and creating a new life for us all, eh?"

Outside the wagon, Minnie could hear her mam talking to some men and actually laughing. Curious, they went out to find Everett, Charlie, and Will holding fiddles up to their chins.

"The Irish songs are the best, don't you know!" Everett declared with a mock Irish brogue, starting to count out a beat. "*One, two, three, and—*" Instantly, he and his little band began fiddling away at an Irish jig, as Mattie grinned from ear to ear.

More than that, her right foot had developed a mind of its own. Tapping slightly at first, it soon bounced up and down, encouraging her hands to clap out a good rhythm while three other men joined the tight, musical group, carrying a fife, a washboard, and a bodrán drum.

Mattie had transformed—her upper torso straight as an arrow, her legs and feet moving up and down, her face flushed with joy as the growing crowd started to follow her lead and join in.

"Me, too, Mam! Me, too!" called out Cora, rushing over to her mother's side.

The crowd gave them a wide berth as the two female Dolans synchronized their dance steps and head tosses, fixing on each other as if they were the only people in the world. Whooping, clapping, and stomping went the crowd, trying to catch up with the mother-daughter team, as the music grew faster and faster. Clamoring for the night never to end, people seemed riveted with Mattie in particular. Her red face flushed, she mimicked a gleeful, mad woman blocking out everything, even her long painful journey from Ireland to this strange new land.

Laughing, Gillian turned to Minnie. "Cora sure loves her mam, no?"

Minnie smiled. "Yes, that's for sure."

"Ach, Minnie," Gillian continued, having seen her half-hearted claps spaced only here and there during the dancing. "Why can't you be as happy as your mam or your sister? Would it kill you to enjoy the moment?"

She looked up at his glowing face. "You're right, Da. 'Tis a *good* thing we're here. I do believe that, I do."

He patted her on her shoulder. "Grand. Now, would you be wanting to take a walk with me? Stretch our legs?"

"Indeed I would. And Da?" she murmured as they began to stroll away from the festivities.

"Yes, me love?"

"Thanks."

He chuckled and placed her arm through his, as the music and shouts grew softer, then almost disappeared.

They sauntered by the rest of the campers going about their business: dinner dishes were being washed and put aside, bed rolls laid out, lamps extinguishing by increments, prayers murmured. Soldiers nearby were conversing in low, gruff tones, their cigar smoke swirling up in wispy puffs.

"Let's ask the soldiers the schedule for tomorrow morning, shall we, Minnie?" Da asked.

"All right, Da. That'd be a good idea." She kept her arm locked up snug against his as they approached the cavalrymen. The night air had shifted, bringing on a heavier breeze than before, and as Minnie wrapped her shawl even tighter around her, just being next to her Da, she could feel her mood lifting.

The soldiers' voices were growing louder, competing less and less against the owls and rolling tumbleweeds. Coming up to a lone bush, Gillian and Minnie could actually hear the men's words as clear as if they were in the same room.

"Those poor buffoons! They have no idea how bad it'll be come tomorrow," one of them commented gruffly.

"Yep, those poor folks, indeed. Only one third of 'em will get themselves some land. Bound to be some accidents as well. It's a damn shame, that's for sure!" another one chimed in.

In the dark, Minnie and Gillian turned to each other, her eyes wide, his wary eyes scaring her even more.

"Da?"

"Husssshhhh!" he hissed, placing his index finger across her lips. "That won't be us, it surely won't! We're going to make it, we will!"

They were about to move forward toward the soldiers to ask about time, when a third one piped up and gave them their answer. "So, we're all set for nine o'clock, right?"

"Yes, we are," the second soldier said. "No later. We've got to make sure there's order first, then we'll be up on the ridge ready to shoot our rifles."

The walk back to the Dolan wagon was slow, the two of them cloaked in their own thoughts. By the time they arrived, the music was already winding down, the fiddlers and dancers tired, and with the soldiers encouraging everyone to get some sleep, the crowd was drifting off to their own wagons.

Mattie, still flushed from the evening, called out to the fiddlers, "Thank you so much! Now I feel as if I'm a real Irish pioneer woman!"

The musicians' laughter echoed across the camp like distant waves of thunder. But later, as the Dolans snuggled down onto their bedrolls inside their main wagon, each one stayed silent. Minnie could only imagine what Cora, her little hand resting over her heart, was thinking. Was it about how Mam looked that night, finally confident about her new life? And Da, was he scared but determined to make sure all went smoothly the next day by securing the straps and reins on both teams one more time?

She tried to stop her mind from whirling and speculating, but couldn't. Not until she started to count sheep, anything to calm her real feelings of impending doom.

* *

The next morning an eerie, almost ghostlike presence blanketed the camp. Families, singing and dancing the night before, now hastily chowed down their breakfasts. Horses snorted softly, mules stifled their brays, and settlers gently clicked at their steeds while checking for loose horseshoes. Tightened straps around toolboxes were given a final inspection and bedrolls on packsaddles were secured, but not a single word was uttered.

To Minnie, the stillness only enhanced her sense of doom, and as she looked out on the vast, daunting, exciting plains that stretched before them, just ready for the taking, her heart fluttered faster than a hummingbird's wings.

"Stay in your places, folks! Stay in your places! If anyone starts before the white flag drop and gun salute, they will be disqualified," barked several cavalrymen making their rounds through the rows of hopefuls.

Wiping his brow, Gillian stopped one of them in passing. "Excuse me, Sir," he said, "what if we are not one of the frontrunners? They'll not be any land left."

"There are also lots close by to settle on," came the clipped reply.

"But those ain't good for farmin'," hollered a disgruntled man across the way.

"Again, there are also lots close by to settle on," the solider replied gruffly, in no mood to be argued with.

"Da, is that like the map of parceled land we saw in the newspapers before we left?" Minnie asked.

"Ay, that it is. But don't worry, I'm going to make sure we're one of the ones who gets the rich farmin' land. That's a promise!"

Mam started biting her lower lip as Minnie had seen her do a hundred times. "Gillian, I don't think I can drive the mules that fast."

"Don't worry, Love. I'll charge ahead, you follow the best you can." His arm covered her thin shoulders before he turned to his oldest daughter. "And Minnie, you follow your mam, and don't you be coming after me."

"But I'm not saddled down with a wagon, Da. Shouldn't *I* be the one chargin' ahead?"

"Girl, you're *not* going to try me patience on this day of all days! For the love of God, do as you're told!"

As Minnie glowered, Mam bit, and Gillian grumbled, Cora shifted from one foot to another.

Bradford Jones appeared from out of nowhere. "Hello! How 'bout a picture of you all before the big rush?"

It was a couple of seconds before Da found his voice. "Why, that's grand of you, Bradford. Very kind, indeed. Isn't it, Mattie! *Isn't* it, Minnie?"

Directing them professionally, Bradford lined up the family in front of Gillian's wagon, talking nonstop, oblivious to their solemn mood. Unfolding his wooden tripod, he then placed his brand new Fallowfield camera with its fabric bellows and focus lens on top of a ledge and stepped around behind the black curtain attached to the mechanism.

Cora started to giggle. "Look Mam, he's disappeared!"

In spite of themselves, Mattie, Gillian, and Minnie started to laugh. They laughed so hard that Bradford had to reappear to reprimand them. "Listen, no smiling, folks. This is a formal picture. No smiling." But the skin around his eyes crinkled, his grin infectious, and just before he 'disappeared' again to give the camera a quick click, he sent the lot of them a broad wink.

"Before I go up on the ledge with the soldiers to record the entire event, I just want to wish you the best of luck," he said, taking down his equipment.

"What about our *picture?*" Cora exclaimed.

"I'll develop it in town and give it to you afterwards. You can hang it up in your new homestead." After a bow and a wave goodbye, they watched him wend his way over to the northeasterly ledge to position his camera and tripod near a group of soldiers.

Anticipating orders, the cavalrymen had already lined up for the seven-gun salute, their faces and brass buttons reflecting off of the sun's glare, their single white flag poised to drop, while below them the settlers were jockeying for their futures. Despite Minnie's mood, she was impressed.

Suddenly a bugle blared, the white flag dropped, and the rifles cracked over their heads, sending off a frenzy of "Hee-haw's," "We're off!" and "Let's go, let's *go!*" Wagon wheels set their slow churn in motion as horseback riders galloped on ahead, unloading a choking cloud of dust behind.

Da swiveled around in his seat to give one quick wave to Mam before taking off, driving his team with the skill of the best of them. Next to him Cora was holding on for dear life, trying to smile but clenching her teeth instead. Back in the sea of grit came Mam, her reins clutched so tightly her hands would blister in a matter of minutes, while behind their trailing wagon, a frustrated Minnie trotted, her pulse beating so loudly in her ears she thought they would burst.

The first quarter mile out, the human pack was dense, pressed together as a single unit. But very quickly wagons, carts, and dashing contenders spread out, like a stream exploring ways to refill a creviced land. Men on horses were waving their hats and holding onto their claim flags, the fast *glop-glop-glop* of galloping horses intermingling with a fog of dust and dirt, thick enough to produce thunderous coughs everywhere.

Out of the corner of her eye, Minnie took in a few of the cavalrymen, their single-shot military rifles nestled in their side cases, their barking orders to "Maintain order, maintain order!" useless in the tumultuous din. All at once, the flat prairie turf had turned into a rough, sinewy terrain, jostling the wagons even more vigorously and instantly sending one settler flying.

"God all mighty!" Minnie heard her mam scream, as she doubled up on her reins and watched the settler scramble for his life.

Off to one side, a large chuck wagon hit a boulder, throwing both the driver and horse to the ground. While Minnie watched in horror, a tangle of both man and horse legs flailed helplessly as the oncoming rigs swerved sharply to the right or the left, in an all-out effort to miss the struggling mass. Powdery dirt rose up, veiling the air with tiny particles that stung Minnie's eyes and made Mam sob.

"I can't see anything, I *can't*," she wailed, just as an oncoming wagon trampled over the settler and his animal, leaving them both writhing in agony.

Another horse buckled under from the rough ground, screeching in pain, and as she rode by, Minnie saw its owner yank out his pistol and shoot the horse in its head.

"Why in the world would you *do* that?" she yelled at him.

"He ain't no good to me now," was his answer as more and more wagons, carts, and stagecoaches streamed by.

In no time at all, their once clear path was now strewn with scattered supplies, flung wide from the wagons and adding to the bumpiness. Straddlers on the sides of stagecoaches, clinging to anything within reach, were being thrown off at an alarming rate, and each time they dropped, a gasp and a groan partnered their thud as they landed, only to be hit or trampled on seconds later.

Pete, the poetic snake oil man, came next, ambling along on his horse as calm as could be.

"Aren't you in a rush, Mr. Pete?" Minnie asked, shouting loud enough to be heard over the ruckus.

"I figure there won't be any farmland left for the likes of us tag-a-longs, so I'll probably end up in the two-street town they call South Benton, anyhow," he shouted back, tipping his hat to Mattie as he slow-gaited with her for a while before moving on.

Suddenly, a slight wind cropped up, blowing the circulating dust even farther into eyes and noses. Abandoned barrels lay everywhere as Minnie watched her mam trudge on, barely able to see. When Minnie pulled up beside her, Mam shaded her eyes and gave a stoic nod as if to say, 'I'll be all right. Everything's gonna be all right.' Her daughter smiled, and was still smiling when her mother's right front wheel hit a boulder the size of one of their suitcases, tilted, and flipped over.

Time stood still as Minnie watched her mother being hurled from her front seat, flung a good five yards, and then crushed by the very dresser she cherished. Drawing up short, Minnie dropped down to the ground, screaming for help while desperately trying to pull the heavy furniture off her motionless mother. But no one stopped. All the noise drowned out her pleas; the race for land, too vital.

From out of nowhere, Pete appeared.

"Lordy, lordy, dear girl!" he exclaimed as he jumped off his horse and ran over to her mam. Tugging and lifting, he and Minnie managed to free Mam from the dresser, her prized possession, but it was too late. Her bleeding and indented skull spoke volumes. After Pete measured her pulse, he turned solemnly to tell Minnie what was all too clear. The Irish pioneer woman was no more.

By the time the race had ended and the dust settled, the plains were strewn with broken wagons, supplies, horses, and bodies. Faint moans and soft pants now filled the same surroundings that just hours before had housed eager shouts and big dreams.

Gillian and Cora were finally slowly making their way back to their family, unable to have claimed any land. But as they approached the twosome standing by the Dolan's other wagon, they sped up, once again racing for the second time that day.

Leaping onto the ground, Da rushed over. "What in the world? What happened?" he hollered before he spied his wife on the ground. "Oh, no! Oh, *no*..." he wailed, kneeling down next to her, cradling her in his arms.

"Da, she hit a rock. It was so awful!" Minnie whispered at his elbow.

"It was your job to watch over your mam, it was!" he hissed, then stopped when he looked at his daughter's tortured face. "I'm sorry, Love. I know you couldn't help her. No one could." He looked up into the sky, his tears mixing with a trail of spittle from his mouth. "Oh, God, it's me own fault, it is!"

Rocking his wife back and forth, he began sobbing and railing at himself and the world as Cora clung to Minnie, her ten-year-old thumb finding its way into her mouth, her eyes dulled. Pete stood a respectful distance off to one side, but a few settlers, either returning to look for closer parcels or claim their good farming land, began to form a tight circle of condolence around them.

Still on the ground, Minnie first gazed up at the supporters, then at her da. "Oh, Lord, I wish with all me heart we'd never come, I do, I surely *do!*"

* *

Pete stopped talking, stared into the distance and sniffled twice.

"Oh, my Lord! That's *terrible*, Pete? How old was Cora back then?"

"Just ten, I believe."

"No wonder she's been so sad at times. No wonder." He wiped one eye with his shirtsleeve. "Please, go on, Pete. What happened next? What happened to their da? How did she and Minnie end up at Madam Ana's?"

Pete held up his hand. "Wait, you'll see…"

* *

At first, after burying Mattie in an unmarked grave in the only cemetery in South Benton, Gillian did try. He managed to fix breakfast for his girls in their two adjoining rooms above the local Water Stop Saloon. He cooked suppers as well, with the sounds of laughter and honky-tonk music drifting upstairs, serenading them as they ate. Minnie would tap her fork in time to the rhythms or hum a bar or two before Gillian gave her a stern eye. Cora usually ate in silence, watching these interchanges, but unlike her older sister, never drove Da any further to distraction.

His dreams of farming thwarted, he nabbed the only available job—sweeping and mopping up floors for the saloon owner downstairs. A sparse, wood-planked, whistle stop with a tuneless piano, the saloon served its basic function: to likker up anyone who came in. Gillian's days—and sometimes nights—consisted of cleaning up spilled drinks, food, and vomit, while he listened to local cowboys and drifters boast about their powerful cattle driving abilities or how they were as good as any hired gun for sale.

But after a few weeks, the girls began asking him questions. They both noticed butter was being replaced by lard, eggs by pigs' feet, red peppers by chard, and their plates, once full, now held at most, meager portions, not fit for growing children.

"Da, we need to make more money," remarked Minnie, the pragmatist, one night at supper. "I could work downstairs at the saloon, I could."

He looked at her in horror. "No daughter of mine will be working in such a hell-hole!" he barked, as he slammed his fist down on the table and flipped their plates up a good quarter inch.

The girls said nothing. But as if lit on fire, their father jumped up, headed downstairs, and marched across the street, straight to Madam Ana's, where he pleaded with the notorious madam to give him a part-time job. The tough, but kind-hearted woman, who knew full well about his motherless girls, instantly gave him some work, then as the months passed, watched the light slowly leave his eyes.

Finally, she had had enough. "Gillian, your Mattie is gone. She is no more. So vhy you forget your girls, huh? *They* are here. *They* are alive and they *need* you!" she clucked, placing a gentle hand onto his back.

He gave her a slow, thoughtful nod. "You're right, Mrs. Ana. Of course you're right," he said, promising to do right by his daughters from here on in, but he knew he wouldn't—he was too lost, too broken.

When he left her a letter on the parlor's mantelpiece early one morning, as the cold October rains pelted down in sheets and the rest of the household was sound asleep, he was already far away, completing his mission.

It was a short note, but the madam couldn't finish reading it.

"What *is* it, Madam Ana?" Becky entered, her eyes wide.

"Read it, just read it," Ana whispered, collapsing on the settee and dabbing at her eyes with her handkerchief.

Picking it up, Becky started reading out loud with a groggy, morning croak:

> *Dear Mrs. Ana,*
> *I am truly thankful for your kindness these past months.*
> *You saved my family from God only knows what. Please forgive me, but I'll be needing your help once again.*
> *Tomorrow I'll be going away to a better place. A place where I can be together with my Mattie forever, up in Heaven.*
> *Please take care of my little girls, because I'm never coming back.*
>
> *With much appreciation and trust,*
> *I am your grateful servant, Gillian Dolan*

* *

Thomas leaned back against the tree. "He abandoned them. Her ma was dead, and he abandoned them."

"He was a tragic figure, my boy."

"I don't care, Pete! I would *never* do that to my children." His eyes grew fierce. "And that's why I'm not going to abandon Cora."

"You have *no* choice! If you love her, you will stay away. That's what she wants. Do you have enough love to do that, my boy?"

Thomas stared at the would-be bard a couple of seconds, and drew a deep breath. "Yes," he half-whispered. "If that's what she wants. Yes, I love her that much."

CHAPTER THREE
1861 – 1871: harsh realities

The morning after Wes attacked her, Cora woke up to one eye swollen shut, a pounding head, and a bruised face and body that ached all over. With a hot water bottle wedged up against her womb, she tried to prop herself up onto her freshly laundered pillows, but it was no use. Even the tiniest movement brought excruciating pain.

But what lay inside her head was far worse. Every hour, every minute, was filled with Wes. Wes, unbuttoning his vest; Wes, putting his gun down on the side table; Wes' hot breath on her back and neck as he chased her through the house. And always, always, the sound of Wes' pants sliding down his legs.

From down the hall came routine morning sounds: Mrs. Ana setting out dishes around the kitchen table, the doves trudging downstairs and slowly shuffling toward the kitchen to line up for the madam's famously strong coffee, while endless wagons rolled by on the street. To Cora, these noises would normally seem pleasant, but now, just listening to them all, she had to stop and hold her head, it hurt so badly.

But as Minnie held her hand, she managed to utter her first words. "Where's Thomas? I need him. Where is he?"

Minnie stroked her face with a cold, wet cloth. "Honey, he had to go away. To the army."

"But Thomas…"

"Army. He's gone to fight, Cora."

Cora closed her eyes.

After a week, she could actually sit up in her bed, just in time to hear her sister and Ana conversing in the hall.

"The doctor says she'll make full recovery. All she needs is good, long bed rest," Ana told Minnie. "Thanks to you, dear girl. You stayed vit your sister all day, all night."

"Glad to hear it," the tough, twenty-year-old said. "But I'm *never* going to let anything happen to her ever again!"

"Minnie, you're such good sister, you make my heart glad," Ana said, and continued pouring coffee.

Cora could hear the clink of coffee mugs, dishes clattering, and silverware being plunked down onto the table.

For Cora, bed rest was easy at first. With such low energy and great pain, that was all she could manage. But several days and nights passed, and she began improving more than anyone thought possible.

At least, physically.

"What's that noise, Minnie? It's a man, isn't it?" Cora kept crying out from their bed, her pupils dilated, her favorite dime novels strewn out on either side of her.

"No, honey, like I told you an hour ago, that's not a man. I think it's Becky this time," Minnie reassured her. "Remember, all the men are in the main parlor, far away from here."

"But I swear, I *heard* it. It was a man's strange footstep, like…" She bit her lip ferociously.

"Wes is long gone, Cora, and he won't be back any time soon, I can guarantee you that. The posse looked high 'n low for him for weeks. Trust me, he's *gone*."

Nodding, Cora gulped. "If you say so. Are you sure?"

Minnie sighed.

Two weeks later, Cora was taking little baby steps around the back of the house, her face bruises paled to a slight green. A week after that, she was almost walking normally.

She didn't even mind when she overheard the doctor getting personal about her with Ana.

"Because she was a virgin, Mrs. Ana, her vaginal tears were significant, but she's healing nicely, so you'll see a marked difference in her walking."

Yet the phantom noises continued. "Oh, Mrs. Ana, surely you heard *that*," she exclaimed one morning in the kitchen, then promptly threw up in the sink.

Minnie came running. "Mrs. Ana, what's wrong with her, do you think?"

The madam shrugged, but looked concerned. Turning to Cora she said gently, "Cora, vee need to have doctor come again to check on tings."

"But just a few days ago he said I was healing nicely. *You* told me that!"

"It's time for another visit," Ana repeated firmly.

By nightfall, the doctor had come and gone leaving his patient wide-eyed in horror.

"Me? *Pregnant?* But it *can't* be!" Her voice trailed off.

"Oh, honey," Minnie murmured as her sister started to sob. "It'll be all right, I promise. Mrs. Ana and I are here for you. Don't worry, please."

"Be *all right?*" she almost screamed through her tears. *"How* will it be all right? How can I raise a child? *His* child?" A moment later, her anger turned to fear. "I'm so ashamed. How can I face people in town? How will Thomas ever love me again?"

Each day, Minnie kept on repeating, "It'll be all right. We're here for you," but Cora soon stopped listening.

As the sixteen-year-old became increasingly tense, the doctor concocted a special tincture to use as a sleep aid. It seemed to work. Cora's dark circles slowly disappeared, as her belly steadily grew. In time, the phantom sounds also dissipated, and Minnie whispered more than a few *Thank goodnesses.*

But not for long. Nightmares came next. Nightmares that featured Wes in a starring role and jolted Cora awake in the middle of the night, drenched in a body-soaked sweat.

"Tell me about it, Cora," Ana coaxed one morning when the doves were sleeping in, and Cora quaked in fear.

Cora gulped. "It's always the same. He's chasing me around the house. I can smell his breath right up against my neck, that disgusting alcohol breath. And his sweat, so wretched."

Ana put her arm around the girl's shoulders and led her to the parlor's settee. "Go on, talk, child. It's good for you."

Nodding, Cora continued. "Then he's hitting me over and over again and laughing. Always laughing. And then when I'm heading toward a big faint, or goodness knows what else, I can hear him putting his gun on the side table and unbuttoning." She started to cry again. "Unbuttoning his pants. That's when I wake up," she ended, two lines of tears running down her cheeks and dribbling onto her nightgown.

"Oh, *where* is Thomas?" she wailed.

"It vill pass, *kotick*. I promise all this vill pass for you."

* *

By Cora's seventh month, she decided to face the world. Arm-in-arm with Minnie, the two girls proceeded to Mr. Mahoney's as a hopeful replay of more innocent days. He was as kind as ever.

"Well, well, well. If it ain't Miss Cora. How *are* you?" he asked solicitously, avoiding looking at her belly.

"Fine, thank you Mr. Mahoney," she answered, nervously scoping out other customers.

The first person she laid her eyes on was Matthew Johnson, the postmaster's son.

He stared at her swollen front for an awkward moment or two, then, looking into her nervous eyes, stretched out his hand.

"Nice to see you, Cora," he said with a grin.

Grateful, Cora performed a little dip of her head and smiled back, as Minnie muttered, "That's one more person we can count on."

Three well-dressed women didn't follow suit. Noses in the air, sniffing loudly, they not only refused to look at Cora, they put their heads together in a tight cluster to gossip.

"Pay no mind about them, Cora," Mr. Mahoney said, placing his large, gnarly hand on her arm. "Pay no mind."

She nodded gratefully and accepted his free gift of one of the new dime novels that had just arrived that morning.

But she did mind. Minded enough to tell Minnie and Ana she wouldn't go out again until after the baby came and minded enough to add on another disturbing behavior.

"Cora, honey, how's the new dime novel?" Minnie asked several weeks later.

"All right," Cora answered flatly.

"Just all right? It looks like a good one, all about Jesse James and the Younger boys."

"It's all right," the expectant mother repeated, staring blankly at the book in her hands.

Minnie studied her for a few seconds, nodded, and immediately sought out Ana.

"I think we've headed into new territory with Cora," she told the madam, fighting back tears.

"Vhat now, Minnie?"

After relating the scene, Ana shook her head and sighed. "I tink everything too much for our girl now. She's broken, you know."

"Will she ever come back to us?" Minnie asked softly.

"I hope so, Minnie. I hope to God so."

"Hope to God so, what?" Pete asked, as he entered the room.

They recounted what had happened.

"Leave this to me," he said thoughtfully. "I'll get her back. I owe her that much."

"Oh, Pete. Just remember, Wes would've done what Wes wanted to do, no matter who was there," Minnie said, reaching out toward their old friend.

He drew a deep sigh. "I owe her that, Minnie."

* *

A few days later, Pete knocked on Cora and Minnie's bedroom door. "Are you decent, my girl?"

Cora quickly opened up. "Yes, of course. What is it, Pete?"

"Oh, my..." he started, staring at her dark circles and pinched face. One fast gulp, and he continued. "Sweetheart, I have a special surprise for you."

"Surprise? Oh *no*," she moaned, her eyes filled with apprehension.

He reached out to her. "My dear girl! It's a *good* surprise, I promise you." When she didn't react, he added, "As Lord Byron would say:

> *There be bright faces in the busy hall,*
> *Bowls on the board, and banners on the wall;'*

Still, no reaction.

"Let me show you, Cora. I *promise* you'll like it." He gently took her arm and guided her into the parlor.

There, a fiddler was smiling broadly as he tuned up his instrument. "I hear tell you like Irish jigs, Missy!" he exclaimed and began bowing a tune.

Immediately, Minnie and an Irish dove named Daria began to dance, their torsos straight as arrows, their chins uplifted and Irish proud.

Forming a wide circle around them, Ana and a few of the doves started clapping in time to the music, hesitantly at first, but as the rest of the doves,

Pete, and the male customers joined in, it became a wall of sound. Drinks were held up high as stamping, laughing, and cheering were all added to the mix. When the tune ended, everyone applauded with whoops and hollers.

All except Cora. As people turned toward her, they were met by a pleasant, but unmoved face.

"Didn't you like that Cora, honey?" Minnie asked.

"It was fine, thank you," her sister replied. "I'm tired. I think I'll return to our bedroom if you don't mind," and she waddled away.

Ana looked over at Minnie. "I tink she's in big trouble."

* *

Although strong winds hammered the pelting rain against the windowpanes at a furious pace, no one at Madam Ana's was paying any attention. As Minnie stood vigil at her sister's side, Cora was in the midst of labor, and her yelps and screams had been keeping everyone in the household on edge for hours.

What few customers had come there on such a frightful night had been immediately sent home, and when Charlotte, the midwife, at last arrived, frazzled doves and a terrified Minnie met her at the door.

"Thank God, you're here!" they all exclaimed, clearing a pathway through the parlor so the woman could complete her job at the back of the house.

Cora, spread-eagled on the bed looked up at the newcomer and moaned weakly, "Help me, please."

Minnie rushed to her and took her hand.

Another contraction came, and with it, a blood-curdling yell.

"Let me see her!" Charlotte barked at Ana, who pushed Minnie out of the way, yanked off the covers, and rolled up the girl's nightgown.

"It's breeched," the midwife commented, and instantly went into action. When she muttered, "Water," like a well-trained nurse, Ana handed her a bowl of water, soap, and a towel.

After a fast hand wash, Charlotte placed her right hand up inside Cora's womb while her left hand was gently placed on top of the girl's enormous belly. Wiggling and prodding, the seasoned midwife managed to manipulate the baby around, repeating every few seconds, "Not much longer, love, not much longer."

Ana, gripping Cora's hand the entire time, watched this miracle worker performer her magic. She had seen it all before.

"It's turned around now so I want you to push," Charlotte urged.

Cora shook her head. "I can't, I just can't."

"Yes, you *can!* Do it for me, darlink," Ana said. When Cora didn't move, she leaned in. *"Do it now!"*

"Yes, *do* it Cora!" Minnie called out.

Mustering every ounce of strength she had left, Cora gave one last big push and howled.

First a head appeared, then little shoulders, and soon the complete body slithered out mewling and crying.

From the parlor came applause and cheers, but Cora could barely move as Ana took the baby girl, swaddled it in a warm blanket, and offered it to the teenager. "Here's your little daughter, Cora."

Cora turned her head away toward the wall. "I don't want her," she stated simply.

Horrified, Minnie stepped in toward her sister. "Now, Cora..." but she was stopped by Ana's 'Leave her be look.'

For days, the new mother refused to be with her baby. Each time it was for a different reason—"I'm too tired," "I need to heal," "I'll hold her when I'm ready." Finally, she admitted, "It's *his* baby! Not mine," and left it at that.

Minnie stepped up to try and give the infant some fresh milk from their neighbor's cow, but she knew that wasn't the best thing for the baby.

Finally, Ana took charge. "It's time to be a mother, Cora. No matter how you feel, it's time. It's your milk and it's *your* baby. *Yours!"*

When the madam handed the tiny, gurgling infant into the mother's arms, Cora pleaded with her eyes, but Ana ignored everything, grabbed Minnie's arm, and strode out of the room, leaving the door slightly ajar. She hastened away, but halfway down the hall, she stopped, put an index finger to her lips, and pulling Minnie along with her, tiptoed back toward the bedroom where they pressed against the wall just outside its door.

The silence seemed to last for quite a while. Then the baby cried, and Minnie and Ana looked at each other, holding their breaths.

"Ssh-ssh-ssh, little Eleanor. You want some milk?"

Silence. Then came a slight, suckling noise. "There. Is that better?" Cora cooed in baby talk.

Mouthing *"Eleanor?"* to each other, Minnie and Ana grinned and snuck back into the parlor.

* *

Four years later, a battled had emerged between the two sisters.

"It's Eleanor. *El–lea–nor!*" Cora enunciated.

"Ellie suits her far better. Just *look* at her, Cora," Minnie said.

They both turned toward the pretty little girl chasing after two neighborhood boys in a circle, flailing her arms and yelling, "I'm gonna get you!"

Minnie chuckled. "This is *not* an Eleanor. This is an Ellie."

"I just want her to be treated with the respect she deserves," Cora stated, thinking of the week before—just one of several similar encounters.

It had started out as an ordinary day. A trip to Mahoney's where Eleanor was treated to some fine candy, then off to the post office. Entering the main room, Cora and Eleanor stopped at the counter.

"Has my package arrived yet, Mr. Johnson?" Cora asked.

"Yes, it has Mrs. Cora. And how are *you*, Miss Eleanor?" he asked as the girl flashed her teeth and curtseyed.

"Fine 'n dandy," she replied, making him laugh.

"That's a live one you've got there, Mrs. Cora. My son Matthew thinks the world of her. And you," he added.

With a tight smile, Cora acknowledged the compliment. "Does he now," she said, and pulling Eleanor along with her, exited with a short "Good day to you, Mr. Johnson."

Out on the street a group of fancy-hatted, well-dressed women were passing by, their parasols all tilted in tandem.

Staring at the little girl, one of them sniped, "You know *her* story, don't you?"

"Yes, such a shame," another one answered, maintaining the same intonation. "She's a pretty little thing, but she'll *never* amount to anything in this town."

As soon as they reached home, Eleanor peeked into the parlor, hoping for a free dove to play with.

"Eleanor, stop that!" Cora snapped.

"Stop what, Mama?"

"I don't want you to go in there anymore."

"What's wrong, Cora?" Minnie asked, entering with a ledger tucked under her arm.

Cora's cold face spoke volumes. "Eleanor, please go to your room."

She waited for the sisters to be alone. As soon as Eleanor left, she said, "They did it again."

"They did, eh? Well, who *cares* what those old biddies think," Minnie scoffed.

"I suppose I do. If not for myself, for Eleanor." She bit her lower lip.

"I doubt if Ellie—if Eleanor even cares."

"Perhaps not now, but some day she might. I just want her to have a chance, Minnie." Cora blinked and turned away. Her face started to pinch. "I wouldn't care so much if Thomas…"

Minnie shook her head. "Not *that* again. The war's only just over. Who knows what's happened to him, Cora. You're probably waiting on a ghost."

* *

Almost a year later, when Cora told Minnie that Matthew Johnson had asked her to go with him to the upcoming big dance, she was surprised at her sister's reaction.

"Cora, you know he cares for you different than how you care for him," Minnie said one evening, as the sisters both rocked back and forth on the front porch, the setting sun deepening its colors in the changing sky.

"I realize that, but he's been a good friend, and that's what I need right now," Cora said, rubbing the back of her neck with a vengeance. "So I told him I would go. Besides, I deserve to be happy, don't I? And if Thomas isn't…you know."

"Coming back?"

"Yes, coming back. I need something in my life."

"Well, I suppose that's true, honey. Be happy, 'cause chances are what with the war 'n all, Thomas is not comin' back. He'd be back for sure if he had made it through."

The church committee had made the barn more than festive. Quilts hung from the rafters, tables were covered in colorful, cotton-dyed cloths and laden with baskets of food, whiskey jugs, plates, utensils, and napkins.

When Cora and Matthew walked in, arm-in-arm, Cora couldn't believe her eyes.

"This is wonderful!" she exclaimed and tightened her hold.

As two fiddlers entertained the growing crowd chowing down their food and guzzling their likker, young children poked their heads around their mothers' skirts, men roared with laughter over the latest cowboy joke, women swapped recipes, as young men shyly—and not so shyly—asked young ladies to dance.

Matthew turned to Cora. "Dance?"

"Perhaps later. I'm starving."

"Of course. I'll get us some food, shall I?" After depositing her on a chair, he darted off toward the food tables.

She sat there, tapping her right toe to the music and thinking how good it felt to get out and be a part of things. Suddenly across the way, she saw someone she recognized. What was his name? She returned his stare. She broke her gaze, and looking down, suddenly remembered who he was. William, yes, that was his name. A friend of Thomas'. Haven't seen him for a while.

When she glanced over again, she noticed he was deep in a conversation with Matthew. At one point, they both turned toward her, still chatting away.

"That man you were talking to was William, was it not? What were you two talking about?"

"Nothing much. He's back from the war and was just visiting his folks. Just talk is all, nothin' special."

"Back from the war. Hmmm, I wonder..." she started, then caught sight of Matthew's face. His eyes were searching hers as his body stiffened. She didn't finish.

"Yes, he's goin' back to Chicago soon."

Later, they danced, twirling around the floor, with blurred, happy faces surrounding them, some supportive, and others familiar with disdainful expressions, but she didn't care. She was having a bit of fun. Finally, flushed, sweaty, and in high spirits, everyone applauded.

"You've been a good friend to me, Matthew," she said, as they stepped up onto Ana's porch. The owls were beginning to hoot, and the horses snickered softly in their barn.

"Just a friend?" he asked, gripping her by the shoulders. "Just a friend?" he repeated, so close to her, she could feel his breath on her face. He shoved his lips forward and tried to kiss her.

She jerked away. "Matthew! Please, your friendship means a lot to me, but..."

His eyes narrowed. "But I'm not Thomas, *am* I?"

"I'm so so-sor...ry," she stammered and quickly opened up the front door.

Inside Eleanor, took a running leap into her mother's arms.

"Mama, you're home!" she shouted.

Cora held her for a second then gently, yet firmly, put her back down. "Eleanor, calm down. That behavior just isn't…just isn't…"

"What, Mama?" she asked, her little face flushed with confusion and hurt.

"It's just not seemly," Cora said. Ellie ran to her aunt.

Turning away, she didn't even care that Minnie, with Ellie nestled in her arms, sniped, *"Seemly?* Oh, Cora."

* *

At ten, Eleanor told everyone her name was Ellie, despite what her mother claimed. After school, she visited their two horses as much as possible, and she and Minnie had carefully worked out a secret code system.

Whenever Cora was out, Ellie knew Minnie would allow her access to the parlor. The doves loved her and she them. If she had her way, she would spend even more time there, lapping up their colorful stories, risqué or not.

She soon figured out that all the doves were also a part of a pact Minnie had dreamed up. As soon as one of them heard Cora coming up the front walk, they would all rush the girl out of the back end of the parlor so she could scurry down the hall toward her bedroom, plop down on her bed, and Cora would be none the wiser.

In fact, all in all, everything appeared, as Ellie would say, "fine 'n dandy."

Until Madam Ana fell ill.

At first, everyone assumed it was a bad cold that had laid her up for a week. But that week stretched into two weeks, then three. The doctor was finally summoned, notwithstanding Ana's resistance, and when the exam result was declared, it was not good.

"Pneumonia, plain and simple. I'm afraid your lungs are in dire need of drainage. In addition, your heartbeat sounds too irregular," he announced to the madam and a couple of doves present in her bedroom.

Prescriptions, instructions, and warnings were dispensed, and within days, she did seem to improve a little. Still, the Dolan sisters were called into her bedroom at eleven o'clock one stormy night.

"Come in, girls. I vant to talk to you."

Sitting down across from her, the sisters reached for each other's hand.

"First, I know you were both so sad when we never could find your papa.

Never could give him a proper funeral. And I know, Cora, life has not been so good for you."

She drew a ragged breath and immediately coughed so hard, a spot of blood appeared on her imported Russian handkerchief. When her spasm subsided, she looked at the two pairs of stricken eyes staring at her and continued.

"But I also know you love each other, and I love you. So, I have put you both in my vill. If I don't make it, I give you my business, free and clear."

Cora looked at her sister, who stared back at her, displaying the same horror Cora felt.

"But…" Minnie began.

Ana held up one hand. "No buts. Is already written by lawyer. It's done. You have no choice."

When the girls came over to the bed and encircled the madam in their arms, they both began to cry.

Sniffling, the older woman cleared her throat. "By the vay, you are the daughters I never had. God bless you."

But the madam managed to cling on a little while longer, giving everyone hope. Pete even stopped drinking for a week or two, his recitations filled with faith and salvation, and all seemed right in the house again.

Until the doves made a fatal mistake. It was a Saturday afternoon, lazy, uneventful, with Cora about to go to Mr. Mahoney's, Minnie at the stables, and Ana holed up in the office going over the books.

One dove swore later that she saw Cora leaving, another did not, but when Ellie entered the parlor and asked the doves where babies came from, their lecture was loud and decidedly non-clinical.

"Becky," Ellie asked, sucking on a candy, "What do you mean when you talk about getting some good loving?"

The dove smiled. "All I can say, Ellie, is when a man touches you there, it gets you all inflamed, like you want him to never stop touchin' you down there, and other places, too."

"What other places?" the young girl asked, wide-eyed.

Susannah laughed. "Like your titties for one thing, and your…"

Josephine leaned in. "Your snatchbox, your…"

She never finished. From the doorway, the wheeze of horror escaping from Cora's mouth was palpable.

All heads pivoted toward her in time to see her march over to Ellie, grab her hand, and snarl, "That's *it!* I'm sending you back east to school!"

Ellie's tiny protests fell on deaf ears, and three weeks later, she had stopped trying to make new ones as she, Cora, Minnie, Pete, and a frail Ana all waited for the Wells Fargo & Co stagecoach to arrive.

When it did, Ellie was guided into the coach, the driver given careful instructions in regards to the schoolgirl, and the only emotion Ellie saw her mother show was a steely-eyed determination.

Her fingers curled over the rim of the half-open window, the little girl eyed the foursome through her tears. Ana was sitting on a bench, blowing her a kiss, and Minnie's scrunched up face looked like their old hound dog, Billy, after he had stepped on a burr. Pete was openly crying, his shoulders twitching up and down, and Cora, although stone-faced, was biting her lower lip, refusing to meet her daughter's eye.

"Oh, *please*, Mama," Ellie tried one last time as the driver secured her bag atop the luggage rack, climbed up into the driver's seat, snatched the reins, and released the foot brake lever.

"Please don't send me away!" she sobbed.

But her cries were swallowed up by the click-click of the driver, the coach shifting, the six-teamed horses snorting, and the wheels starting their slow, rattling grind out of town.

CHAPTER FOUR
Returning Home: 1883

Over the next few years, Cora had developed a habit of telling any new dove about the importance of order always being maintained in the establishment she and Minnie had inherited. Cleanliness was tantamount to godliness, compliance to the customers understood—unless they became too unruly—and everyone was to expect the unexpected at every turn.

As one of the madams, she was proud of her standards. Proud of how she always tried to protect her girls, along with her life-experience motto, *Expect the Unexpected*. But one routine Monday, when instead of Ellie's monthly letter coming from back east, a telegram arrived and was handed over to her in their office, she read it, and nearly choked on her morning coffee.

> RETURNING HOME TO STAY. STOP. BEEN HIRED BY SOUTH BENTON SCHOOL COMMITTEE. STOP. WILL ARRIVE NEXT TUESDAY ON THE 2PM TRAIN. STOP. LOVE TO YOU AND AUNTIE. STOP. ELLIE"

"Minnie, come here quickly!" Cora hollered.

Minnie came running. "What in the *world?*"

"Take...take a look," Cora stammered.

Minnie picked up the paper and mouthed the words. "My, oh my! Ain't this wonderful!"

Cora cleared her throat. "I'm not so sure. Remember, I went to considerable trouble to get Eleanor *away* from this place, so she could become a real lady."

"Look, Cora, I know you've gone through hell and back. I also know that you have always worried a damn sight more about what those holier-than-thou town women think than about keeping your own daughter here, close to us!"

"*You* know that wasn't all of it, not by a long shot," Cora snapped as she massaged the nape of her neck.

"That was a long time ago, Cora. Honestly, for all your smarts, you don't have the sense of a bag of hornets. Don't be such a fool. For goodness sake, just enjoy your daughter. And by the way, as you well know, she wants to be called *Ellie*, not your hoity-toity Eleanor that only *you* have insisted on calling her."

The two sisters shifted into their usual standoff poses: Cora annoyed, self-righteous, her hands on her hips; Minnie, wiry, know-it-all, breathing hard.

Just then, one of their ladies entered. "Mrs. Cora, Miss Minnie, there's a problem out on the floor."

Cora sighed. "What *now*, Marlena?"

The soiled dove gulped before answering. "One of our customers, the old geezer one, is having a fit. Gettin' real ornery, too."

In recognition of a regular happenstance, the two sisters looked at each other and grimaced.

"Need any help?" Minnie asked Cora as she stood up.

"Nope, I have it under control. Thanks, Sis," Cora replied and headed out the door, Ellie and her homecoming temporarily forgotten.

Out in the main parlor, the girls had already formed a wide circle around old Pete. Corsets, bustles, crinolines, pantaloons, and camisoles intermingled with a whiskey-stained suit, a grimy vest, and mud-caked boots. He was no match for them. As they gleefully shoved and tickled him, his fury rose with each breath, while his face ripened into the color of raw meat. Finally, when he could take it no longer, he sputtered, "She-devils!" which produced gales of laughter.

"Ladies, *ladies*. Enough. Leave the man alone," Cora said, placing a concerned arm around the smelly habitué. "There, there, Pete. They meant you no harm."

"As Mercutio proclaimed in *Romeo and Juliet*, ... *'tis not so deep as a well, nor so wide as a church door, but 'tis enough, 'twill serve. Ask for me tomorrow and you shall find me a grave man*. All I wanted was a little love, Cora. I swear it!" He sniffled pathetically as the girls giggled.

With a dirty glance aimed at the group's ringleader, Charity, Cora turned back to Pete. "You did produce some money, right, love?"

He looked down.

"Now, Pete, you know the rules."

"I just wanted a little love. As Henry David Thoreau said, *There is no remedy for love but to love more*. He also said..."

"Now, Pete, enough about Thoreau," she interrupted, gently angling him toward the door. As soon as he left with a snort and an "After all we've been through together," Cora shook her head and turned back to face her employees.

"Ladies, she said, "some women in this town may look down on us, but I do have my standards. Gentility is most important, above all else. I thought I had made myself perfectly clear."

A few head nods and corset scratching was all she got before Marlena stepped forward. "Ah, Mrs. Cora?"

Placing one hand on her hip, Cora sighed. "*Now* what?"

"He was full as a tick, that one was. He almost fell down twice."

Cora squinted her eyes, assessing her new employee. "I don't care how drunk he was. He, Miss Minnie, and I go way back."

"But you tossed out a feller from Fanny's bed just the other night. I reckon he wasn't half as likkered up as that ol' coot."

Cora frowned. "I could tell the man with Fanny was going to be big trouble."

"Yes, zat one very, very scared me," Suzette, the resident French girl affirmed. "I zink Mrs. Cora maybe saved Fanny's life."

"Trust Mrs. Cora," Rosie interjected. "She'll always watch your back, or at least your backside!" There was an explosion of laughter.

"All right, all right. Get a wiggle on, ladies," Cora continued, her eyes sweeping over them. "I heard a group of cowboys are ridin' through town, maybe even this afternoon. Now, go, *go!*" Her two claps, echoing through the room like claps of thunder, reminded her of Madam Ana in her prime, before she got sick and died, before the Dolan sisters inherited this enterprise, whether they had a hankering for it or not.

She could hear the girls whispering as they retreated up the winding, red-carpeted staircase to their various rooms, and soon, the parlor's sudden calm brought her back to a scene she wanted to forget.

> "…*All I can say, Ellie, is when a man touches you there, it gets you all inflamed, like you want him to never stop touchin' you there, and other places, too.*"
> "*What other places, Becky?*"
> Susannah laughed. "*Like your titties, for one thing, and your—*"
> Josephine leaned in. "*Your snatchbox, your——*"
> "*That's enough! She's only a child…*" cried Cora, immediately turning to Ellie.
> "*That's it! You're going to back to school back east, young lady.*"
> "*But Mama, I don't want to. Please don't make me! Oh, Mama, pleeeeeeease.*"

After plumping up a few stray pillows on Madam Ana's center settee, resetting chairs in strategic positions, leveling a gilt-framed painting on the wall, and glancing up at the prized crystal chandelier, she slowly returned to her office to think.

It was a much more cheerful room now than when Mrs. Ana had occupied it. Filled with personal objects that might mean little to most people, to the Dolan girls, they were treasured assets: Ellie's first report card, framed (all As of course), the gingham-clothed doll from their mother Mattie, several dime novels she refused to let her daughter read as a child, two dented brass lamps her parents had brought from Missouri, *Buffalo Gals*, *Old Dan Tucker*, and *Sweet Betsy from Pike* sheet music for their friend Everett to play when the customers wanted to lean against the piano and sing, and most prominently displayed, their family portrait taken that fateful 1856 morning, so long ago.

She could feel her mind tip-toeing back toward the dark times—*the sound of Wes unbuttoning his pants, the metal clink of his notched gun on the side table, Pete's muffled cries, the blast of Minnie's shotgun, the…*

"Cora!" Minnie exclaimed, bursting in. "You've *got* to accept her coming, that's all there is to it. Stop that lip biting right now!"

"I'm just fine, thank you," Cora muttered, straightening up the already organized papers on the desk and running a finger over one of the lamps to check for dust.

She softened. "I just want her to be everything I'm not. Is that so difficult to understand?"

"No, it ain't. All's I'm sayin' is let the girl live. She's back here with an important job. A job with respect, I might add." Minnie chuckled. "After all, somebody's gotta tame all those little savages and with one teacher after another skedaddling, she just might be South Benton's only hope."

Cora nodded slowly.

"All right then," Minnie said. "We'll meet her at the train station. Pete will want to come too, of course. I'll put ol' Becky in charge."

Cora wrinkled up her nose. "Becky?"

"Cora, she'll do just fine."

* *

The two o'clock train from New York was more than an hour late. While Cora walked over to the stationmaster to complain, Minnie regaled Pete with a story a drunken cowboy had shared the night before, and by the time Cora returned, the bard was howling with laughter.

"That's a good one, Minnie. Reminds me of…"

"Mr. Waterford says it'll be here any time now," Cora cut in. "Trains have been running late these days," she muttered, thoroughly massaging the back of her neck.

"That's interesting," Pete said, and suddenly knelt down. He laid his right ear directly onto one of the tracks.

"What are you doing, Pete? What will people think of us?" Cora blurted out, checking the platform for people's reactions.

"Great idea, Pete," countered Minnie.

Pete stayed low, his face thoughtful, as if in a trance.

"Did you hear me?" Cora asked.

Minnie shook her head and turned away. "Lord help us."

"I can feel it, I can feel it!" Pete announced. He stood up and dusted himself off. "We'll hear the whistle any second now."

Sure enough, within seconds, a lone, haunting wail echoed somewhere off in the distance. Thick plumes of black smoke suddenly appeared, rising up into the light blue sky as a train made its slow approach, the repeated clang of its locomotive bell growing louder and louder as it completely dominated the otherwise calm air. When the train finally entered the station, the locomotive's side-rods rattled, and jets of steam hissed out venomously from its cylinders, blocking everyone's view. Now that South Benton's railroad commerce was expanding, at least seven or eight people had stepped off the

'Iron Horse' before they caught sight of Ellie on the platform, three cars down.

Cora took a sharp intake of air. Her daughter was a sight to behold.

With auburn hair and hour-glass proportions, Ellie cut a perfect ladylike figure in her tan and black brocaded traveling suit, bustle, matching boots and parasol; everything Cora could ever ask for in a daughter. As the trio trotted toward her, Cora thought she heard Minnie's "We've got a real lady on our hands now!" and Pete's "As Alexander Pope would say, *Fair tresses man's imperial race ensnare; And beauty draw us with a single hair,*" but she couldn't be sure. Her heart was beating so hard, she thought it would surely burst out of her chest.

Colliding together in a mass of hugs and tears, the four of them paused only to lean back from each other and laugh.

"Lordy, lordy, if you aren't the prettiest thing I've ever seen," Pete exclaimed.

"Oh, Pete, you 'ol flatterer, you." Ellie giggled, flinging her arm over his shoulders.

"It's true, you *are* a sight for sore eyes, Ellie," Minnie added, then turned to Cora. "Isn't that so, Sis?"

Cora beamed. "She sure is. Welcome home, Eleanor."

A slight shadow crossed Ellie's face. "It's Ellie, Mama, remember? Ellie."

Minnie and Pete exchanged looks, while Cora stood still, giving her lower lip a good couple of bites.

"Ellie," she said finally, and tried a smile.

Minnie rubbed her hands together and drew Ellie close. "Well, let's go home, shall we? We made sure your room is nice and cheerful. Why, your mama even picked a big bunch of flowers for you just this morning."

Leaning into her aunt, Ellie smiled. "Oh, Auntie, you haven't changed a bit. So good to see you!" Arm in arm, they walked on ahead as their chatter wafted back toward Pete and Cora.

"She sure is lovely, Cora. You must be so proud." Pete's grin stretched from one ear to another.

Again, Cora managed a tight smile. "Now, Pete, when we get back, I need you to cut down on the liquor cabinet. There's no need for Elean—Ellie's first night home to be…"

"A total den of iniquity?"

She sighed. "Yes, something on that order."

* *

That night, the liquor consumption was a bit low, but teasing and merriment certainly weren't. Surrounded by all the doves—new as well as a couple of the old—the now adult Ellie easily waltzed around the parlor with Minnie and Pete to Everett's lively piano accompaniment. The customers present were regulars and trustworthy, the food flowed even if drinks didn't, and the noise reverberated off the walls like a John Phillips Sousa marching band.

Off on the sidelines, Cora watched the festivities, deep in the past.

> *Next to their wagon, Mattie had transformed—her upper torso straight as an arrow, her legs and feet moving up and down, her face flushed with joy as the growing crowd started to follow her lead and join in.*
>
> *"Me, too, Mam! Me, too!" called out little Cora, rushing over to her mother's side. The Land Rush crowd gave them a wide berth as the two female Dolans synchronized their dance steps and head tosses, fixing on each other like they were the only people in the world.*

When the grandfather clock struck eleven, Cora took charge. "This is the last dance, everyone. We have a lot to do tomorrow."

Ellie was in mid-twirl with Pete. "That's my mama," she muttered.

As they all wandered off to their rooms, and Pete to his horse outside, Minnie drew Cora aside.

"Tread a little lighter with her, Cora," she warned. "Just show her your heart."

"I think I know what to do with my own daughter," Cora snapped, blowing out kerosene lamps and briskly plumping up pillows.

Minnie expelled a deep breath. "Lord have mercy."

* *

In the back of the house, Ellie lay in her old bed, her fresh nightgown pressed, her hair brushed, her latest Charles Dickens' novel on the bedside table, her mind churning. Was coming back a mistake, after all?

The next morning, she awoke to a rooster's first crow and the sun's slow, upwards arc. A quick stretch, and she was out of bed, splashing water on her face from a nearby porcelain bowl and putting on her new riding outfit:

bloomers under a simple tunic, perfect for riding horses. As she softly padded downstairs, the household was still cloaked in deep slumber, and with her old jacket tucked under her arm, she grabbed some carrots from the kitchen and left.

Inside the weathered barn, the hay smelled fresh, the two horses looked sound and well cared for, and both were definitely curious. When they spied the fresh carrots, they inched forward in their stalls and angled their necks out toward her.

"Hey, hey, hey," she murmured as she stroked each one's soft nose. Then, feeding carrots to first one then the other one, she chuckled at the glopping noises they both made as they munched. By the time they finished, she had chosen the sorrel. Fifteen hands tall, his rich, coppery red tones served as the perfect backdrop to a snippet of white on his forehead, and when she hoisted herself up into the saddle, he sighed and exhaled a deep, fluttery breath out through his nostrils.

Riding out of town, she noticed how much it had changed. Before she had left it had seemed so small, so dirty. Now, the town's center played only a small, albeit significant, part in the thriving community. In true grid fashion, street after street had been established to accommodate hotels, saloons, a sheriff's office, yet another church, a larger post office, and of course, Madam Ana's and its three competitors. Wood-planked sidewalks and hard, mud-packed streets made walking—or, for the refined ladies, strolling—far more pleasurable than ever before.

Reaching the town's outskirts now took longer than it once did, and with an encouraging 'click-click' to the sorrel, their steady pace turned into a trot, then a light canter. The land was as open as ever, and as the horse broke into a gallop, Ellie closed her eyes, laughed, and reveled in the breeze whipping through her loose hair. No tight bun today, no binding corset, no cumbersome petticoat under a dress.

She let the red-coated steed go full force. Soon, both rider and horse were one as they blazed through the flatlands and hills, the tumbleweeds and sparse trees, the rocks, and an occasional stream. Still, in spite of having spent many years in an eastern city, she was well aware of a horse's limitations. She gently pulled in the reins so the sorrel wouldn't feel the pressure of the bridle, slowed him to an amble, and patted him softly on his neck.

"Good boy, good boy," she cooed, as she turned him around to head back toward town and the new schoolhouse the committee had mentioned in their offer. Within minutes they had arrived.

It certainly appeared to be brand new, the wood so fresh she could smell it fifty yards away. Once she tied her ride to a post, she stepped up to the main door and entered.

At first glance, it looked like a teacher's dream. Rows of clean, organized desks covered a puncheon floor, and upon further investigation, she noticed each desk contained a small journal, a pencil, and unfortunately, an obsolete primer. At one end of the large main room was a rock-stick-and-mud fireplace filled with more freshly cut wood. Empty bookshelves spread out against the back walls along with framed, embroidered signs that read, *Health Is Wealth, Never Say Fail, Look Before you Leap,* and *A Stitch in Time Saves Nine.*

She shook her head. It definitely needed more books on those shelves and more helpful primers in the desks. But first off, she needed to remove those silly signs. Soon, her mind was spilling over with new plans and new book titles.

Behind her a gruff, "Excuse me, ma'am," almost knocked her off her feet.

She spun around. Facing her was a disheveled homesteader, his slouch hat in his hands, his overalls coated with fertilized soil.

"Don't mean to disturb you, but are you the new schoolmarm?"

Touched by his deference, she stretched out her hand. "Yes, I am. My name's Ellie Dolan. Pleased to make your acquaintance."

He wiped off his right hand on the front of his jean bib before clasping hers.

"Yessum, I know who you are, ma'am. Yes, indeedy! My name's Paul Wentworth. Proud to know you, Miss Dolan. The missus and me, we're lookin' forward to you teachin' our youngins some good book learnin' *and* some manners. Matter of fact, we *all* are lookin' forward to that. All them other teachers weren't worth warm spit—pardon me—weren't worth anything." Embarrassed, his face turned as bright a red as any rose.

"I'll do my very best, Mr. Wentworth," Ellie said, watching him nod, replace his hat, and step out.

Half an hour later, she had hung up the horse gear in the barn and was facing an agitated Cora at the back entrance.

"Just where have you been?" she asked.

"Good morning to *you*, Mama." She chuckled. "I went out riding, you know, to relive my childhood, so to speak."

"Oh. Well, you must be hungry. Come on into the kitchen. Minnie and

Pete are waiting for you. What in the *world* are you wearing?" she added as her daughter walked by.

Ellie paused for a brief moment, took a deep breath, adjusted her collar, and entered the kitchen with a tremendous smile. "Good morning," she announced gaily to her aunt and Pete.

"Darlin', did you have a good ride?" Minnie asked.

"Why, yes, I did. Thanks, Auntie."

"That's quite an outfit," Pete added. "Turn around so we can take a better look."

Minnie was intrigued. "Now, *that's* what I call perfect for ridin'. I'm gonna get me one of those."

Cora stayed silent.

"Mama obviously doesn't approve of it, do you, Mama?"

"Well, fiddle-dee-dee. It looks mighty comfortable to me," Minnie declared.

"Oh, Minnie, you are the best!" Ellie cried, giving her aunt a big hug.

Turning toward the stove, Cora mumbled something unintelligible.

"What was that, Cora?" Minnie asked, winking at Ellie.

"That outfit she wore yesterday was so beautiful, that's all." She turned around and faced Ellie. "You looked so elegant."

"Sure she did. But she can't very well ride a horse in it, *can* she?" Minnie said.

As Ellie placed her arm around Minnie, she gave her a soft kiss on the cheek.

Cora, setting some biscuits on the table, paused. "I was just hoping maybe you and I could go into town early this morning, Ellie. So I could show you off. That's all."

Ellie put down her fork and smiled. "Oh, Mama."

* *

Later at the store, people showered the new teacher with hugs, pats, and good cheer. Compliments were abundant: "What a beautiful young woman," "My, she turned out real well, Cora," and "Pretty, oh so pretty!" filtered throughout the room as Cora checked on her latest order of *Harper's Bazaar* and *M'me. Demorest's Magazine*.

"Yes, she certainly is," Cora nodded proudly, so happy for her beautiful daughter. But when she passed by a mirror toward the back of the store, she caught her own reflection and paused wistfully. Who is that tired looking woman? Was it really her?

She could see Ellie was fast developing her own patterns. Early mornings were spent galloping through the countryside followed by a big breakfast in the kitchen. Afternoons were reserved for school preparations. In very short order, her daughter's schedule grew so regular, her enjoyment of Minnie and Pete so evident, Cora stopped worrying about her lingering in the parlor, joking with the ladies and customers like old times. It was clear her daughter was no longer a little girl.

Indeed, on her second day back, Ellie grinned when Minnie, her former partner in crime, had commented, "You're a grown woman now. Your mother even mentioned to me you can be in the parlor anytime you want."

As for Pete, he had now become a permanent fixture in the household as he belted out poems and sneaked a poke into the liquor cabinet when no one was looking.

"Pete, can you recite an entire poem for us?" Ellie asked him one night after Cora had coordinated a packed parlor to celebrate her sister's birthday and a general 'Here's How' toast to Minnie had finished. Everyone was present—the girls, Pete, Ellie, some regulars and a few new customers tolerating the festivities as a means to a good end upstairs.

Pete stood up, happy to play the gallery, and holding a single shot glass up toward the ceiling, he commenced with Edgar Allen Poe's *The Raven*.

He didn't get very far. *"Once upon a midnight dreary, while I pondered, weak and weary, Over many a…many a…"*

"Quaint," Ellie said gently.

"Yes, of course! *Many a quaint and curious…curious…"*

"Volume," Ellie offered.

"Volume of…" he paused. "Let me start again. Isn't that the damndest thing, it escapes me," he muttered, his face bloated and shiny.

"That's all right, Pete, really it is. You don't have to," Ellie said softly, stroking his arm.

"Yes, I do. Let me do it! I'm gonna do it correctly." His eyes started welling up.

"Pete, can you help me with something in the office?" Cora quickly asked.

After they left, Ellie turned to Minnie. "Is Pete not well?"

"A lifetime of drinkin' will do that to you." She sighed. "Your mama has been really patient with him, Ellie."

"That's good to know. Now, if she'd just be a little more patient with me."

Minnie put her arm around the new teacher's shoulders. "Give her time, Ellie. Just give her time."

* *

September had arrived, and within three days' time, the start of South Benton's school year. At Madam Ana's, a fine cornbread breakfast with a slab of bacon filled stomachs and heartened outlooks. Ellie noted even her mother seemed peaceful. According to the general store owner, the finest French dress materials were easier than ever to order and the thought of making up the newest *haute coutour* fashions for Ellie practically made her hum.

"Now, Ellie, dear, did you sew in those weights like I asked you to?" Cora asked, serving up a large portion of cornbread. Ellie rolled her eyes, as Minnie paused mid-bite.

"What in the world are you talking about, Sis?" the older madam asked.

"Weights, Auntie. I had to sew in weights on the bottom of my hem, in case a wind picks up and blows my skirt up," Ellie answered, sighing.

Turning to Cora, Minnie crossed her arms. "This is a joke, right?"

"Of course not. *Harper's Bazaar* claims real ladies should do this."

"Well, I don't give a *hoot* about that magazine. Pardon me, I mean your bible. For God's sake, Cora. *Weights?* What's next?"

"Now, Minnie, you must understand," Cora said, shaking her index finger. "If Ellie is back here, she has to maintain some decorum, unlike the girls and…"

Minnie laughed. "And me?"

"I didn't say that. I only meant…"

All of a sudden, Marlena entered the kitchen, holding a piece of paper in one hand.

"Mrs. Cora, Miss Minnie? Some feller outside gist gave this to me. Said to make sure it got to you both," she announced.

Cora grabbed the notice, and reading it through, handed it over to Minnie. "Oh, my God, it can't be true!"

"What? *What?*" Minnie asked, perusing the sheet herself. "My goodness." She shook her head. "I guess your dream is coming true, Sis!" she remarked, chuckling.

"It sure is. Imagine that. Buffalo Bill in Omaha. Who would have thought?" Cora's eyes sparkled as her face stretched into a broad grin.

"Glad to see you happy, Cora," Minnie said, adding softly, "Finally."

She turned to her niece. "Ain't that right, Ellie?"

Ellie nodded vehemently. Maybe now her mother would have something else to occupy her time instead of nitpicking with her on every little detail of her life.

CHAPTER FIVE
Taming All Devils: 1883

"By the time I count to fifty, you *know* what I'm gonna do!" Ellie called out, cupping her hands over her eyes and listening to her students scatter. Ever since she had introduced this game two weeks before, even the unruliest scamps had begun to cooperate in class.

Next came her slow 'one-two-three-four-five count.' Instantly, several of the older students began tugging helpless five- and six-year-olds along with them, carrying the littlest ones on their backs so they could squeeze into the best, secret spots in the school yard. Stifling their giggles, the most unlikely companions ran hand in hand. Even the meanest one of all, Joshua, Judge Endicott's son, had scooped up a fallen girl in his path, gently promising her a good place to hide.

"Fifty! Here I come, ready or not!" Ellie declared, beginning her search. "Now, where could they all be?" She projected her voice, much like Sarah Bernhardt emoting on stage back east. "Are they here?" She mocked-searched, stooping down next to the old, mildewed well.

Slight giggles.

"Are they behind the outhouse?" she asked, ignoring a hiccup followed by a collective "Sssshhh!"

"Well, are they…" she started.

Behind her a distinguished man in a three-piece suit and a silk cravat loudly cleared his throat.

She looked up. "Hello, and you are?"

"Mr. Townsend from the South Benton School Committee," he announced, displaying all the earmarks of the northeastern haughtiness she had been so anxious to leave. "Now, what is going *on* here? Is this not a school for learning?"

"Of course, it is," she said, smoothing her skirt and attempting forbearance. "We're just taking a little break to play Hide 'n Seek."

"Might I remind you this is supposed to be only for the edification and modification of the students?"

Edification and modification, indeed. "Of course, Mr. Townsend."

He straightened his cravat and turned to walk away.

"Mr. Townsend, we really do need more books."

He turned around slowly. "Feel free to bring that little matter up in front of the committee."

"When will that be, pray tell?" Ellie asked, lifting up her chin.

"Believe me, you'll be hearing from them soon." He looked her up and down, then over at the assembling students. "*Very* soon."

After he left, some students clustered around her, patting her on her shoulders and asking her when they could finish the game. Her answer was a simple sigh and a "Not now." So back they all marched into the school, making sure they rubbed their dust-encrusted boots on the doormat Ellie had provided, and settling down at each one's desk, began their afternoon lessons.

That evening, as Ellie fumed about Mr. Townsend, Cora was humming. Lamps, tables, and counters were cleaned with quick, haphazard strokes, each swipe never truly meeting its mark. Finally, she stopped in front of the recent notice she had so prominently displayed in the main parlor.

COME ONE, COME ALL!!!!
Buffalo Bill's Wild West Show
Coming to Omaha
In Four weeks!

"You can die happy now." Minnie laughed, standing next to her.

"Stop. I know you're just as thrilled as I am," Cora countered.

Minnie nodded and winked. "Yup, it sure is exciting. They say there's nothing like it."

"Nothing like what?" Ellie asked.

"Buffalo Bill's Wild West Show," Cora and Minnie rang out

simultaneously.

"Oh, that. That'll be nice for you, Mama," she said with a slight giggle.

"What's so funny?" Cora asked.

"I remember seeing all those Buffalo Bill novels hidden under the bed years ago."

"*What?*" Cora crossed her arms over her chest.

Grinning, Ellie winked at her aunt. "I guess I was a curious child."

Minnie chuckled. "And obviously a clever one at that."

Ellie nodded. "I'll leave you two ladies with Buffalo Bill. As for me, I'm going to bed with Charles Dickens."

* *

The new schoolteacher sat directly across from the school committee in one of her most staid dresses: high collared, gingham-printed, no bustle, no adornments. Opposite her in rigid formation, seven men and three women had assembled on one side of a long table, somber, watchful. Mr. Townsend was shuffling papers officiously, and one of the women had a nervous tick in her right eye.

Mr. Townsend looked up at the teacher facing them. "Miss Dolan, I have seen firsthand your little play methods, and I must say I was *not* impressed. We offered you this position based on your school's reputation and your glowing recommendations. What do you have to say for yourself, young lady?"

Her back turned ramrod straight. "With all due respect, Mr. Townsend, you did indeed see my 'play' methods, but that was all it was. Perhaps if you had stayed longer, you would have witnessed my learning methods as well."

Murmurs rippled down the table.

"Besides," she continued, "due to the inauspicious parade of overly strict, incompetent teachers your committee had previously employed, I decided to win over these students' trust with a few harmless games."

"Do you dare to," sputtered a man behind the plaque labeled Judge Endicott.

"Mr. Townsend," she interrupted, ignoring the judge, "when you were at the school, I believe you asked me to bring up the matter of new books. Perhaps having better resources would enhance my learning methods."

Silence.

"Yes, books," he mumbled, as she pulled out a folded piece of paper.

"Here is my invoiced list for necessary books for the classroom. I'll read it to you now:

Stories of Greece and Rome
Illustrated Bibles
Arabian Nights
Goethe's poems
The Life of Thomas Franklin
Shakespeare
Spenser, Coleridge, Burns, and Shelley
The Encyclopedia of Britannica

"And by the way, I took the liberty of ordering them a few weeks ago. According to the telegram I just received, they are due tomorrow on the noon mail coach," she added, handing the list over to them.

Mr. Townsend cleared his throat. "Impressive list, I must say, but…"

"On whose orders?" Judge Endicott's mouth smacked closed like a snapping turtle.

"My own, sir. I happen to know what's needed."

"This is *not* acceptable, Miss Dolan," inserted a rather plump woman in a broad-brimmed, black-feathered hat sitting next to the judge. "You should have requested these books in writing."

"Indeed. Thank you very kindly. I'll certainly know that for the next time around," Ellie answered, rising. "Please do forgive me, ladies and gentlemen, I need to go home now to help with supper."

Judge Endicott stood up. "Miss Dolan, before you go, hear me out. It appears I shall be attending school tomorrow with my son, Joshua. Make no mistake about this visit. If indeed, I find your techniques as bad as our colleague here claims, I shall send you back to New York myself."

"And I'll be accompanying you, my dear," agreed the black-hatted Mrs. Endicott. "After all, we did all take a chance on the daughter of a…"

"Yes, enough said," the judge muttered to his wife, with a wave of his hand. He then turned to face the committee and Ellie. "You may expect a full report of Mrs. Endicott's and my visit tomorrow," he ended, as he gathered up his papers and stormed out, his wife trying hard to keep up with him.

* *

The next day, after pushing their son Joshua toward the school grounds, the couple stayed out of sight behind a large bush to observe. The school bell was clanging, parents were busy giving directives to their children for the day, and Ellie was greeting each student with a smile and an encouraging word. Girls in pinafores and boys sporting knickers, knee-high socks, and black boots all bobbed their heads enthusiastically, as they proceeded to file up the wooden steps and enter the front door.

Both Endicotts continued watching as their irascible boy, the one various servants had left over, took off his hat, nodded to Ellie, wiped his hands on his knickers, rubbed his boots on a large mat, and guided two of the younger children inside.

Mrs. Endicott turned to the judge. "Well, I never..."

"Hmm," he said. "Let's wait another five minutes before entering. Catch her in her act, so to speak."

"Yes, dear. Good idea." She adjusted her new bonnet and fingered her top two buttons. That morning she had chosen her most dignified outfit for the occasion, aiming for respect and indeed, some intimidation. After all, this girl, this upstart, the daughter of a whorehouse madam, for goodness sake, had *not* been her first choice by any stretch of the imagination. But after reading the girl's high-end school's many glowing letters of recommendations, her husband had been sold.

Judge Endicott entered first. Then, at a respectable distance, Mrs. Endicott followed him in, more than expecting the worst. Just inside the doorway, they stood together, stock still, surveying the room. The walls exploded with ABC charts, grammar rules, famous quotations, and student papers. The students themselves were concentrating on their journals, all except Joshua, who stood at the front of the room, assisting Ellie, his face calm, peaceful, purposeful.

Ellie glanced over at the visitors and without speaking, nodded, then pointed to several empty chairs at the back of the room. No announcement of their presence, no recognition of their societal stature.

"Now, class, who remembers what we discussed yesterday?"

Hands shot up.

"Joshua?" she asked.

"Yes, we talked about different continents and the oceans separating them."

"Very good, Joshua. Now, who can remember some of the oceans mentioned?"

Students clamored for Miss Dolan to choose them.

She smiled calmly, reminded them that shouting out didn't always get good results, and called on one timid little girl on the far end of the back row. The child's face was dirtier than most, and her hair, obviously not brushed that morning, contained flecks of dried leaves in it, but when she gave her soft answer, Ellie clapped her hands and praised her as if she had just solved the most difficult mathematical problem imaginable. The girl sat up a little taller and beamed.

Next, Ellie brought their attention to the chalkboard where she had written assignments in ascending grade level order. In her hand, was a small pewter bell, and as she jingled it, the students instantly took their cue. They opened up their desks, pulled out their pencils and leafing through their new journals, began their school work, as Ellie circulated around the room, scrutinizing each student's writing, quickly correcting it, and ending each conference with a gentle pat on the shoulder.

Joshua suddenly stood up. To his parents' amazement, he made his way over to his teacher, and asked as clear as a bell, "May I be your teacher's aide again this week? I surely would enjoy that."

She gave him a fast nod, and without further ado, he strode over to the younger grade levels. There, he bent down next to each young student, his voice patient, giving. Apparently, his efforts were not wasted. After he finished helping each young boy or girl, he or she would gaze up at him with nothing less than total adoration.

The Endicotts stared at each other in stunned silence.

* *

That night, Madam Ana's parlor was packed and buzzing. Cowboys coveted their whiskey shot glasses as if they were precious jewels, regulars in their bowlers and vests were slapping each other on the back, and the doves intermingled throughout, stroking arms, and sidling up against any man deemed a potential customer. In the middle of the soirée sat a couple of strangers talking loudly, and as their volume increased, the entire room soon stilled, everyone giving these men their rapt attention.

Hailed from the Buffalo Bill's Wild West Show, they described a few of the acts that would be offered and how this high-toned spectacle was sure to fetch audiences the likes of which no one had ever seen before.

"No doubt it'll also fetch a pretty penny for Buffalo Bill Cody," Minnie commented when they had finished.

Cora, who had been 'oohing and ahhing' off to one side, took over the floor. She cupped her hand around her mouth like a megaphone.

"And there you have it, ladies and gentlemen. Our next excursion, on to Omaha in just a few weeks," she announced.

Cora noticed Ellie enter, just as the cheers became deafening.

One of the Wild West Show men stood up and called out, "Wait! There's more."

Everyone shifted toward him.

"And as fer our horses?" he began, "why, you ain't never seen what a horse kin do 'til you see them in our show, and it's all 'cause of our bronco buster! His name's Brett Parker, and he's the best horse trainer there is, no doubt 'bout it."

"Ellie," Cora beamed, clapping her hands. "Isn't this the most exciting thing in the world?"

Seeing her mother's flushed face, Ellie smiled. "It *is* exciting—for you, Mama."

It was like the time she had snapped at her girlhood friend, Charlene, who had bragged about getting an 'A' on a paper when Ellie got an 'A-'. The second the words slipped out of her mouth, she knew she'd made a mistake.

Cora's eyes darkened. "It *is* exciting, Ellie, not just for me but for everyone else in the room, am I right?" She swiveled toward the crowd.

A stillness hung over the room for several seconds, broken only by a single cough from Pete.

The Wild West Show cowboy cleared his throat. "As I was sayin', that trainer, Brett Parker is his name, well, he kin git a horse that's chute crazy 'n startin' to break in two, then turn him 'round to be gentle as a lamb. He's a miracle worker, that's fer sure."

"Amen to that!" his friend concurred, reaching for his last swig before following the various customers drifting off leisurely into the cool night air.

Meanwhile, Cora and Minnie set into motion their closin' up routine. Glasses were collected and put into soapy water, chairs were repositioned, the settee primed, and finally, lamp wicks were extinguished, using either a quick puff of breath or a two-calloused finger snuff out.

"Mama," Ellie said, gently placing her hand on her mother's arm. "I was wondering if you would like to come with me tomorrow to pick up my books.

They're due to arrive on the Omaha mail stagecoach, and I know how much you enjoy seeing what else arrives. Maybe a gazette or those dress patterns you love so much?"

Cora nodded. "Perhaps. Let's see how I feel in the morning. Good night, Ellie. Sleep well."

A good night's rest faired well with Cora. By early morning, she and Minnie were calmly eating a hearty breakfast of biscuits, eggs, and ham when Ellie wandered into the kitchen.

"Ellie, my girl. Looks like I'm coming with you and your mama this mornin'," Minnie said, her mouth stuffed with food. One look from Cora, and she dabbed her lips with a fresh linen napkin before taking another sip of coffee.

"That's just fine—a family outing," Ellie answered, looking over at Cora. "Excellent breakfast, Mama."

They were, as Pete often claimed, a collective force to be reckoned with. Cora, with her new elegant parasol, Minnie, slap-dashed into whatever dress was handy, and Ellie, in one of her teaching dresses, her hair swept up into a soft, bun, two long wisps framing her face completed the trio.

The grimy red and black Wells Fargo & Co. Overland Stage coach, with its tarnished yellow wheels, dusty front boot, rusted out luggage and cargo rack, and broken running lamps, had seen better days, yet that was of small consequence to the eager crowd, anxiously waiting for their packages.

Seeing the three of them approach, Mr. Crowe, the driver, tipped his hat.

"Why, good morning ladies. Mrs. Cora, Miss Minnie, Miss Ellie. What're you here for?"

"My books, Mr. Crowe, my books. I told you about them a few days ago, remember?"

His brow wrinkled. "I do remember you tellin' me that, but I don't recall seein' any box marked 'books' on this load. Sorry."

"That can't be! I received a telegram from the book company saying they would be on this very coach. They *must* be here!"

She leaned into the coach's back and started shifting packages.

"Whoah, *whoah*, Miss Ellie! Please don't do that."

The schoolmarm didn't even slow down. "I'm sorry, I need those books. I'll just take another minute or so."

"Ellie, please," Cora warned, glancing at a couple of well-dressed women in their fine, 'Lilly toque' hats.

"Now, what's in these burlap bags? Look! Here they are."

Mr. Crowe cleared his throat, as Ellie pulled out two rope-tied piles of books from the bag. Clutched against her side, she couldn't resist running one finger over the various books' edges.

"Double-double, toil and trouble, Fire burn and Caldron bubble," came a deep, male voice next to her. Looking up, she took a catch breath. Two of the darkest slate-blue eyes she had ever seen were boring a hole into her.

Minnie laughed. "Ah, there's an educated man in our midst, and it ain't even Pete."

She thrust out her hand to him, introduced her sister, and while they performed a round of introductions, Ellie snagged a second look at him. With his shoulder length dark brown hair and clean-shaven face, he appeared handsome, intelligent even, but his broad shoulders and large gnarled hands read rough, like he was no stranger to a hard day's work.

Now, why would someone like that know Shakespeare?

"Yes, this is my niece, Ellie Dolan," Minnie started, as he took the bundles from Ellie and offered her his hand.

"Miss Dolan? Pleased to meet you. By the way, I admire your determination. My name's Brett. Brett Parker."

The miracle-working broncobuster she'd heard about the night before. She outstretched her gloved hand. "Nice to meet you." Their hands stayed connected for another beat or two, until Ellie heard Minnie chuckle and Cora sniff.

"I've heard about you, Mr. Parker," she managed finally, withdrawing her hand.

"All lies," he answered with a wink.

Ellie tossed out a sudden loud, unladylike laugh. "Undoubtedly," she bantered, taking back her books and noticing a few lines crinkling around his eyes. "You are here to pick up something today?"

"Yup. A bridle bit for the horse I'll be training."

"And where will you be doing that?" Minnie asked.

"I'm stayin' in a room at Mr. Hanson's stable, so I can work there every morning, at least 'til the show starts. Then, it's whatever is needed for the other horses."

"So, what's your official title, Mr. Parker?" Cora inquired, as Ellie and Minnie both shook their heads.

"Title? Hmm. Not exactly sure, ma'am. Some say wrangler, some broncobuster. For me, I guess I just know how to train horses, is all."

"Well, good-day to you, Mr. Parker. I wish you the best of luck," Cora said.

He turned to Ellie. "You leaving as well?"

Glancing down at the ground, she measured her next words. "I suppose we are."

"Sure hope to see you again," she thought she heard him say softly, but she wasn't sure. She was too busy being pulled away by her mother and listening to her pulse beat up into her ears.

Around the corner, in front of the hardware store, Minnie started the conversation Ellie was already thinking about. "Now, *that* was a cool oasis in the middle of a desert."

"If you like that rough, cowboy type," Cora remarked. Turning to her daughter, she added, "You could do better."

"He quoted Shakespeare, Mama," Ellie said softly.

Minnie looked at her niece, smiled, and shook her head. "She's a goner," she sang as low as a baby's lullaby.

Just then, several of the more 'respectable' women in town approached them from across the street. Carefully lifting up their dress edges to avoid the hard packed dirt, their bonnet steamers fluttered in the breeze, and their calfskin gloves, most probably direct from England, lent an elegant air. Ellie noticed her mother instantly turn to study the store windows, and Minnie's spine arch backward in a defiant gesture.

"You are Miss Ellie Dolan, are you not?" one of the ladies said to Ellie, performing an ever so slight curtsey.

"Why yes, I am. And you are?"

"I am Mrs. Burnside, and these are my friends, Mrs. Wright and Mrs. Pollock."

"Pleased to make your acquaintances, ladies. This is my mother, Cora Dolan, and my aunt, Minnie Dolan," she announced, politely trying to ignore Cora's slit eyes and Minnie's one raised eyebrow.

The women did their best, but their disdainful faces were transparent. It was clear Ellie was the only one they were anxious to meet.

"Miss Dolan, I have to tell you, nowadays my son is ever so excited about attending school." Mrs. Burnside began.

"Yes, the same with my daughter, Millicent," Mrs. Wright said. "Now, she practically leaps out of bed first thing in the morning!"

Mrs. Pollock chimed in. "Yes. Might I add that you are nothing short of miraculous! A true credit to our town."

Miracle worker, like the broncobuster? "Thank you, kindly. I must say, your children are a pleasure to teach. So smart, so capable," Ellie added sincerely, yet knowing full well the effect of her words.

The three women, puffed up like peacocks, chortled proudly, nodded to her, gave half-nods in the general direction of her aunt and mother, and moved on. As they sauntered away, the three Dolans stood and watched. All of a sudden, Minnie and she doubled over in unison, trying to suppress their cackles, but Cora remained quiet, drifting back in time:

> *She had felt so happy, so proud to be out in the town on a Saturday morning, arm-in-arm with Madam Ana. Up ahead a carriage jostled down the street toward them, its windows dusty, its wheels and underbelly mud-splattered. Just as it stopped in front of them, one of the female passengers leaned out of the window and caught sight of Mrs. Ana. Instantly the inside curtains dropped down with a light thunk.*
>
> *"Why did the curtains go down?" Cora asked.*
>
> *Mrs. Ana's body turned rigid. "Because they don't vant to see me and my place of biznees, child."*
>
> *"Why in the world not?"*
>
> *The madam looked down into the confused girl's face and gently stroked her hair. "You're too young now, kotik. I vill tell you ven you're older..."*

* *

That night in the parlor, the pace was slow; the mood, curiously somber. All in all, it had been a sluggish day and night. A lot of the cowboys had wandered over to a local horse auction, several of the 'regulars' had chosen to stay home with their wives and children, and the few 'potentials' had fallen flat. The girls, bored and frustrated, had taken to playing cards and lapping up real whiskey, not the usual sugared tea they used with clients, while Minnie stayed in the kitchen amongst the pots and pans, thinking up menus for the following week.

"Is Ellie already in bed?" Cora asked Pete as she straightened up.

"I do believe she said she wanted to retire extra early so she could get up at the crack of dawn. The early bird catches the worm, so to speak."

"But why so early? Perhaps she has papers to correct."

"What is it, Cora? Between you and me, you seem a bit long in the mouth. *Such a blue inner light from her eyelids outbroke, You looked at her silence and fancied she spoke.*"

She looked over at him. "And who wrote that?"

He patted the settee pillows and motioned her over. "Elizabeth Barret Browning. Now, sit, and tell me what's on your mind."

She took a seat beside him and gave out a long sigh. "I've been thinking recently."

"That's good."

"Well, no, not really. I've been thinking about Thomas. I mean, I sometimes still wonder why…I mean, I wonder what he's up to now," she finished, unable to ask her real question out loud. Why had he abandoned her right when she needed him so badly?

"Ah, Cora, my dear, dear girl. You know, after you had your, well, you know." He started to sniff.

"Oh, Pete. I've *never* blamed you for what happened."

He looked at her for a second and sighed. "You're a truly good girl, then. Better than most. As I was saying, I heard somewhere that when Thomas signed up, he was assigned to an outfit that ended up fighting the Texas Rangers. Now, to me, there's no fiercer group than those fellows. Word came out Thomas' troop got wiped out. In other words, I'm certain he never made it, Cora." He paused. "I'm truly sorry."

She dabbed at one eye with her embroidered handkerchief.

Putting his arm around her, he gave her a light peck on her cheek.

"Time to move on, Cora, honey," Minnie said softly from the doorjamb. "Time to move on from ghosts."

CHAPTER SIX
1883: Different Encounters

By the time Ellie made her way over to the stables, the sun was well above the horizon. That morning, a couple of the doves had remarked how the chilly air signaled their summer might be ending sooner rather than later, but she firmly believed in the age-old adage, "only time will tell." With that phrase in mind, she approached the complex of barns. A horse whinnied nearby, and from its loud presence, she figured it must be stationed in the main corral, not holed up in one of the warm, snug barns.

Leaning against the main corral's fence, a lone male figure stood with his back to her. Immediately, she recognized Brett from his broad stance and the same hat he had worn the day before, but within seconds, the horse he was observing also captured her full attention. A magnificent looking palomino, it was one of the prettiest she'd ever seen. Its movements were jerky, almost frenzied, as it shook his head and pawed the dirt with its right front hoof, and when Brett climbed up onto the corral's fence, she leaned in, eyeing both man and beast carefully. For the longest time, the broncobuster sat there on top of the wood railing, and she wondered if he was even aware of her presence, but he never turned around, so she stayed put and watched, curious.

All of a sudden, Brett dropped down into the corral and the Palomino backed up with a loud snort, its ears twitching slightly and pointed so far back, they almost lay flat against his head. Ellie waited to see what the trainer's first move would be as he leaned against the fence assessing the horse, his hat cocked off to one side, his right hand cupping his eyes against the rising sun.

Her only memory of someone breaking a horse had not been pleasant. Ropes, whips, and a wide sycamore stick had been integral parts of the trainer's equipment, as he lashed out at a wild mustang. To this day, she could still remember the bronc fighter's red, blustery face, the horse's wide-eyed terror, and how, at the time, she had let out a sharp cry.

Her stomach now in knots, she steeled herself against what was sure to follow and waited for the worst. But Brett surprised her. Approaching the golden horse bare handed, he alternated between soft clicking sounds and "hey fella, hey fella" with long pauses in-between. Every time he saw the horse's ears curl forward, he would take another step. If they flipped backward, he would pause his stride. Forward. Stop. Forward. Stop. He advanced, adjusting his pace as if there were at least forty-eight hours in a day.

Finally, he simply stood next to the horse, humming some song in a low, seductive timbre. When the horse snickered, he did the unthinkable. He leaned against the palomino's side. No commands, no hits, not even a rolled-tongue clicking sound, just the gentle pressure of his body on the horse's belly. Slowly, he placed both his palms on its side, then inched them up toward its neck. The horse's ears stayed vertical, so he ventured further. He stroked its neck repeatedly, until the horse tossed out a big sigh. With that, Brett slowly heaved his body perpendicularly across the horse's back. Then, although there was no protest, he slipped back down again to wait for any negative reactions. When none came, he hoisted himself up again, only this time, he used some clicks and grabbed a hold of the mane. When the horse's ears shifted backwards, he lowered himself onto the ground again and waited. But the horse tried to nudge him tentatively, so he hoisted himself onto the horse's back again and held onto the mane.

"That's why Buffalo Bill Cody hired him, you know," came a soft, feminine voice from behind Ellie.

"I beg your pardon?" Ellie turned to face a pretty young woman dressed in a plain, no-frills beige dress topped off by a cowboy hat.

"He sure is bone-seasoned," the woman added. "Why, everyone knows he's the best in the business." Her smile was as infectious as her smooth, ladylike voice.

"Business?"

Her chuckle was reminiscent of delicate chimes. "Why, the horse wrangling business. I wouldn't have any other feller take care of my horses, I can tell you that."

"Interesting. Are you part of the new Wild West show?"

"Yes, as a matter of fact, I am."

"How about that! What do you do for the show, might I ask?"

"I guess I do a little target shooting." Her little, genteel wink was even more infectious, and as Ellie extended her hand, Brett came over.

"Done for the day, Brett?" the woman asked.

"Yes, no need to push him any further," he answered, his eyes locked on Ellie as he tipped his hat.

The woman noticed his new focus. "Planning on using that big corral up on the ridge Bill got for you?"

"Yes," he answered, nodding. "As soon as the horses are ready to walk around and try some tricks, I'll take 'em up there. That's where I'll do the heavy trainin' while we're here."

"What big corral? Where?" Ellie asked.

The woman and Brett pointed collectively toward a ridge in the distance.

"That's the Ambrose place," Ellie said. "Folks say they got the best spread during the 1856 Land Rush, but frankly, I'm surprised they offered it to you, even for an hour, much less a week or two."

"Some money did exchange hands. That always helps, doesn't it?" the woman laughed and extended her hand. "Annie's the name. Annie Oakley."

Ellie gaped at the woman. "*The* Annie Oakley? My mother is your biggest fan! Isn't *that* a coincidence?"

"Well, ladies, I do have to get this horse fed." Brett again tipped his hat, his eyes still centered on Ellie.

"His patience is remarkable, I must say," Ellie said casually as he walked away. Inside, she wasn't so calm. Goodness gracious. Those eyes. That face. Those shoulders.

"This is nothing," Annie said. "Just wait and see what else he does. Every morning he'll be out here, getting that horse ready to be one of our best."

"I don't think I will be able to be here to see it," Ellie replied, her breath still a little shaky.

"Oh?"

"Teaching. I teach every morning."

Annie laughed. "At five or six in the morning? My goodness, your school starts earlier here than where I come from. All I can say is, don't miss him; it's a sight to see, it truly is."

"Perhaps," Ellie murmured glancing off toward the barn before she wandered off.

* *

Sure enough, the next morning as Ellie nestled into a secret spot behind a hollowed out peephole, Brett had already begun his training. Hitched under his arm was some sort of roped bridle, so crude it looked more like a child's toy. When he approached the horse, he made a different sound from the day before, but she knew he had earned the horse's trust because it remained tranquil.

Ellie expected him to toss the bridle over the horse's neck next. That's what she would do, but it didn't happen. Instead, he looked up toward the sky, clicking and muttering, with a slight hold on the horse's mane.

The horse angled back toward him, but he ignored the move. He simply patted the horse's neck and began cooing, as the horse blew air out of its nostrils and eyeballed him, as docile as a branded cow. Again, Brett looked skywards, this time raising his left hand, and while the animal stood idle, waiting, he quickly pitched the bridle over the horse's head and clamped the roped bit around his mouth.

"There, boy; there, boy," he coaxed, still gentle, still soothing.

Ellie grinned. A little psychological distraction goes a long way. He fascinated her.

Once the rope was on, Brett had some control. If the horse turned away from him, he softly guided him back toward him by pulling the rope in the opposite direction. Over and over again, the broncobuster repeated this move, still patient, but more and more in charge. With the sun now well settled in the sky, she quietly turned and tiptoed away, her mind filled not with lesson plans or students, but with the unique techniques she had just witnessed. And who performed them.

The next morning, he put the bridle over the horse's neck in no time and within seconds the horse was being led around the corral as if he were the wrangler's well-seasoned stud. Having learned Brett's slow patterns, her eyes now strayed over to the rider's movements—strong, confident, yet always low-key. He stroked the horse's neck as he slowly hoisted himself onto its bare back, humming his songs. The horse gave a loud snort, and Ellie froze, but the ears were still forward, so she figured all was well.

By the fourth morning, a full saddle and bridle were in place along with plenty of "Good fella, good boy." She was tempted to lean out from her hiding place, but didn't. Better not to let him know she was there, she reasoned. But when she took out Pete's old watch and read six forty-five, she quickly gathered her wrap and stepped out of the barn to hurry away.

"Miss Dolan. Hope after all this, you'll at least see this horse at the show," he called out, getting down from the horse.

She pivoted slowly around and faced him. "I didn't mean to bother you."

He sauntered over, removed his hat, and stood a mere two feet from her. "No need to explain. You watching me's all right. More than all right," he added, his blue eyes drawing her in.

Fiddling with her collar, she cleared her throat. "Your patience is admirable, Mr. Parker. Pray tell, how do you manage it when other bronco busters don't seem to be able to?"

"I suppose to me, it's all about the horse figuring out if and when I can ride him or not. Some things are just not meant to be pushed. Kind of like people, you know?"

She couldn't help smiling. "Like people? Which people would you be referring to?"

His hat replaced, he tipped two fingers to it and before he turned away, his wink instantly lodged itself under her skin.

The audacity! How cocky he is with women! Then, without warning, "Oh, dear Lord," escaped her lips.

* *

The next morning she decided a solo ride by herself would be just the right thing. No need to give him the impression of being so available.

The sorrel knew her signals by heart, and as they galloped through the countryside, she soon forgot about the horseman. She had so many things to be grateful for: the students, Minnie, Pete, the ladies, and most of all, as difficult as she was sometimes, her mother, Cora.

Riding full force, the wind biting her cheeks and lips, she was suddenly transported back in time:

> *Oh, please, Mama." She tried one last time as the driver climbed aboard the stagecoach and grabbed the reins. "Please don't send me*

away!"

The last three words were swallowed up by the click-click of the driver, the coach shifting, the team of horses snorting, and the wheels starting their slow grind out of town.

Confused by its rider's lack of guidance, the sorrel slowed to a light canter. Ellie, her face streaked with tears and paying little attention to their path, didn't notice the upcoming low tree branches directly in their path. Before she knew what was happening, she was swiped off the horse, and her mount, catching its hoof in a slight hole, fell headlong onto the ground.

She lay still in the dirt, dizzy and disoriented, as she listened to the high-pitched squeal of the horse. Turning her head, she could see it lying on its side, groaning, its right leg crumpled under its left, making her instantly fear the worst—a broken limb.

Distant galloping hooves grew louder, becoming thunderous as it neared. Someone called out in a worried voice, "Miss Dolan! Are you all right?"

Looking up, she saw Brett jump down from his steed and race over to her. As he knelt down on the ground beside her, she was surprised to see such concern painted across his face as he examined her.

"Are you hurt? Can you move?" he uttered so tenderly, it made her blush.

"I'm all right but my horse..." she choked, her eyes welling up.

"I'll see to him, but first, you. Can you sit up?"

She took his outstretched hands, and when she let him pull her into a sitting position, their roughness felt surprisingly warm and comforting.

"My horse. Please, my horse," she whispered.

"All right. Stay where you are," he directed, before heading toward the half snorting, half neighing, red mount.

The sorrel was quiet now, its eyes half-closed, its nostrils flaring with labored, uneven breaths. As Brett ran his hand over its legs to check for damage, it tried to nuzzle him until he touched the right leg. Then it let out another screech of pain. "There, fella, there, there," he soothed.

"Are you going to shoot it?" Ellie asked.

"Of course not! Why would you even *say* that?"

"Isn't that what people do when horses' legs get broken?"

He nodded. "Yep, they do. But look here," he said, pointing to the horse's rapidly swelling leg. "See? It's not broke, it's only sprained."

From out of his back pants' pocket he withdrew a bandana, and fetching his saddle canteen, first poured water over the cloth until it was fully soaked, then firmly tied it around the wounded leg.

He continued to stroke the horse for a few minutes before standing up. "That oughta stop the inflammation. We'll take this fella back with us to Mr. Hanson's stable where I can keep an eye on him. I'm also gettin' you into town to see a doctor."

"All right, thank you. And thanks about the horse."

"Well, we can't leave him here."

Visualizing her students waiting for her, she started to protest about not letting them know about her, but one look at his determined face, and she kept quiet. Her students would just have to wait. Drained, she allowed him to lift her up and cradle her for a couple of seconds before placing her carefully onto his horse's saddle and handing her the reins. Then, coaxing the sorrel up, he took those reins and slowly, slowly walked them all to town.

On the way back, every few minutes he'd pause and ask the same question. "How you doin'?" Then check the sorrel's leg.

She'd nod or hold her thumb up, but her mind was busy, thinking about how wonderful he was to the sorrel, and wondering if her unsupervised students would behave. She also thought about being snuggled up against his chest, and how sturdy his arms felt as he hoisted her atop of his horse.

"By the way, how did you know I was in trouble?"

He took his hat off and combed through his long hair with his fingers. "I was up on the ridge taking a short break when I happened to look down and see you. Thank goodness."

"Yes, thank goodness, and thank Mr. Ambrose for being greedy enough to rent his property to your boss."

They both laughed.

She commanded herself to speak, trying not to stare into his eyes for too long. "Can we at least go past the school so I can tell them there won't be any classes today?" she managed.

"Can I trust you not to change your mind and teach?"

"Yes, sir!" She gave him a slight soldier's salute.

No longer jovial, he stopped and placed his hand gently on her right boot. "Ellie, this is for your own good, and the good of your horse."

She hung her head. "I'm sorry. That was uncalled for. We'll head for the doctor and the stable. Thank you, Mr. Parker."

"Brett, please."

"Thank you, Brett. You've been very kind." She chuckled when he give her a thumbs up and extended a tiny smile.

That night was filled with bed rest and sharing compliments for her rescuer. As she lay under the covers, exhausted, Minnie and Pete gathered around, hailing the wrangler as a conquering hero.

Even Cora seemed grateful, although she couldn't resist saying, "I suppose he did act like a gentleman. Not bad for a cowboy."

"Remember, Mama, he's friends with Annie Oakley," Ellie murmured seconds before she fell into a much needed, sound sleep.

The next day Ellie was back at school, regaling her students all about her clumsiness and how being alert would have saved her, her horse, and everyone else a whole lot of trouble.

"Remember," she said, using her mother's mandate, "always expect the unexpected."

* *

"Miss Dolan, Miss Dolan, William just pulled one of my pigtails!"

Ellie shook her head. Lately, classroom decorum had fallen by the wayside. The children, once so obedient, so eager, now seemed endlessly needful of her undivided attention. Had she created monsters? She couldn't say. All she knew was these days she had trouble concentrating on anything. Her teaching, her homework corrections, her lesson planning, even her morning rides with the other horse, all seemed less important than they did before.

Minnie and Cora must have noticed the change, because the night before, they both had become quite vocal.

"You've fallen for that feller, I can *feel* it," Minnie declared, lining up shot glasses on top of the credenza.

Cora, her inventory list in hand, had scoffed. "Nonsense, it's the accident. Perhaps you should see the doctor again, Ellie. Don't you *dare* laugh," she snapped as Minnie chortled.

In the classroom, Ellie now drew her attention back to William, who was fully enjoying his power. But when he caught sight of his teacher moving up his aisle like a hurricane, he dropped the girl's pigtail and held up his hands like a train robbery victim. Much to the delight of his fellow classmates, he hollered, "I give up! I give up!"

"Now, William," Ellie stood over him and scolded, "this is not like you. What's gotten into you?"

All of a sudden, several children started yelling, "School's over! School's over!" pointing to the grandfather clock against the northeast wall.

Sighing, Ellie glanced over to the expensive gift that the grateful Judge and Mrs. Endicott had given her and nodded. School was indeed over. Were they so anxious to leave? Had she become like the other spinster schoolmarms they so detested? As they picked up their school bags and filed out, as much as she tried thinking of better lesson plans, the urge to not only check on the sorrel, but also to visit Brett in the stable's tackle room to thank him, flooded her like a greedy child clamoring for a new toy.

* *

Just shy of the stables, a good wind kicked up, a sure fire sign her lightweight shawl would be no match for the early evening's sting. Hugging the sheath closer, she entered the stables and called out his name. At first, all she could hear was the sound of horses in their stalls, snorting, pawing, and munching, and she hurried over to them to see how her horse was faring. He still had a light bandage wrapped around his leg, but the swelling had all but disappeared, and his spirits seemed high. She was stroking the sorrel's head and cooing when she heard a couple of bridle clicks.

Brett had entered the room, his opened shirt only partly covering his muscular chest.

"Ellie, excuse me," he said, buttoning up his shirt and tucking it into his pants as fast as he could. "I didn't expect you."

She stared at his upper torso for a couple of seconds, then focused on the floor. Crossing her arms over her chest, she shivered.

"You cold?" he asked.

"I'm all right," she answered automatically, but the trembling wasn't stopping.

He pulled his jacket off a nearby hook, stepped in close, and carefully draped it over her shoulders, her scent of rosewater reeling him in. Scouring her face, he waited for a sign, some sort of go-ahead, but her eyes darted sideways and her hands stayed molded against her body, so he took a pace back. She wasn't ready.

"I came to check on my horse, and to thank you again for the other day," she managed. Oh Lord, how pathetic.

He paused, gauging her a beat before moving in close again. He couldn't help it. Resting his large hands on her petite shoulders, he said, "No need for thanks, Ellie. I saw you in trouble and I acted, that's all. Well, that's not *really* all."

She offered a tiny half-smile, and he could feel her slackening under his hold. When she tilted her face up, it caught the early twilight's glow, softening her features. With her beauty so close, his breath became jagged, as he carefully angled her chin—and lips—toward his.

"Brett, we will need you to…oh, dear, I'm *truly* sorry." Annie's urgent voice turned apologetic.

Under his breath Brett muttered, "Dang," while Ellie fidgeted with his jacket, drawing it off her shoulders and handing it back to him.

"Miss Dolan, Brett, please don't mind me." Dipping her head, Annie scurried out the door.

"I suppose I should go," Ellie said.

"Wait, don't go yet," he urged, dropping his jacket onto the floor and reaching out for her right arm.

Inexperienced in these matters, she stood frozen, but like his horse wrangling, he surprised her. Leaning over and cupping her face with his hands, he bypassed her lips and kissed her softly on the cheek before letting her go. When she raised one eyebrow, he shrugged. "Had to kiss you at least once, didn't I?"

Her open laugh ricocheted off the stalls, as the horses looked up lazily to watch.

"Ellie, tomorrow's Saturday, so no school. Would you care to meet me up at the corral and get a preview of the horses' show steps? I'm sure you could use one of Annie's horses. We could take a ride together afterwards."

No longer fidgeting, she nodded, already looking forward to the next day.

* *

The same palomino that had been so wild, so raw, was now, inside of a week, prancing, cantering, sidestepping, and rearing up on cue. Once Brett and the horse trotted out, some of his additional techniques surfaced. Before each side step, he would draw the reins in using just one hand, not both, finessing the horse's head with a quick neck pat to guide its hooves, and when he reared up, no spurs were used. He simply leaned back in the saddle with his legs slightly forward, tapped on its rump once, and much like connecting dots on a triangle, the horse wondrously stood up only on its hind legs.

After a time, he gaited over to where Ellie was standing. "Ready for our ride?" he asked.

Their horses were given full rein. Still up on the ridge, they let them canter at a fast clip, then move into a full gallop, then back to a canter before slowing them down again to a controlled amble. As they walked side by side, they chatted about the nature of horses and people.

Taking in the scenery, Ellie remarked first, "It's such a beautiful day, isn't it?" She lifted her head up to soak in the full sun's warmth.

He watched her intently for a moment, then scanned the panoramic view stretched below them. "It sure is. Let's go down."

They singled out a shady area beneath a thick cluster of trees. A light stream was trickling nearby, and the breeze rustling through the leaves serenaded their ears. Their horses tied together, Brett extracted a rolled-up blanket from his saddle pack, and spreading it out, they both sat down a foot apart, drinking in their lush surroundings.

"*Shall I compare thee to a summer's day?*" the wrangler said softly.

She turned to him. "I'm really curious about something."

"What?"

"It's just that..." Being so near to him was disconcerting.

"Yes? As my mother would say, 'A penny for your thoughts.'"

"How come you know Shakespeare so well?"

He laughed. "For just a wrangler, you mean."

"I didn't mean any harm." She could feel her face warming by the second.

"Don't worry. No harm done. My ma used to read to me every night, is all. I kind of took to it, I guess." When he shrugged, she again noticed how broad his shoulders were.

"You would *definitely* get along fine and dandy with Pete," she said.

"Pete?"

"An old family friend who loves the poets. I was also wondering..."

"Something else on your mind?" Although his tone teased, his eyes were still intense.

She drew a deep breath. "I'm curious. I heard you were from the South, but I don't detect a strong accent."

He cocked his head. "Virginia. If your next question is whether my father fought for the Confederate cause or not, I can tell you right off, yes, he did."

Beet-red, she blurted out, "I didn't mean to pry." She looked down then up again. "Did he own slaves?"

"Not pryin' huh?" He laughed, then grew serious. "No, like most southern folk, we couldn't afford them, just horses. Just another misunderstanding from the North, I suppose."

"I really didn't mean anything by it. Just conversation," she muttered, touching his arm with the lightest of touches. "The war's over. I just wonder if that was where you fell in love with horses." His eyes felt like magnets, rendering her breath shaky.

"I suppose so," he answered. "Even when I was young I got all fired up around them, felt a kinship somehow. But you should understand that. It's like you and your books, and why you became a teacher."

She shook her head. "Actually, that wasn't my calling." Her eyebrows knitted. "No, I was sent away at too early an age because of my mother. She had this ridiculous idea her ladies, the 'doves,' might teach me too much."

He reached over and covered her hand. "Maybe your ma was just being protective. I respect that."

"But at what cost? A fine education back east hardly replaces a mother's love. And as for a father to talk to, that's an even darker story I found out about. No, I only had a mother who assumed I couldn't handle myself, so basically, she sent me away." A tear gathered in her right eye, threatening to slide down her cheek.

"Oh, Ellie," he murmured, leaning against her, shoulder to shoulder. "You're here now. No one's gonna hurt you, I promise."

When he pulled her against him, her first thought was how warm his chest and arms felt. "It's all right, it's all right," he whispered.

She could feel her body relaxing—her arms, her chest, her legs—as she melted into him. Involuntarily, she let out a loud sigh, so audible that the palomino standing next to the horse she had borrowed looked at them, then shook his head. Normally, she would laugh, but the thought of kissing Brett was what guided her, and as he turned her face around, she pressed her lips against his to render her first real kiss, ever.

The consummate wrangler, he understood timing versus nature. He met her lips full on but softly, tenderly, as he tried to downplay his male instincts. Within seconds he drew back long enough to ask, "You all right?" but his words were never voiced. He had seen her face—the half-closed lids, the parted mouth, the need to continue.

His embrace strengthened, his kiss intensified, and his hands started roaming over her back and her hips, drawing her into him as he battled the consequences in his mind. This was not simply a dove he could easily afford, or a saloon girl ready for a tryst; this was something different, possibly life altering.

"Ellie, we should stop, before…" he murmured, tilting back slowly.

He eyed her loosened, wispy hair, the rose circles spreading on her cheeks, her chest rising and falling as he shook his head.

"Brett. I never," she began, then stopped.

He clasped her hand. "Don't worry. I just think it's time for you to go home."

Their trip back to the stables seemed to last a week. Talking lightly about how he could get them ringside seats for the Buffalo Bill Wild West Show through Annie, he remained friendly as ever, even after he put the bridle and saddle away and gave the horses some feed. She quickly checked on the sorrel, and then let him take her back to Madam Ana's.

On the front porch, she was close to tears. "Brett, if I did anything wrong, please tell me. I'm not…I've never…"

"My God, Ellie! Is that what you thought?" He cradled her in his arms. "No, as a matter of fact, you did everything *right*. Wondrously right. I just had to stop before I…well, you know…" He half groaned. "Ellie, Ellie, you and your kisses are…what can I say?" An almost mischievous look came over him. *"Alack, there lies more peril in thine eye than twenty of their swords."*

"You're actually quoting *Romeo and Juliet*?" she smiled, somewhat restored. "So, I'm that powerful to you, huh?"

"Yes, especially when you tempt me." He started to angle in for another kiss, but hearing female chortles coming from inside, drew back. "I guess that means a good-night. I'll be seeing you soon," he added lamely, and stepping off the porch, disappeared into the night.

"Someone's got a new feller!" one of the doves teased as soon as she walked in.

"A new feller all right. And *what* a feller. He's a handsome devil, he is. Why, I'd bed him down faster than you can say Jack Rabbit!"

Soon, she was surrounded by a ring of doves dancing around her, pointing to her disheveled hair, poking at her bodice, and cackling hard.

"What's this nonsense I'm hearing?" Cora hissed, crossing over to her daughter and yanking her riding crop out of her hands. "Ellie, have you forgotten you were going to help me with one of the girl's legal papers this afternoon?"

"Sorry, Mama."

"Cora, Cora, let her be," Minnie broke in. "She's here now. Why, she just had some fun." She paused dramatically. "With a feller!"

Screams of laughter and a mock toast from Pete turned Cora's face dark. *"You* two," she snapped at them. "Where were you earlier when I needed your help?" Turning to the parlor's assembly, she ordered, "Remember everyone, we were gonna close early tonight."

The doves, Ellie, Pete, and the customers took one look at her and scattered.

"What's going on, Cora?" Minnie asked later, seeing her sister's nightly cleaning routine now done cavalry style—dishes clanged together, the credenza wiped down as if she were scrubbing laundry in a creek, the settee pillows plumped up like a pugilist throwing punches.

Just as she finished, a lone cowboy, one of the last to leave, collided with her, almost knocking her down.

"Oh, he's just had a little too much who-hit-John, is all," Minnie said, chuckling.

"*I'll* give him a little too much who-hit-John," Cora retorted, grabbing a broom and whacking the cowpoke on his rear. *Wham!* she smacked. "Get out! We don't want any more drunk cowboys in here!"

Stunned, he stumbled out onto the porch before falling face down into the street.

Cora stared at his inert body. "Just leave him alone. Serves him right," she snarled. Spent, she sank down on the settee. A light kiss on her cheek startled her and looking up, she saw Minnie sitting down beside her, an odd expression on her face.

"What's that for?" Cora asked.

"I just figured you could use a little love, that's all." Another quick peck on her sister's cheek, and she was gone, leaving Cora alone with her thoughts.

* *

No Dickens that night for Ellie. Snuggled up in bed, the lamp extinguished, she closed her eyes and smiled, stroking the satin comforter over and over as the wind increased its whispers and whooshes. She pictured Brett in his bunk at the stables in his long johns, perhaps completely barechested, as he read one poem after another. She tried to imagine the words he might be reading, but the only thing that came to mind was what the doves had told her so long ago:

"All I can say, Ellie, is when a man touches you there, it gets you all inflamed, like you want him to never stop touchin' you there, and other places, too."

"What other places, Becky?"

Susannah laughed. "Like your titties, for one thing, and your—"

Josephine leaned in. "Your snatchbox, your—"

Down the hall, in the room they still shared, Cora climbed into bed next to her gently snoring sister. The full moon was beaming in strips of light through the lightly banging shutters as she tried to think of all the things she should be grateful for. Her daughter was back home. Their establishment, now turning a fine profit. Her sister—her rock, her Blarney Stone—lying next to her. But as Minnie's snores grew more intense, Cora stared up at the ceiling, a single tear making its way down her cheek and onto her neck.

Damn you, Thomas.

CHAPTER SEVEN
Buffalo Bill and Beyond

Cora had never been so excited. At the first crack of dawn, she was in the parlor ready to go, dressed in one of her smartest travel outfits. By the time everyone else started preparing for their trip to Omaha, she had unfolded, read, and refolded their official invitation—signed by none other than Annie Oakley—at least ten times before it made its way into her purse.

"I see the envelope was addressed to Ellie, not me." She had initially pouted a little about that, then rethought it. A special invitation was a special invitation, after all. Brett had brought it over several nights before, reassuring them that they would all be treated 'right'—*more* than right, but even though her eyes sparkled when Brett mentioned that Buffalo Bill and Annie Oakley were inviting them all to dinner after the show, she had trouble concealing her annoyance at the messenger. No sooner had he closed the door on his way out, she voiced her thoughts.

"He must think he's mighty fine to be the deliverer of such a worthy invitation. After all, he's just a glorified cowboy. He's *not* on the same level as Annie Oakley, for goodness sake!"

"Cora, if you don't stop," Minnie warned, as Ellie threw up her hands and left the room.

The week before, after much discussion, Cora and Minnie decided that in order to diminish costs, most of the doves would be lodged at a slightly lower-end hotel down the street. But then Cora came up with a unique idea. To make the excursion even more exciting, why not create a lottery, to garner even more enthusiasm? That way, Ellie, Pete, and the two winners of their 'Wild West lottery' would all get to visit the Omaha Grand, where the sophisticates stayed at outrageous prices. Amidst bated breath and crossed fingers, the lottery took place late one night in their parlor, and when Marlena and Rosie won it, folks claimed their shrieks could be heard for several blocks.

As the sun slowly edged upwards, Cora double-clapped. "Let's get going, everyone," she announced, her voice at fever pitch. "It'll take us about two hours to get there."

Within minutes, the household was busy checking carpetbags, bringing the buggy around, and climbing into a neighbor's borrowed wagon. The temperature at a balmy sixty degrees helped. The trip went smoothly, until they hit Omaha and all the Wild West show traffic. Carefully maneuvering their doves into a slightly dingy hotel, the madams made sure they were all safely housed before continuing on to bigger and better things.

Registration at the Omaha Grand was an experience in and of itself. As soon as they entered the main lobby, they could see a young, stiff-collared, tight-suited clerk from behind the front desk give them the once-over, then appeared extraordinarily preoccupied with his paperwork. Up close, they were completely ignored until Minnie harrumphed, at which point he put down his pen to address no one else but Pete.

"I presume you have a reservation for your party?" he said.

"You presume right, sonny," Minnie replied, bristling.

Cora leaned against the counter. "Yes, we most certainly do. It's under the name Dolan."

The clerk wrinkled his nose at the two doves standing off to one side, then started quickly running one finger down the thick reservation ledger. "Let me see. McMillan, Swathmore, Markham, Smith, Cullen. No, I'm afraid I don't see Dolan."

"Do check again," said Cora, her gloved hand clamped over his, her voice like ice.

"Yes, I believe my friend, Miss Annie Oakley, made the reservation. *Do* check it again," Ellie chimed in.

"Miss Oakley? Let me see." He did a more thorough search this time, his finger slowly gravitating down the list. "Ah, here it is, reserved by a Miss Oakley and Mr. Butler. My, oh, my," he mouthed, ogling them with renewed respect.

Cora drew herself up, slightly irked by Ellie's statement. How *dare* Ellie mention only her knowing Annie! It's just not fair. She doesn't even care about Buffalo Bill, not the way Cora did.

Minnie cleared her throat. "And our room numbers are?"

Eyeing the doves, he paused. "I've put you on the second floor; rooms 210 – 214. But, one second."

He bent over the counter and whispered to Cora, "Excuse me."

"Yes, *now* what?" she replied, two fingers tapping triple time.

"Are they who I think they are?" He jerked his head toward the doves' general direction.

Festooned in their brightly colored satin dresses, boa-feathered wraps, and low-cut bodices, Marlene and Rosie stood by awkwardly, fidgeting with their purses and trying to look nonchalant. Upon first entering the lobby, the doves had already created a small sensation amongst the guests, especially from the men. The women—presumably their wives or mistresses—immediately set their noses up in the air and actively disregarded the entire South Benton entourage.

"They are *paying* customers. That's *all* you need to know, young man," Cora said, using her most autocratic voice. "Will it be necessary to speak to your superior?"

"No need, no need," the clerk sputtered, palm-slapping the counter bell. From out of nowhere, two bellhops instantly appeared, and in a matter of seconds, they were all ushered upstairs.

Traipsing through the hallway on the second floor, they admired the beautiful floral wallpaper, the long, lush carpet, and commented on how just a hint of lavender was lingering in the air. Halfway down the corridor, the bellhops opened a few doors for them, but it was just shy of Cora and Minnie's two-roomed adjoining suite that Rosie stopped and flung her arms around the younger madam.

"Mrs. Cora, you are always there for us. May God look kindly on you," she blurted out, wiping away a tear.

"Of course, Rosie, of course," Cora nodded, patting the girl's arm, but it wasn't until she and Minnie had entered their double rooms that she remarked, "A little help from God would be nice."

Closing the outer door to Cora's room, Minnie chuckled. "Amen to that."

Cora dropped her bag and surveyed their suite. Her room was the very epitome of elegance. Plush chairs, expensive carpets, ornate glass lamps, two brocade-covered settees, as well as large, mahogany desks made their jaws drop, but it was the elegant four-poster bed, covered in gold damask, that bowled her over. Cora immediately went over to it, and lying down, spread her arms out like angel wings.

"Now *this* is the life, isn't it?" she purred.

"Don't get too comfortable, Cora," Minnie said snickering from their joint doorway. "We have to get to the show soon. We didn't come here to lie around all day on a bed, now did we?"

Her remark triggered a frown from Cora, but inside of ten minutes, they were down in the lobby next to Ellie, Pete, Marlena, and Rosie. A quick hand signal to the now humble clerk promptly brought their buggy around to the front entrance, and after meeting up with the other doves, they were off.

Just outside the makeshift show gates, Cora was awestruck by all the colorful signage. Posters of Buffalo Bill were everywhere—Buffalo Bill stopping a stampede of wild Indians, Buffalo Bill on his steed next to Napoleon, Buffalo Bill's face superimposed on a running buffalo, Buffalo Bill facing a group of docile Indians. Annie's portraits were prominently displayed as well, Cora noted. One was with her and Sitting Bull, another one with her posed with her rifle, her dress, and her curls.

Excitement rippled through the audience as the Dolan contingent parked their rides, filed through the main gate, and settled into their reserved seats. Looking across the corral, Cora could see along the south side, the public wooden benches rapidly filling up cheek to jowl, with jostling, talking, and laughing ticket holders.

"It seems Annie and Brett really *did* take care of us," Minnie exclaimed, patting her cushioned seat and viewing the noisy throng across the way.

Cora wasn't listening. She was too busy looking around, soaking up the atmosphere.

When a bugle heralded its first notes and an American flag was slowly raised by a couple of cavalrymen, a hush fell over the crowd. All eyes were riveted on a gray-haired, well-dressed man clutching a megaphone as he walked out of the front door of a cabin placed in the middle of the corral. He paused theatrically.

"Ladies and gentlemen, boys and girls," he announced. "Welcome to the first ever Buffalo Bill's Wild West Show. My name is Nate Salsbury, and today you shall see the most tremendous, the most audacious, the most authentic re-enactment of the Wild West you will ever have the good fortune to see!"

A thunderous cheer erupted as Cora leaned forward intensely with an odd little smile.

Suddenly, visions of her pouring over each newly bought dime novel so many years ago were washing over her now with a vengeance. How could she possibly explain to her seatmates about her excitement, as she had lain nestled in bed, studying Buffalo Bill's every move, Annie's every shot?

Mr. Salisbury continued. "What you are about to witness today is nothing short of a masterpiece. Each act has been carefully designed and choreographed to render a true flavor of the Wild West and the people who lived, and indeed, still live in it. So, without further ado, just sit back and enjoy the show!"

His last two words were drowned out by a tremendous applause as a 'family' of plainspeople suddenly appeared and positioned themselves around the log cabin. The mother and daughter were in gingham prairie dresses, the father in work clothes, and the young sons in knickers, high woolen socks, and boots. All in all, a most peaceful scene as the audience waited, quiet, unsuspecting.

Without warning, a row of war-painted Indians appeared on the upper ridge just beyond the corral, raising their bows in the air and whooping furiously as they headed down toward the cabin.

The audience let out a collective gasp. "Look out!" they shrieked, as mothers tried to calm their children, and everyone watched in horror. Round and round the tribal 'savages' rode, encircling the terrified family, closing in slowly, the feathers in their war bonnets shaking and their tomahawks, raised to strike.

The sound of heavy powwow drums rumbled through the air, enveloping everyone with a sense of doom. A musical band, dressed in cream-colored, woolly cowboy chaps off to one side, commenced playing, and none other than Buffalo Bill, garbed in white on his white galloping steed, swooped in with his men to save the day. The crowd went wild. Stamping, cheering, and applauding, they rose up to give the Great White Savior and his team of expert marksmen a standing ovation.

Cora rose up with them, practically pounding her hands together as she yelled, "Bravo! Bravo! "

Glancing down again at Minnie and Ellie, she was appalled to hear her daughter mutter, "I wouldn't say that this is entirely accurate, would you, Minnie?"

"Hush! It's Buffalo Bill, for goodness sake!" Cora snapped.

Once the act was over, a team of men pulled the cabin away as people all around them commented, "Isn't this grand?" "I guess *he* showed them!" "Such good theater!"

The crowd was more than ready for the next act: *The Best Little Shot in the West*.

"Look, it's Annie!" Ellie called out, as Pete guzzled the contents of his flask, the doves oohed and aahed, and Cora leaned forward so far her elbows rested on her knees.

There she was, perky in her tan outfit, her tan woolen leggings, and her tan hat with her little signature silver star on the inside brim. Shouldering just a .22 Marling rifle and a mirror, she strolled out to the center of the corral and waited for her husband, Frank Butler, to come out and set up targets in varying sites—some high, some low.

Next, she positioned the mirror in front of her with one hand, and with the other, adjusted the rifle backwards on her shoulder. Everyone stopped breathing. *Crack-crack-crack-crack! Crack-crack-crack-crack!* went the rifle, shattering each target into bits and pieces.

People were on their feet, cheering, whistling, and screaming. Bowing magnanimously, she held out her right palm, her 'wait' signal, as her husband retrieved the mirror and brought out her horse and a shotgun.

"A *shot gun*?" Cora exclaimed. "Why, she's much too small for such a big gun!"

Ellie was more specific. "Why, that's the palomino Brett trained," she said, but no one was paying attention to her.

All eyes were on the pint-sized lady being helped up onto the palomino. Her shotgun in a sheath and riding side-saddled, she took the reins and began trotting around the corral to thunderous applause. Out came Nate Salsbury again, his megaphone tucked under his arm, and when he issued his next announcement in a manufactured Western twang, "Wait, ladies and gents! You ain't see nothin' yet!" the crowd roared their approval.

In the middle of the corral, Frank Butler stood with a clay pigeon launcher. As Annie picked up speed, he launched the first clay piece. High into the air it went as Annie shouldered her shotgun, still going at a fast clip. She aimed, shot, and down the object came, raining tiny fragments of clay. Butler launched another one. Annie aimed and shot. Another pigeon came crashing down in pieces. Soon the palomino shifted into a full gallop, and with every new launch, Annie aimed, shot, and hit each target full on.

"I just can't believe it, can you?" Cora asked Minnie, not even waiting for any answer before turning back to the show.

With the crowd in a near frenzy, the young woman slowed to a standstill, sheathed her shotgun, climbed off of the horse, and gave the cutest little curtsey imaginable. Then, as laughter and applause rippled through the corral, a team of red-bandanaed, black-shirted cowboys rode around her, holding their cowboy hats up in the air and hollering flamboyantly to all the visitors.

No sooner had Annie and Frank walked off, then the cowboys started their trick riding by sidestepping, rearing their horses up on their hind legs, doing fancy hoof work, and looping lassos in coordinated circles.

"Ellie, you're missing everything!" Cora said angrily, watching Ellie's eyes turn toward the sidelines where Brett was taking care of Annie's horse as it left the main ring.

"Yessiree, Ellie, ish gonna be grand, just like Ulyssessh," Pete slurred, his face bright red, his nose more bulbous than ever.

"Hush, you two! *Watch!*" Minnie yelled over the applause, winking at Ellie.

It was bandits this time. Dressed in black dusters, black hats, shirts, pants, and carrying six shooters, they were violently taking over a Wells Fargo & Co. stagecoach filled with passengers and their driver, a hired shot-gunner, riding on top. The crowd yielded a collective gasp while one woman shrieked. But her scream morphed into a "Thank *God!*" as once again, Buffalo Bill came to the rescue.

With his long hair flowing behind him, his white steed galloping effortlessly, he and his men started shooting blanks as the well-rehearsed actors fell each time the bullets 'hit' them. Before long, the strewn bodies on the ground were up and smiling, the passengers were out of the stagecoach acknowledging their liberators, and the Great White Savior, like true royalty, sat back in his saddle and waved to the delirious crowd.

"My hands are gonna fall off from all this clappin'," Marlena announced, as the full cast and crew came out onto the field to take their final bows.

"Best day of me life," Rosie shouted, wrapping her feathered boa more securely around her.

Cora remained silent, but when she turned toward the others, her face was nothing short of glowing.

"Oh, Mama." Ellie smiled.

The crowd was beginning to leave. Their pace, once lively, was now sluggish as the tired homesteaders, well-dressed patrons, and visiting dignitaries slowly made their way toward the exit. Amidst the crowd, a young man was holding up a sign that read "Dolan."

Cora made her way over to him. "We are the Dolans," she said. "And you are?"

"The name's Ambrose, ma'am. I'm here to invite all of you to the Peachside Drinkery. In an hour's time, Mr. Buffalo Bill will be hosting a special dinner."

"And Annie Oakley?" Ellie asked.

He grinned. "You betcha!" and handed her a small map.

An hour gave them ample time to walk through the camp. It was as if they had entered a small tent city, like the 'Hell On Wheels' they had all heard of during the early railroad building days. Complete with cooks preparing food, a blacksmith, costume seamstresses, and a large pen housing horses, goats, and pigs. Further off to the north was a small corral, with a couple of buffalos and beyond that, various teepees.

"*Buffalos!*" Minnie exclaimed. "That's interestin', seeing as how I read Buffalo Bill was famous for killing so many of 'em."

"Along with Injuns, I might add," Pete agreed, looking less red but still holding onto Minnie. He hiccupped. "You know, this camp reminds me of when we gathered at the sshtart of the land russsh, when we…"

"Pete!" Minnie warned.

Cora swirled around violently, tears forming. "Listen, you are *not* going to spoil this day for me! You hear me?" She charged ahead.

Ellie sped up to walk beside her. "Mama, it's all so grand. Just think, they have everything they need right here, don't they? Just like a little village. I'm so looking forward to meeting Buffalo Bill tonight, aren't you?"

"Thank you, Ellie," Cora said, her eyes growing soft. "Thank you for supporting me."

Before they knew it, they had reached the Peachside Drinkery. Ambrose greeted them at the door and quickly ushered them toward a back room. There, several long tables had been set up with candles, baskets of bread, and an abundance of whiskey bottles and shot glasses. As more and more Wild West show people entered, the Dolan cluster stood off to one side, waiting for directions. Suddenly Annie, Frank Butler, Brett, Nate, and the great buffalo hunter, Bill Cody appeared.

"Where's Mrs. Cora?" Annie asked loudly. When Cora gingerly raised her hand, the sharpshooter laughed and steered her way over. "So nice to meet you. I have heard *such* good things about you! It would be a great honor if you sat between me and Bill Cody tonight. Won't you please follow me?"

Everyone laughed at Cora's stunned reaction. As Annie guided her toward Bill Cody at the head of the table, the madam's eyes were practically popping out of their sockets. With the clatter of chairs moving over a wooden floor, the clink of shot glasses, and loud chatter filling the room, Brett quietly grabbed Ellie's arm and maneuvered her toward the other end of the table where they cuddled up so close, they appeared as one. Pete and Minnie sat across from Cora, with Pete next to Nate, Minnie on the other side, and the doves were all nicely distributed amongst admiring cowboys, musicians, and actors.

The door swung open with a bang. "Bradford!" Bill broadcasted. "Glad you could make it, fella! Hope you brought your camera! Come, sit here," he said, sweeping his hand toward an empty seat next to Minnie.

All heads rotated toward the newcomer as Pete, Minnie, and Cora cried out, "Bradford Jones, the *photographer?*"

A look of bewilderment crossed his face.

Minnie rang out, "Remember us, the Dolans? Nebraska Land of '56? Small world." Minnie giggled, as he sat down next to her and gave her a quick peck on the cheek.

"My, oh, my," he agreed, with a sizeable wink. "To think, you were just a girl the last time I saw you. 1856 Land Rush, right? And now? Well." He glanced across at Cora, then looked Minnie up and down. "Let's just say, you both turned out just fine."

Blushing, Minnie almost choked on her whiskey.

Across the table, Buffalo Bill was drinking his and holding court. "Mrs. Dolan, I do hope you enjoyed our show today," he said, pouring himself another shot.

"Indeed I did, Mr. Cody," she said, beaming.

Annie placed her hand lightly onto Cora's. "I'm so glad. This is our first real go at it, and we were all a little nervous about it."

"Speak for yourself, Annie, speak for yourself," Bill said, his face reddening with each new drink.

"Oh, dear, here we go again," Annie mumbled.

"Why, I've fought Indians, for Pete's sake. Today was *nothing!*" He leaned in toward Cora. "Mrs. Dolan, do you know how many scalps I've taken?"

Cora stared at him. "Well, according to those novels about you…"

"Damn those dime novels! No, I got me at least…"

"Excuse me, Bill. Perhaps now's the time to take some photographs," Annie interjected. Cora noticed her jaw was slightly clenched.

Bill paused, his glass mid-air, and nodded. "Yes, yes, you're correct. Bradford?"

Bradford and Minnie were head to head, laughing.

"I say, Bradford." Bill raised his voice. "Can you take some pictures right now before everyone gets too roostered up?"

Bradford, still chuckling, nodded reluctantly, and stood up to retrieve his equipment. "Of course, Bill, whatever you say."

Cora leaned in toward Annie. "Is he always so likkered up?"

"You have *no* idea."

"But he's so famous. A legend in his own time."

"He's also a man, isn't he?" the markswoman said, shrugging.

Cora sighed. "Yes, I know all about men who disappoint. Men who love you then never come back."

She could feel Annie's eyes studying her.

"So sorry, Cora," the shooter said softly, as she placed her hand over the madam's. "But you mustn't…"

A buzz of excitement overtook the room as Bradford returned, his fascinating, wooden camera *obscura*, dry plates, and tripod ready to go. "Which grouping should go first?"

"How about one of me and Cora?" Annie said, standing up and pulling Cora up after her.

Cora couldn't stop grinning. Was this truly happening to her? If she pinched herself would all of this go away? As Annie hooked arms, Cora forced herself not to cry.

"You know, I grew up reading all about you all. Read so many dime novels. They were my great escape, my treasures."

Annie smiled and pulled her in close. "Oh, Cora, you are a dear. Now, smile for the cameras."

Bradford came over, positioned the camera facing the two women, and behind a curtain directed, "Now, on the count of three…One-two-*three!*" He clicked, producing a bright flash, followed by a white-ash chemical smell.

"Next, Bill?"

"Why, one of me with the same gal!" he answered, his voice beginning to slur. He got up and put his arm around an uncomfortable Cora.

"Ready, little lady?" he asked, his grin lopsided, his alcohol breath overpowering.

Suddenly, Cora felt a chill. *Wes.* No, mustn't think about him now. Still, she inched away slightly from Buffalo Bill's drunken hold.

"Ready, Bradford?" Another click and flash, then one of the doves called out, "How 'bout just the Dolan girls?"

"The Dolan girls! The Dolan girls!" several more of the doves chanted, accompanied by lots of male whistles.

To a background of "Ain't they the best?" and "Dolan, Dolan, Dolan!" Cora motioned Minnie and Ellie over to her. Together, the three ladies locked arms and stood shoulder-to-shoulder as Bradford clicked and flashed several times.

When they finished, Ellie pulled Minnie aside.

"Look at Mama. Just look at her. Now, if only she could be this relaxed and happy all the time. Why does she have to be so ..."

"Nervous? Crabby?" Minnie sighed. "She wasn't always like this, Ellie. Years ago before you were born, she was wonderful. Maybe someday things will be different. Who knows?"

Cora came over. "Who knows what?"

"Hey, look. They're taking more pictures," Minnie said, and turned toward Bradford next to his camera, fiddling with his lens.

Other group photos followed, and then the serious drinking began. Seeing the men gulp down one shot after another, Cora decided it was time to retire. Turning to Annie, she thanked her profusely as Brett quietly whispered something in Minnie's ear.

"Oh, Annie, thank you so much for having me sit with you and Mr. Cody."

The 'Best Little Shot in the West' smiled at her seatmate.

"You should really thank Brett, Cora. He was the one who insisted that you and your entourage be invited here tonight, and what's more, he asked that you be seated between Bill and me."

"He did?"

She paused. A cowboy. Her daughter was going to end up with a cowboy, even if he quoted Shakespeare. And after all she had done to protect her. After feeling relieved to see the town ladies accept Ellie so readily. Still, he did go to a lot of trouble. Perhaps he might be worthy. Time will tell.

THE DOLAN GIRLS

She turned toward Brett's end of the table to smile at him, but he was nowhere to be seen. Nor was Ellie. Where in the world could they have gone?

Minnie appeared on Bradford's arm.

"I saw you looking for them. Let the girl be escorted home by a good man, Cora. Heaven knows, they're hard to come by. Besides, a little fun won't hurt her, you know." Her older sister's face flushed, as she turned to the photographer and stretched out her hand.

"Grand to see you again, Mr. Jones."

"Good to see *you*, Miss Dolan, Mrs. Dolan," he answered with a tiny bow, but before he turned away, Cora thought she caught a fast wink aimed at Minnie. What is going *on* around here?

By the time the madams returned to the Omaha Grand, the lobby was almost empty and their adjoining rooms well-lit by a gloriously full moon.

"Well, goodnight, Cora. Sweet dreams," Minnie said, before closing their joint door.

Cora lay on her bed, still dressed. As soft and luxurious as it was, it felt so empty without Minnie or without someone else beside her. She closed her eyes, the events of the day spinning around in her mind. Eyes still shut, she smiled at the thought of Annie, then frowned at the great Buffalo Bill, her all-time hero, being a little more human than she cared for.

She glanced over toward the glow filtering into the room, and again, thought about how bright the moon was that night. *Was it the moon that was making her feel so crazy* raced through her brain as she slowly moved over to the window and parted the curtains. She remembered how Thomas and she always loved to watch the moon. How wonderful it was staring up at the iridescent globe together, his arms around her, his warm breath on her neck.

Suddenly, her attention was drawn downward toward the street, down toward something happening in the not-so-dark shadows.

* *

"It's beautiful tonight. Let's walk back, shall we?" Brett suggested two hours earlier, offering his arm.

"What about Mama?"

He smiled. "I told your aunt about us returning to the hotel separately, and she seemed fine with that."

"So you didn't tell my mother?" She looked up and grinned.

As they strolled, her arm through his, the full moon was illuminating everything in its path: streets, boardwalks, buildings, and hitching posts. And although Brett had mentioned that the street lamps almost seemed redundant, Ellie exclaimed, "The lamps made it seem like we're strolling through the streets of a Dickens' novel."

Under the night's shiny orb, they talked. She told him all about her school experience back east, the patronizing air of the headmasters who always scoffed at her, and the singular non-acceptance of her 'Wild West' heritage by teachers and classmates alike. He talked about how his father's loud, angry drinking had made him corrupt of heart, but at the same time, by owning horses, he had given his young son, Brett, some beauty in the world. When she mentioned how neglected she had felt being sent away from South Benton, his arm gripped her a little tighter. When he told her that as a child he was considered to be a good shot, but because he saw the devastation that guns had caused during the war, he refused to carry one, she nodded and blinked back tears.

Directly across from the Omaha Grand, he took her hand and pulled her into the shadows.

"Ellie," he hummed. Several inches apart, he drew a deep breath, exhaled, and paused.

"Brett, I imagine you've been with many girls before, but you have to understand, I'm well, I'm not experienced."

He shook his head. "It's true I've done some larkin' around, but not as much as you think."

"No? But you're so sure of yourself."

Even in the shadows, she could sense his smile. "Thank you kindly, Miss Dolan. Truth is I could've been with more women, but..." He turned serious. "Frankly, I've always wanted to be with just one girl, someone special."

"Am I special?" She gulped, looking straight up at him.

"Yes, you most definitely are," he said, slowly gathering her in his arms. He could feel her heart fluttering through her chest and when he pressed in to kiss her on her neck, she let out a tiny moan.

Fused together, he sensed her lips rotating around toward his by the feel of their warmth and softness on his face and chin. All along, he made sure his embrace was considerate, non-commanding as he allowed her to guide her lips on her own terms, not his. When she finally placed her lips fully on his, it reminded him of tasting something new and how important that first bite was, so he held back a little, out of respect, and to also savor the moment.

But surprisingly, when she pushed her lips fully on his without any reserve, he gave out a deep groan.

A little voice in his head kept warning him to pull in the reins, to restrain himself, but her responsiveness was something he hadn't bargained on, and soon, all reason was tossed out the window. Kissing her deeply, he stroked her back, waist, and pressed his lower body into hers, trying hard not to envision what lay just beneath her bodice. When she stroked him back, he came close to a growl.

Overwhelmed by sensations, it took the clack of carriage wheels and a horse's loud snort to suddenly jar them apart. "Oh my," Ellie whispered, looking as if she were still in a daze.

Brett grunted, stood back, and caught his breath. That was too close, he thought to himself as he searched Ellie's eyes, oblivious of the second story window in the Omaha Grand. And Cora standing there, watching them.

* *

How *dare* Ellie act so common. Why, she was just like one of the doves! Fuming, Cora burst into her sister's bedroom to share her outrage. Shoving the door open, prepared to unleash a torrent of rightful indignation, she suddenly stopped short, frozen.

Intertwined in a tumble of naked arms, legs, chest, breasts, and buttocks, Minnie and Bradford jerked their heads apart from their embrace. After a couple of stunned beats, Minnie burst out laughing.

"*Minnie!*" Cora croaked, staring down at the floor and backing up into her room. "Could I speak to you a moment?" she said from the doorway.

"What the *hell*, Cora?" Minnie screeched when she entered Cora's room, a sheet wrapped around her like a toga.

"What are you doing?" Cora demanded. "This is *not* setting a good example for Ellie is all I've got to say."

"Cora, Cora. Ellie's doing just fine on her own, thank you very much. Now, if you don't mind, please leave me be." She started to turn around, but at the last second grabbed her sister's arm and looked directly into her eyes. "Frankly, it wouldn't hurt *you* to get some, missy. And for your information, Thomas ain't *never* coming back, so stop pining for him!" She banged the door behind her.

Within seconds, Cora could hear Bradford's chortles and snorts matching those of her sister.

* *

Cora had seen enough. A whirlwind of emotions rushing through her, she checked her hair in the mirror, then quietly stepped downstairs to the lobby, where a new clerk was on duty. Friendly, smiling, he was the antithesis of their earlier experience.

"May I help you, ma'am?" he asked politely.

Cora cleared her throat. "Yes, I realize it's very late, but I was wondering if the restaurant was still open for a glass of sherry?"

"Yes, of course. There are still a few customers in there. Please, do go in." He smiled sweetly, which calmed Cora down. Must tip him handsomely, she thought as she left.

The restaurant was small, elegant, and practically empty except for three tables off to one side.

Within seconds, a waiter approached. "Please do sit down, madam. What can I get for you?" he asked, his eyes tired and half closed, his hair slightly ruffled from too long a shift.

"A sherry, please."

Settling in, she looked around her. The table to her right held four gentlemen deep in conversation; to her left, an elderly couple sat, and beyond that, Nate Salisbury, who saw her and instantly broke into a smile.

"Why, Mrs. Dolan! What a pleasant surprise," he called out. "May I join you?"

She was certainly in no mood for company, least of all Mr. Salsbury, the nonstop showman, but she sighed and nodded. Maybe Minnie was right, and she needed to turn over a new leaf toward men.

Time to just move on.

Salsbury sat down and immediately began a long monologue about the show, and how he was going to turn the already famous Buffalo Bill into an even more famous personality, and how the world was going to be their oyster. Perhaps they would even go to England and perform in front of her majesty, Queen Victoria!

No longer listening to him pontificate, Cora leaned back and started eavesdropping on the men talking at the table next to her. With Salsbury droning on in the background, she quickly became engrossed in their conversation, particularly when one of them remarked, "They say the Soltano Gang from Wyoming is the worst of the lot and monstrous proud of it."

"Yup, I heard that too," said another, puffing on a cigar. I've also heard lots of them other Wyoming outlaws and riffraff are comin' over to Nebraska. Omaha first, then some of them smaller towns."

"Yeah!" The first man inserted. "Why, I bet in no time at all, most of Nebraska will be in hot water. Hell, the streets won't be safe for *anyone!*" He downed a shot glass full of whiskey, poured himself another, and raised it up as a salute. "Gentlemen, it's time for us to clear out 'n head back east!"

CHAPTER EIGHT
Shifting Winds

A slow, undulating breeze ruffled the prairie grassland as the Baltimore & Ohio chugged on toward Cheyenne. High up on a distant ridge, the Soltano gang sat back on their horses and carefully surveyed the scene before starting their drill. Composed of two Mexican-born brothers, seven cohorts, and a new member named Clyde, each man inspected his Winchester rifle or Smith & Wesson, readied his bandanna, and roll-clicked a fast command to his horse before heading downhill toward the Pullman.

On the train, the passengers had been lulled into an exhausted stupor. After days of rhythmic jiggling and wheel clanking, they were looking forward to their final destination in Wyoming. Families, businessmen, and immigrants jostled silently in their seats, while thick dark clouds of smoke blasted past the soot-stained windows.

Down on the plains, the ten-member Soltano gang stretched out in a line, galloping furiously, their torsos bent forward over their saddles, their linen dusters flapping feverishly against the wind.

The train engineer had delivered careful instructions to his fireman, conductor, and brakeman earlier that morning. "Be on high alert today. We've got a safe overloaded with payroll, and we'll be entering Wyoming soon. That's *not* a good combination." Seeing the nervous faces in front of him, he added, "But there'll be a Pinkerton agent riding in the baggage car to protect the money, so there's no cause for alarm. Just be watchful."

The conductor nodded slowly and promised vigilance, but by noon, his predilection for liquor had gotten the better of him. Swaying slightly from side to side, he teetered through each passenger car holding onto seat backs and barely registering the outside world.

As they neared the train, the robbers slowed down long enough to position their bandannas up on their faces and secure their six-shooters. Four of them galloped next to the railroad tracks and stayed in tandem with the last car, four on each side. Two men covered the rear as designated horse wranglers.

The leader, José Soltano, still galloping, rode on ahead and hoisted himself up onto the moving baggage car as his horse dropped away and moved on, riderless. On the other side of the car, his brother Guillermo did the same. Soon, eight of them were onboard with bandanna-covered faces, empty burlap bags, and handguns cocked, ready to go.

Unsuspecting, the drunk conductor had managed to make it up to the baggage car, where he heartily assured the engineer and Pinkerton that all was well, with nothing to fear.

In the caboose, the third-class passenger Renata had plenty to worry about. Startled awake by an odd, rhythmic pounding on the roof, she glanced out of the window and saw two men galloping beside the train, their faces half covered by bandannas, their dusters fluttering. Instinctively, she gasped in horror.

Just then a masked man entered their car. "This is a holdup. Don't be a pack of fools—gist give us what we come fer," he barked.

Another man followed him in, bellowing, "Git out your money and your jewelry. *Now!*"

Renata turned to her seat companions. What were these men saying? Across the aisle, several passengers had the same blank expressions, mixed with fear.

"These folks don't understand nothin'!" the first robber snarled. Charging over to one of the immigrants, he pulled him up, reached into his pockets and produced a few coins. He shoved him down again and roared, "Hell, they ain't worth *nothin'!* Let's move on to the other cars."

The next car was much better. Men were frantically taking out their billfolds or coin purses and handing over any cash they could muster, while chained watches, earrings, necklaces, and bracelets were being tossed into burlap bags as children whimpered and babies cried.

One elegant gentleman sitting near the front of the car looked into the next car and saw a similar scene. Shaking his head, he turned back to the three outlaws in his own car.

"Don't you stare at me all wild!" the last of the outlaws to enter the car called out, taking two strides at a time over to the frightened man.

The bowler-hatted businessman threw up his hands. "I didn't mean any harm. Here, here's my money and my watch."

The thief grabbed the watch and cash, and thrusting them into his own pockets, laughed. "Now, *that's* better. Let's get a-move on."

He turned to open the door but just then, a lady toward the rear, wearing a fancy cornette bonnet, caught his attention. She was holding a small dog and mumbling something to her seat companion. Suddenly, he was standing over her and her stylish hat. Snatching her dog out of her arms, he growled, "Think you're better than me, huh?"

"Run, Aldo, *run!*" she screamed as the dog wriggled out of the robber's arms.

Staring into the bandit's eyes, she shuddered. So lifeless and cold, they made the hairs on the back of her neck stand upright, but at least her dog had escaped.

For a moment, the robber stood still. Then, without warning, he leaned over, slapped her across the face, then staggered up the aisle toward the yelping dog.

"Leave the damn dog alone!" another robber at the front of the car yelled.

But his partner in crime wasn't listening. He caught up with the cowering animal and kicked it so hard it flew up into the air and landed on the floor like a sack of potatoes. The entire car gasped.

"A little dog; it was only a little dog," the woman wailed, as the masked man shook his head and laughed.

Almost strutting, he rubbed his leg once and slowly made his way toward the front of the car, announcing loudly, "Can't abide no damn dogs!"

"Man, you're *cold*, Clyde," the third bandit muttered, as the three entered the next car as a unit.

Several cars forward in the baggage car, the conductor leaned against the safe and watched the Pinkerton detective smoke his pipe. Still reeling from his morning's drinking, he couldn't help but wonder exactly how much money was in their possession, and he was about to ask the detective, when he heard a dull knock against the back end of the car. The agent put down his pipe and slowly stood up.

"Did you hear that?" the conductor asked.

A vigorous nod was his answer, as the Pinkerton tilted his head and held up his right index finger. Several seconds of silence passed before he spoke. "Probably nothing, but just in case, I'll…"

Both locked doors on either end blasted inward, knocking the conductor and detective off their feet and onto the floor. Instantly, both Soltano brothers were in the car, their six shooters aimed at the stunned men lying in the dust and rubble.

"Damn! That dynamite works!" Guillermo exclaimed.

"Open the safe," José snarled at the two men. "Or else!"

"Or else what?" the conductor asked, staring up at the masked men, his voice quavering.

"Pinkerton here knows what else, don't cha?" José smirked as he cocked his gun slowly.

Dazed, the Pinkerton dusted himself off before looking up. "You'll *never* get away with this, you know."

Jamming his Scoffield against the detective's head, José growled, "Oh yes, we will." Then he side-swatted him.

Blood flowed out of the Pinkerton's right nostril, but he didn't miss a beat. Nonchalantly, he wiped it off with his suit sleeve and sniffed. "You're out of luck, fellas. I don't happen to know the combination."

Guillermo turned to the conductor. "Do you?"

"Oh, God, no!" he cried and immediately vomited.

"*Díos mío*, this shouldn't be so hard." Guillermo quickly withdrew a single stick of dynamite out of his pocket and tied it onto the safe's lock. He yanked the men up and pushed them to the back of the car, then with a match, lit the fuse, ducked down, and motioned his brother to do the same.

Boom! The safe was on its side, still intact. Staring at each other in bewilderment, the two brothers shook their heads.

"Let me blast it," Clyde said, stepping into the car. He gripped his scattergun and blew a hole in the safe's front. Another blast and the door gave way and paper money flew up into the air like confetti.

"I can't hear anything!" the conductor screamed, as the Pinkerton reached for his new, double action Model 3.

Clyde swiveled around. "Don't even *think* about it!" He kicked the gun out of the agent's hand as the brothers started stuffing mounds of hard cash into their burlap bags.

Suddenly the sweaty, soot-coated brakeman appeared. "What the hell?" he said before Clyde aimed and shot. Slammed high up against the back wall, the brakeman's lifeless body slid down to the floor.

"That weren't necessary!" Guillermo snarled at the new outlaw, leaning over the dead brakeman as José stepped out onto the car's platform and motioned the other two to follow him.

Outside the baggage car, their partners were howling like coyotes as soon as they saw José's overstuffed burlap bag. The two wranglers led the other horses in close and after the bandits leapt off the still trundling train, they all charged off into the rocky Wyoming hills.

Later that night, Guillermo pulled José aside. "I'm thinkin' maybe we need to get rid of Clyde. He's always the first rattle out of the box. I swear, he ain't right in the head."

José shrugged. "Maybe so, but he got us our money today, now didn't he?"

"I s'pose. Just don't trust him, is all."

CHAPTER NINE
All Manner of Changes

Word usually traveled fast in small towns, but in South Benton it traveled at lightning speed. Inside of two days, everyone and his brother was talking about Buffalo Bill's Wild West Show and how successful it was. They also lamented over the fact that it was leaving Omaha soon and traveling to larger, even more profitable cities.

The doves broke the news to Ellie one evening as she was in the hall, en route to her room.

"Hey, Miss Ellie. You better hold onto your fella any way you can," Rosie advised, by-passing a drunken customer and stepping in front of the schoolmarm.

Ellie's pupils grew large. "What do you mean?"

"I mean, I hear the show is gonna end sooner than we all thought, and that means your handsome Mr. Horse Man will be off to goodness knows where."

"Or who with!" Marlena giggled, then stopped when she caught sight of the shock on Ellie's face.

"He *did* tell you, right?" Rosie asked. "If he didn't, he's a scalawag!"

"Yes, of course he told me. Everything's fine." Ellie looked down at the papers tucked under her arm. "I never expected anything. Now, if you don't mind, I've got some school papers to correct."

Marlena and Rosie exchanged worried looks. "Good night, Miss Ellie," they chorused and started to walk back to the parlor, not looking back at

Ellie, pressed up against the wall, one hand on her mouth, listening to their exchange.

"She's kiddin' herself. She's got it *bad!*" Rosie said.

"She sure does. Poor girl…"

Inside her bedroom, Ellie could barely move. Finally, willing herself to sit down at her desk, she put her students' papers onto her roll-top desk, lit her brass lamp, and pulled both a quill pen and an ink bottle out of one of the top drawers. Carefully reading the first paper, she edited each student's mistakes before marking a grade on the top right-hand corner. The second and third papers got the same treatment. By the fourth paper, her tears had turned each edit mark into more of a water-colored blur than an inked correction. What was she going to do? He came into her life, and now he was leaving. Just like that? She dropped her pen and sobbed.

The next morning, Ellie woke, determined to talk to Brett. Midweek meant he would most likely be back at the stables, either training or taking care of a show horse. The imminent rain had turned the night air chilly and the horses reflected that, with their snorting and pawing. They looked over nervously at Ellie as she passed by them on her way to the tackle room.

Adjusting bridles and polishing saddles, Brett seemed to be moving at half speed when Ellie walked in. When he looked up and saw her, he gave out a huge sigh. "Ellie," he said.

"Is it true? Are you leaving so soon?"

"It seems it was always true. I just didn't know it." He looked away.

She came over to him. "Brett." Her tears were welling up again.

"Oh, Ellie, that's what I do, what the show does. If I could, I would stay." He choked out the last word.

"I know…I just thought…oh, I don't know *what* I thought," she murmured, laying her hand on his arm.

"Please don't make this any harder." He groaned and took her into his arms.

"I've never felt like this before," she cried against his chest, her tears dotting his shirt.

His breath was shaky as he held her, and when she broke his hold and turned to go, he blinked back his own tears. "Ellie, if I had my way," he muttered, but she was already heading for the door. At the last minute, she swiveled around, just in time to see him sitting on a bale of hay, his head in his hands.

"Oh, Brett ..." she choked as she stumbled outside.

Dashing home, she could feel the rain coming down in earnest. Felt the heavy droplets mix in with her tears, as her saturated bodice stayed glued to her torso, and her drenched skirt became heavy enough to make her grunt as she ran. By the time she reached Madam Ana's front porch, she had to hold on to one of the posts, her sobs were so intense. With all her heart, she wished she had never met him.

Finally Minnie came out to pull her in, and guiding her gently into the kitchen, sat her down and handed her a handkerchief.

"Ellie, it's all right. He was your first love. It hurts, I know, it hurts."

The schoolmarm blew her nose and looked up. "Minnie, did this ever happen to you?"

"*Hell* no! Too scared. Knew I'd never git over it if I let someone come that close," she said. "But it sure happened with your mama and many another gal. Happened to our da, and that's why he could never git over our mam's death. In fact..."

"In fact, that's what they *all* do," Cora interjected from the doorway, her face red, her hands clenched.

Ellie both looked up at her questioningly. "What, Mama?"

"Leave you, they all leave you!"

"Thanks, Mama, *that's* helpful!" Ellie said.

"Well, maybe it *is* helpful. Maybe, just maybe, I'm looking out for you!" she snapped, slamming the door behind her.

An hour later, Cora quietly climbed into their bed, so as not to disturb her sleeping sister. Thinking about life and romance, it took her a while to get comfortable. Poor Ellie, she thought finally, and closing her eyes, turned her tear-stained face up toward the moon.

* *

Two days later, they were visited by the local sheriff, claiming he had received a letter from the Cheyenne Pinkerton office, with a letter that pertained to them.

"What in the world?" Minnie asked.

Using Madam Ana's cherished sterling opener, Cora knifed it open and read it aloud.

Dear Sheriff Whitman,

It has recently come to our attention that various unsavory characters may soon be traveling to the state of Nebraska. As your town owns and operates establishments such as Madam Ana's, which might attract such persons, we have taken it upon ourselves to assign one of our top agents to your case, in order to help you protect all your citizens and your assets.

Since this agent will be acting as an undercover bookkeeper, we feel it is in your best interest to have Madam Ana's place an advertisement for said position in your local newspaper, so as not arouse any suspicions.

Our agent shall be arriving by train in two weeks' time. Meanwhile, please deliver this letter to Madam Ana's and have them confirm by telegram they have received this letter as soon as possible.

Cordially yours,

Mr. Mark Latham, Chief Officer, Cheyenne Pinkerton Bureau

Cora turned to Sheriff Whitman. "Why us?"

"Don't know, Mrs. Cora. Maybe there'll be more letters comin' to other places. Now, don't forget to send a telegram to Chief Officer Latham, hmm?"

"Well, I'll be," Minnie said after he had left. "Who do they think we are? A couple of helpless women?"

"I *knew* something like this might happen," Cora muttered.

"What do you mean?"

"While you and Ellie were having yourselves a high ole time in Omaha, I was listening to a group of men at the hotel talking about how Wyoming's riff-raffs were on their way here. They also mentioned something in particular about a Soltano gang."

"Well, I'll be."

"You already *said* that," Cora sniped. "We better go about making up an advertisement. You ask Ellie. She's good with words. Besides, it'll help distract her."

"Why don't *you* ask her?"

Cora gave her a look. "Meantime, I'll go around to Corrigan's to find out if he got any special visits from our sheriff."

The Whiskey House was first on the list. Friendly rivals, Cora felt a slight kinship with John Corrigan, in spite of his insistence on capitalizing on his Irish ancestry. When she walked in, he was leaning against the bar and listening to a female singer auditioning. A 'hootchy-kootchy' type of gal, her voice reminded Cora of the cats in heat outside their bedroom window each spring.

"If it 'tisn't the fair lass from County Cork! Top of the mornin' to ya, Mrs. Cora."

"Hello, John."

"And what do I owe this fine honor, hmm?"

"Do come off it, John. We're in America now."

His eyes slit. "No need to be sassy, gerrl."

"Sorry. I was just passing by and thought I'd come in. How's business? Any trouble? Any sheriff's visits?"

"No, no. Nothin' much at t'all. Why?"

"Oh, just wondering. I must say, your place is looking really grand these days."

Corrigan studied her for a moment. "Lassie, anything you want to tell your ole pal, Corrigan?"

"No, no, just paying a friendly stop. See you around."

That night the two Madam Ana's partners discussed the mysterious letter. "Why us?" Cora kept saying.

"Maybe we're the ones doin' the best business in town."

"I know we've been making good profits this year, but that much?"

Minnie bit into a large piece of steak. "Ellie wrote this here advertisement and told me to give it to you."

Snatching it up, Cora gave it a quick review. "Fine, it's all fine," she muttered and continued her dinner in silence, no longer waiting for the schoolmarm who had stayed holed up in her bedroom for the past two nights.

* *

The first interview happened several days later. The instant Cora and Minnie saw who it was tripping over a stone on their front walk, they both burst out laughing. "Oh, *no!* Not Bill Watts!" Cora said.

Short, portly, Bill Watts had trouble putting one foot in front of the other, much less managing an interview. After taking a seat, he kept licking his lips and playing with the few wisps of hair left on his head.

"Now, Mr. Watts, you understand this is a bookkeeping job, so you do have be good with numbers."

He gazed at Minnie blankly.

"For instance, what's seven-hundred fifty dollars minus fifty dollars, times ten?"

Another blank look was followed by a hiccup.

One more attempt at testing him brought the women to their feet. Cora tried not to giggle, and by the look on Minnie's face, she knew her sister was feeling the same.

"Good day, sir. Best of luck to you," Cora said, watching him stumble off.

The next appointment was an hour later, and at first, the man seemed competent. But when he pointed out that three of his eight children would be accompanying him to work to "help out the missus," he was politely shown the door.

After the sixth interview, Minnie threw up her hands. "Lord help us! How many insane men are *in* this town?"

Cora chuckled. "All right, all right, we'll play this game just a little bit longer. But by the end of next week, we're going to post a sign saying 'Position Filled.'"

"Amen to that!"

* *

Ellie had designated Fridays as 'Geography Day.' Lessons were learned regarding various international countries and their histories, their culture, and their languages. An encyclopedia was passed around and each week, selected students were allowed to point at a large wall map of the world with the teacher's special one-yard pointer. It was indeed an honor to be chosen for this task. It meant the 'honoree' was responsible enough to listen to the different groups summarize what they had learned from books. Then, using this exclusive ruler, the student was to show the class where that particular country lay. It was also understood that being extra well-behaved in class assured students of a faster pathway toward this coveted 'job.'

Usually on these days, the class was particularly alert and eager to please, and on one particular Friday, there was no exception. Until the big fight broke out.

The two boys, Shaun and Samuel were fast friends, but after years of wrassling, fishing, and playing together, they now had a problem. Both of them were taken with Martha, a golden-haired, freckled-faced girl who, at the tender age of twelve, already knew how to manipulate the male persuasion. She applied this talent magnificently, eating lunch with Samuel one day, allowing Shaun to carry her books as he walked her home the next. At first, being good friends, they relinquished any squatter's rights and stepped back. But soon new hormones emerged and with them, male competition reared its ugly head.

Trying hard not to think about Brett, Ellie had forced herself to focus on the children that morning, reminding herself that if it was time to 'move on.' She had no other choice.

"Miss Dolan! Shaun and Samuel, are in the yard *fighting!*" a student yelled.

Running outside with her long ruler, Ellie was horrified to see the two boys punching each other with all their might.

"Boys! Boys! Stop this at *once!*" she cried, trying to pry them apart. Overnight, the boys had changed, and being preoccupied herself, Ellie now realized she must have missed it. No longer companions, with bared teeth and flying fists, they snarled and growled like young men.

She gave each of the boys a good, hard rap on his shoulder with the ruler. Instantly, the fighting stopped as everyone in the room turned to stare in horror at their teacher. Stunned, they gazed at her bright red face and hair hanging down in untidy wisps.

"Miss Dolan," Shaun started.

"*Don't*, just don't," she said, scooping up her flyaway hair and attempting to put it back into a bun.

Samuel added, "I didn't mean to ..."

"*Stop it!* Just *stop it!*" she shouted.

Walking to the front of the room, she dropped the ruler on her desk, and began to straighten the books on the shelves maniacally.

A few of the girls giggled nervously as Joshua raised his hand. "Miss Dolan, can we go on with the geography lesson?"

That did it. "No, Joshua, *No!* We can't!" Feeling as if her head was about to explode, she looked around at all the scared faces. "Class *dismissed!*" she suddenly screeched, then watched them all grab their school bags and run for their lives.

Once they left, the silence was overwhelming. Completely drained, she closed the door and leaning against it, slowly slid down to the floor as deep, silent sobs racked her small frame.

* *

En route to the post office, Cora steeled herself. She knew the moment she stepped into the building, Matthew Johnson, the current postmaster, would be overly attentive. About twice a year, Minnie would comment on what a catch he was, but she always shook her head.

"Matthew Johnson? Oh, please!" she'd scoff.

Entering the post office, she heard the bell tinkle and saw Mr. Johnson look up and beam.

"Why, Cora! What a *wonderful* surprise."

"Yes, well, I have an important telegram to send."

His hurt look reminded her of that night after the dance.

"Of course," he grunted and offered her a pencil and paper. She quickly wrote a confirmation to Latham, then watched him go to his telegraph machine, sit down, and start tapping.

While she waited, she noticed a new 'WANTED' poster of the Soltano Gang. On closer inspection, she inferred that both José and Guillermo Soltano had come from somewhere south of the border. Dark hair, near black eyes, dark handle-bar mustaches, one was wearing an American slouch hat, the other, a black sombrero.

"The whole town's talkin' 'bout 'em, Cora. Scared half out of their wits they are," the postmaster said.

She nodded, frowning.

He continued. "Fact is, don't know what you're up to with them Pinkertons, but it's a good thing, if I get your telegraph right."

She swung around. "Please, Matthew, *please*, you mustn't tell a *soul* about this, do you hear me?"

He stared at her for a couple of seconds, drew his fingers slowly across his mouth, and winked. "My lips are sealed."

Oh, brother. As she left, she knew he was probably following her every movement outside.

* *

That night Ellie admitted to Minnie she was mortified. "I'm just like Mama now. To lose control like that in front of my students was *so* unprofessional, so unlike me," she cried, dabbing her eyes with Minnie's cotton handkerchief.

"Ellie, you're *not* like your mama. Her hurts have been a part of her for a very long time. This pain is new to you, and you're allowed to show a little anger. You're grieving, honey," Minnie cooed, cradling her niece against her bony shoulders as Pete walked in.

He took one look at the two of them and shook his head. "I know this must be a female conversation, and it isn't my business, but could I place an addendum?"

They both looked up at him.

"Ellie, you're a very special young lady, but sometimes love goes astray. As Shakespeare said, *Love is a smoke made with the fume of sighs.*" He thought a moment, then added, "But he also said, *This above all; to thine own self be true.*"

"Good ol', Pete, thank you. I'll try to remember that." Ellie nodded, sniffling.

* *

The incoming storm was fiercer than Cora had expected. Thunder drummed furiously, sheets of rain whipped down at forty-five degree angles, shops closed early, and shutters were locked up tight. Nonetheless, she was surprised to see a few customers make it over to Madam Ana's that night, proving lust outweighed common sense. To Minnie's and Cora's credit, instead of penalizing their girls, they announced that any unchosen dove without a john would be allowed a drink of real whiskey, not their usual cold tea laced with molasses.

Most of the customers there were regulars: Pete, of course, reminiscing about his wife of long ago; Neely, a hired cowpoke who always made a beeline for Marlena, Billy M., who used his forefinger to play 'Eenie Meenie Miney Mo' when choosing a girl for the night, and Malcolm, a bowler-hatted dandy with a penchant for dark-haired gals. For the household, it was a peaceful night. Cora was supervising the parlor, and Minnie ended up telling some of her newest jokes.

"Did you hear the one 'bout the one legged man and his horse?"

"No! *Tell* us!" The entire room roared.

She was about to open her mouth when the front door flew open, making everyone jump. A sopping wet stranger in a black slouch hat and a dripping black duster stood in the foyer, blinking his eyes and wiping his brow.

"*Dang!* It sure is rainin' cats n' dogs out there tonight!" he croaked.

Minnie approached. "It sure is, honey. You look like a fish outa water. Step in by the fire while I hang up your coat and hat."

He was a tall, grizzled man with just a hint of gray, and when he removed his hat and coat, people paused, drinks in hand, and stared. Running down his neck was a long, purple, rope-like scar.

"Now *that's* quite a scar," Pete remarked, already started on a bender.

The man shrugged. "The war. Couldn't help it."

Cora, standing nearby, cocked her head slightly. She wasn't buying it. "Where did you fight in the war?"

"Oh, here and there. What's it to you, lady?"

With respectful nods, the girls went about their business, sashaying coquettishly around the room in their satin and crinoline outfits, angling for an offer. Looking over at Minnie, he tilted his head slightly. "Any whiskey for a worn out stranger?" he asked.

"Sure 'nough, honey, that'll be two bits, unless you wanna make it part of the girl's price."

A cynical smile crept across his face.

"So, you wanna talk biznis right away? Out in Cheyenne, we do it different. Okay, sister, let's deal. How much fer one of these?" He swatted his hand toward the doves. "These here heffers."

Cora saw the girls stiffen. "There aren't any 'heffers' here, mister, just ladies," she said, her eyes narrowed, her voice chilling.

He scrutinized each dove. "I'll take *her!*" He pointed a sinewy finger at Rosie.

Frozen, the girl looked over at Cora wide-eyed, like a lamb headed for slaughter.

Minnie turned to the man. "Honey, she's kinda new. You want someone with more experience, I imagine. Anyone else tickle your fancy?"

He made a fast sweep of the room. "Nope. She's the one. Now, where's my drink?"

Plunking down far more cash than Minnie had quoted, he shuffled over to Rosie, grabbed her arm and yanked her over to where Minnie had begun pouring him his drink. Still clutching the dove, he tossed the whiskey down his gullet without even wincing, then started up the stairs.

"Wait a minute," Cora called out. "You can't just grab her like that."

At the top of landing, he looked down at her and laughed. "Which room, Sister?"

"None. Let the girl go. Right now," Cora snarled.

"Hell, any room will do," and pushing Rosie in front of him, disappeared from sight.

"I don't know, about this, Cora, Minnie," Pete said after several seconds.

Minnie gulped. "Sorry, Cora. He did give a lot of cash, I…"

"That's it!" Cora cried and suddenly left the room.

"Where did Mrs. Cora go? Ain't she gonna help Rosie? He's probably already done something bad to her by now." Marlena said, her voice trembling.

Cora charged back into the room, armed with a shotgun. Shouldering it, she flew up the staircase two steps at a time.

One door after another was flung open, until a scream from the end of the hall pierced through everything.

Running toward the sound, Cora burst into the room.

Rosie was on the bed, her outfit ripped to shreds, her thighs bruised.

"Oh, *no, you DON'T!*" Cora eyeballed his discarded pants and his pistol lying on a side table.

Legs apart, gun firmly held, she stared him down. "Now, get away from her, you bastard."

He wiped his nose with his hand and stepped back a foot from the bed.

"Rosie, get out of the room," Cora commanded.

He smirked. "Now, you *know* you ain't gonna use that shotgun on me."

She pulled the trigger and hit the bedside table four inches from him. "Oh, yeah?" she snarled, watching him flinch. "You wanna bet on that?"

Off to one side, Minnie stood in the doorjamb, a large kitchen knife in her hand.

"All right, all right, I'm leaving!" Jerking on his pants, he started to reach for his gun, but seeing Cora's face, pulled back his hand.

Out on the porch he tried again. "My gun, ma'am." He tipped his hat with mock politeness.

"You can pick it up from the sheriff's tomorrow," Cora said.

"Hell, I want my gun now, you bitch!"

"Start walking," she said and watched him turn around and head off the porch. A few paces out, he turned around.

"Don't you dare," Cora growled and aimed the rifle at him again.

He put up his hands. "All right, all right. I'll get it tomorrow." Turning toward the street again, he quickly vanished into the darkness, his cackling floating behind him.

Cora drew a shaky breath, opened the front door, and went inside.

The parlor exploded with thunderous applause.

"Good for you, Mrs. Cora!"

"Hip-hip-hurray!" surrounded her as Rosie came over. "Thank you from the bottom of my heart." She flung her arms around her employer.

Later, Minnie sat on their bed and sighed. "You see? We can take care of ourselves."

Cora shifted on the bed, still quivering. "We got lucky this time. He was probably just a drifter. But some of those outlaws coming out of Wyoming? We probably could use a Pinkerton, after all."

* *

A week later, the front door bell rang. Ellie, still on tenterhooks, in spite of word about a Wild West Show extension, was teaching, Pete was sleeping it off in one of the upstairs rooms, and Minnie and Cora were busy in their office, bickering over accounting issues.

"Minnie, I've told you a *thousand* times, bookkeepers always use this column for Accounts Payable, *this* column for Accounts Receivable."

"Well, soon, we'll have us a real bookkeeper to help us out," Minnie said.

"No, remember he's mostly here to protect us. He probably won't know a thing about this."

Suddenly, a tall blonde dove named Sasha knocked timidly on their opened door.

"Yes, come in," Cora said, one hand on her hip, the other clasping the ledger book to her chest.

"Ah…" started Sasha, looking like the cat who ate the canary.

"Out with it, Sasha. I haven't got all day."

She cleared her throat. "Mrs. Cora, Miss Minnie, there's a nice gentleman of the first water out on the porch. Says he's your new bookkeeper. Shall I let him in?" she asked. "He sure cuts a good swell, like a real thoroughbred!"

The two sisters eyed each other. "Might as well," Minnie answered. As soon as Sasha left, she turned to Cora. "Let's see what Pinkerton's finest has to offer."

Cora nodded. "Has to be better than the men we've interviewed."

Instantly they broke out laughing. They were still giggling when Sasha returned. Hesitating, the dove stood at their office door and waited.

"Sasha, do bring him in," Cora directed.

As the Pinkerton stepped into the doorframe, Minnie stared at him, wide-eyed, and Cora had to sit down.

CHAPTER TEN
"We Never Sleep"

The last twenty-plus years had been kind to Thomas Garrett, or so he'd been told. He had survived the gripping horrors of war and evaded the ravages of disease so many of his fellow soldiers could not. Yet throughout, he never escaped the growing ache in his heart, planted so many years before. Solid and sturdy as an eighteen-year-old, at forty, he was robust and muscular under his crisp black suit, stiff collar, and string cravat. With his Pinkerton regulation-length hair and a dark, close-cropped beard, he cut a dashing figure that often gave the ladies pause.

But he barely noticed their glances. He was too hell bent on hunting down outlaws, while he avoided facing his empty life. Relentless, he was known to work twenty-four hour days, interview key witnesses in the driving rain, and if need be, forego holiday festivities. It all paid off. His superior, Chief Deputy James Prather, recognizing quality, rewarded him at every step as he climbed the organizational ladder, and by 1880, he became Head Agent at the Springfield, Illinois branch of the Chicago Pinkerton Detective Agency.

In certain districts, he had become a bit of a celebrity, leading to both compliments and resentments. So when he dragged himself in one morning, bleary-eyed from an all-night surveillance, he had mixed feelings about the 'good' news he had received.

"Do you have a moment, Agent Garrett?" Prather called out from his office.

Nodding, Thomas walked past two male secretaries, who stopped sorting papers to grin up at him.

"Have a seat. I assume you have received the Chief's letter from Chicago?"

"Yes."

"Quite an honor, wouldn't you say?" his supervisor remarked, leaning back in his new leather chair.

Thomas tried hard to look enthusiastic. "Of course, sir. Looking forward to it."

"Good. By the way, I have received word about your appointed interview time with the *Chicago Tribune* journalist. It has been scheduled for next Tuesday evening at Susannah's Place on Halsted Street. Seven o'clock. Any questions?"

"Yes, I do. If I may, what is the reason for this article?"

"I've told the head office all about you, Garrett, and even Alan Pinkerton himself thought it might be a good strategy to let the people of Chicago know a little more about an agent who represents us Pinkertons so well, an agent who keeps them all safe."

"I don't really think I'm the best person to do this, sir."

"Look, Garrett," he persisted, "after the Pinkerton fiasco with the Younger Brothers' house burning down and killing their little brother, the agency needs all the good publicity they can get."

"I understand, but…"

"Agent Garrett. I know you are not, shall we say, pleased, with Pinkerton's 'The end justifies the means' philosophy, but frankly, at this juncture, you're needed, so if you wish to continue working in this agency, you'll do the interview. Understood?"

Thomas shifted in his seat. "Trust me, sir, I'm very grateful to this agency. I'm just a little concerned about his sons who are taking it in another direction by cracking the heads of some labor leaders."

"Yes, those incidents were regrettable." Prather started shuffling papers. "I *know* you can handle this, Agent Garrett. Just answer the questions and don't make us look bad. That should be simple enough, right?"

Susannah's Place was aptly named. Above the carved mahogany bar hung a gold-framed painting of a mermaid, smoking a pipe with a small brass plaque underneath that read, 'Susannah lives here.'

Thomas gaped at the unique painting for a few seconds before scouring the room for the journalist. Embossed metal ceilings, wide crown moldings, and wooden floors surrounded him while off to one side, a lone fiddler was softly playing *Oh Susannah*. Men in bowlers, derbies, top hats, Stetsons, and homburgs sat on the bar stools guzzling one whiskey after another as he spied two men sitting at a corner table set against a far wall. They motioned him over.

After he sat down, one of them opened the conversation. "Let me introduce myself. My name is Elijah Mohr, sent over from the *Chicago Tribune* to write an article about you. Mr. Bradford Jones here is going to take a few photographs afterwards. Any questions before we begin?"

"Yes. Why me?"

Taken aback, Mohr turned to his companion. "A modest fellow, isn't he?" He chuckled. "Word has it you have an excellent reputation, Mr. Garrett, so my paper would like to share parts of your story with the good people of Chicago."

"There isn't much to tell."

"I doubt that," Mohr said. He took out a pen and several sheets of paper from his satchel. "For example, did you participate in the war?"

"Yes, of course."

"Can you be more specific?"

Thomas cleared his throat. "I was part of the 10th regiment, out of Illinois."

"So you're from around there, then?"

A shadow crossed the Pinkerton's face. "No, I didn't *say* that. I just signed up there in '61, that's all."

"All right. What was your rank in the 10th?"

"At first, private."

"What fighting did you experience as a private?"

"I partook in the First Bull Run."

"Exciting!"

"Not really," Thomas said, grabbing one of the filled shot glasses in front of him and taking a swig.

"Why don't you tell us about it, then?"

Sighing, Thomas began. "I remember, both sides were in a state of panic. Green as grass we all were and shaking in our boots. To make matters worse, everyone was certain, whether you were a Reb or a Yankee, they'd all be going home soon, victorious." He drifted back in time. "I can still remember what a searing hot July day it was, the air so thick we choked on it."

He looked over at Mohr's ink-stained finger scribbling furiously. "We had spent weeks doing drills. In fact, I still can recite those drills in my sleep." His voice rose. "*Shoulder arms. Company by the left flank! March! Right oblique! March! Forward march! Right wheel march!*"

Startled, the *Chicago Tribune* duo, along with several other customers, all gawked at him.

"And of course, the firing drill," he continued, starting to breathe hard. "*Company load! Fire by files! Ready…aim…Commence firing! Cease fire!*"

Bradford poured another round of shots.

"Then came time for the battle. I can tell you, we saw the elephant."

Both men nodded knowingly.

"But just before the very first shot rang out, I happened to look up toward a nearby ridge and saw a crowd of people having a picnic."

"*What?* What in the world do you mean?" Mohr asked.

"Yes, ladies sat there in their fine dresses, men in their top hats, laughing and chatting away as if they were about to watch a new play, and we were the actors."

He paused and gave them a long hard look. "But all that soon changed."

The two men sat back.

"All this God forsaken training, and when the final hour came, everyone lost their nerve. *Both* sides!" He shook his head. "But we were worse than the Rebs. We simply fell apart and went into full retreat. And those fine Washington folk, they were in a panic as well. When we hightailed it back to the city, our troops ran headlong into all those fancy carriages with the fancy Washingtonians in them. I remember the clouds of dust, the horses screaming, women screeching. *Lord*, it was a nightmare!"

The pause seemed to last forever as Mohr feverishly added more notes.

"Where did you go from there?" he asked.

"Here and there. Was at Gettysburg. You know there was only civilian casualty during the Battle of Gettysburg, and my good friend, Clem, was the one who caused it."

Suddenly, the men at the bar grew boisterous, the music swelled, and another bottle of whiskey was ordered for their table. When it arrived, the three of them chugged down the next round in unison.

"You say your friend killed a man, the civilian?"

Thomas's eyes grew sad. "No, it wasn't a man. It was a young girl, only fifteen years old."

Both men gasped. "How'd *that* happen?" Mohr asked.

"By the time we arrived in Gettysburg, we were sick of the stench of war. Fed up with killing men and bone weary from all the diseases that devoured so many of us in camp. And always, the men missing their families something terrible.

"But oddly enough, it was one of those unusually calm mornings. Peaceful, eerie, really, like just before a storm is gonna hit, and the dense air feels like it's about to burst. We all knew that at any moment, we could catch a load of bullets. Most folks were hiding in their cellars 'cause even with us Yankees positioned in Gettysburg with them, they knew the Rebs were hiding in the fields, just outside of town, itching to come in and raise hell. So we waited, sweltering in our wool uniforms and boots.

"After days of no real fighting, I'm sure the Rebs were starving, but we were lucky. We had fresh baked bread each morning from a Mrs. Wade and her daughter, Jennie. They'd bake loaf after loaf of bread, then bring it out to their front yard where our troop was resting. If I close my eyes, I can still smell it." He closed his eyes.

"How fortunate for you all."

"For us, maybe, but not for her." Thomas reached for another swallow. "My friend, Clem? While everyone was waiting for that fine bread first thing in the morning, he thought he heard a noise. Then it happened."

The men tilted forward.

"When we saw a Reb dash across the road, Clem, using his 1860 Henry rifle, aimed and fired. He was taking no chances."

"*And?*" Mohr asked.

"When the Reb didn't fall, we knew something was wrong. Clem *never* missed. Suddenly, our blood ran cold."

"What *happened?*" Jones wanted to know.

Shoulders slumped, the agent reached for the whiskey bottle. "We heard a woman's scream from inside the house. Then the door flung open, and Mrs. Wade let out the most blood-curdling sound I'd ever heard. 'My *girl*, they got my girl!' she wailed. And Clem? He never recovered. He still shot at the Rebs. In fact, when we were facing the tough Texas Rangers, and most of our troop was being massacred, he picked off quite a few of those sons of bitches before he got killed, but his heart wasn't in it."

"You mentioned the Texas Rangers," Mohr started.

"Yeah. My outfit went further south and came up against the Texas

Rangers."

The photographer cut in. "You said your outfit was mostly wiped out?"

"Yes, they were. All except me and one other soldier from my hometown."

The two men leaned in, their eyes the size of quarters.

"It was almost the end of the war and by some miracle, we managed to make it. We almost didn't though. The Rebels had left us for dead, but we crawled our way northward bit by bit and got picked up by a Union troop, thank the Lord."

"And then?"

"Then we were transported by train up to Washington D.C., where I was laid up in a hospital for a long time, almost a year."

"That's a long time," Mohr commented.

"Yes, indeed." Thomas took another swig.

Just then, the fiddler started playing *Ashokan Farewell*. Lyrical, haunting, the entire room turned to listen. Lost in the past, a few of the older men sniffled, a couple more blew their noses self-consciously with crumpled handkerchiefs. When the musician finished, the applause was thunderous.

"How'd you become a Pinkerton? That's quite a transition."

Thomas nodded. "I was always good with maps and figures. So when I had finally gotten out of the hospital, my former captain came to visit. He asked me if I could decipher a map code for someone named Alan Pinkerton."

"And?" Mohr asked.

"It was easy for me. I unraveled it within minutes, and not knowing where I was going next, I accepted a job at the Pinkerton Agency out of Chicago, assigned to deciphering messages. I also performed the agency's new practice of compiling photographs—mug shots, they called them—and put those together with newspaper clippings to build a more complete profile for different outlaws."

"You mean like Jesse James and the Younger brothers?"

"Yes, exactly. Those profiles were very helpful."

"So did you get to know Pinkerton well?"

"At the beginning, I'd say he sort of took me under his wing. Said I reminded him of how he was at my age. Told me…"

"Yes, what did he tell you?" Mohr's pen was poised in the air.

The room was beginning to sway slightly as Thomas tried to level his eyes on his interviewer. "I don't think I should."

Mohr pushed his notes across the table. "Look, no notes. Off the record, I promise," he said, motioning to the barkeep to bring another round.

"Well," the agent began, "he told me that he had had a falling out with the President years before. So when Lincoln was killed that fateful night in 1865, Pinkerton felt it was because he wasn't there to protect him. Never forgave himself."

Mohr shrugged. "We all have our regrets, don't we?"

"We certainly do." Thomas fingered his glass.

Bradford shot a warning glance at Mohr.

"Just a couple more questions, Mr. Garrett, I promise." He checked through his notes. "You entered the army at a young age. Did you return home? Have you ever been married?"

The Pinkerton's face hardened. "No. I had hoped to go home and get married but found out there was no reason to return." He stood up. "Interview's over, gentlemen."

Mohr rose unsteadily. "Wait, Jones here needs to take a good likeness of you. He's set up his camera in a side room. Please, Mr. Garrett, follow him."

The photographer and interviewee slowly wended their way through the crowd of drunken, staggering customers as a player piano clanged loudly, and the crash of glass splintered across the floor.

The side room had already been prepared, with a curtain at one end, a high barstool, and two side tables at the other. While Bradford fidgeted with his lenses, Thomas, slightly recovered, waited, deep in thought. All this fuss and bother, and for what? Still have no one to share this with.

"I'll be ready in a minute, Mr. Garrett." Bradford popped his head out into the open. "After we're finished, I have some of my other photographs on the back table in case you're interested. Ready? Here we go."

Click–*flash!* Click-*flash!* The smell of white ash suddenly filled the room.

After the last film plate was done, Thomas blinked and tried to adjust his eyes to normal light.

"Would you care to see those pictures now?" the photographer asked.

It was the last thing the agent wanted to do, but Chief Deputy Prather's 'If you want to continue working at this agency' loomed large. Stepping over to the back table with Bradford, he was shown the photographer's oldest pictures first.

One by one, Thomas studied the images of factories, carriages, railroad cars, and all manner of houses, marveling at—in spite of himself—the photographic skill displayed along with the story they each presented. Continuing on, he paused. "When was this picture taken?" he asked, cocking his head slightly.

Bradford looked down at the photograph. "Yes, that was taken at the start of the Nebraska Land Rush of 1856, why?"

The agent leaned in closer over the print. "A couple of people look familiar," he muttered, pointing to a teenage Minnie and a very young Cora.

"Let me show you my most recent ones," Bradford said proudly, oblivious to the agent's quizzical expression.

Extracting several more photos from a leather portfolio, he spread them out on the second table. "Here we are. Now, these were taken at the famous Buffalo Bill Wild West Show in Omaha, just a week ago."

"Interesting," the Pinkerton observed, scrutinizing the first two. When he came to the third one, he turned pale. "And this woman?"

Bradford stood next to him. "That was taken at a dinner celebration after the show. Yes, these ladies are definitely special. Actually, they were in that other Land Rush photograph. The Dolan girls: Minnie, Cora, and Cora's daughter, Ellie. Why do you ask?"

Thomas' voice turned husky. "Where are they living now, do you know? Is Cora married?"

"They're living in South Benton, and no, she is not married."

"Are you sure? I heard a long time ago she was getting married."

"No, never been, according to Minnie. Do you *know* them? Here, I have an extra print of the ladies. Please take it. It's my gift to you."

Thomas took the photo, his eyes sparkling. "Thank you, Mr. Jones, it's been a real pleasure!" Gripping the photographer's hand and shaking it enthusiastically, he then fast-paced it out the door.

* *

"You wanted to discuss my promotion with me, sir?"

Prather nodded. "Yes, Agent Garrett, I do. We need to work out some of the details."

"And those would be?"

"First of all, this promotion comes with a tremendous amount of responsibility, more than you've had before. In fact, a great deal is riding on your performance."

Thomas cleared his throat. "What are you trying to tell me, Sir?"

"Agent Garrett, as you well know, the entire west is now rife with outlaws. Because of this, my current orders are to start up smaller, secondary offices in towns all across the area to control this menace." He walked over to a large wall map and pinpointed various spots. "Towns such as Cody, Bear River City, Harville, and Cheyenne here were mentioned. If you were to choose one, which would it be?"

Thomas attempted to appear casual. "Hmm. How about Cheyenne?"

A hop, skip, and a jump from South Benton.

"Cheyenne it is, then." Sitting down again, Prather continued. "You'll have to begin packing immediately. Arrangements will be made as far as hotel accommodations are concerned, but once you're fully installed in the new office, we will send you several agents. Oh, and while you're waiting for further instructions, get a feel for the community. Check out the local banks and saloons. See how secure they are. Also the whorehouses, if necessary." He cleared his throat. "All in good time on those, all in good time."

Prather stared at the paperwork on his desk for a few seconds. "Within a month or so, I will be giving you more procedural information. He stood up.

Smiling, Thomas did the same. "Thank you, sir, for this great opportunity."

"Not at all, not at all. I know you'll do an excellent job. Bon voyage, agent, as the French say."

Thomas turned to go.

"And agent?"

"Yes?"

"Remember our motto: *We Never Sleep.*"

* *

In all his years, Thomas had never seen so many saloons, not even in Chicago, where the population far outweighed that of Cheyenne's. Before he left, Prather had never bothered to mention this fact, but the new head agent of the Cheyenne Pinkerton office soon discovered these cheek-to-jowl establishments on his regular evening walks through town.

Highly organized, the powers that be had made certain that there were several saloons for each station in life. Cowboys, after a grueling day of herding cattle, lumbered into their own designated watering holes, where the cheap whiskey and nighttime dancing lasted well into the wee hours of the morning. Miners gratefully entered their taverns, covered from head to toe in soot and choking back tiny black particles permanently embedded in their lungs. Soldiers had their own niche as well, as they swilled down shot glasses of substandard whiskey and complained endlessly about 'Injun trouble.'

Businessmen and successful merchants were a pampered lot. As more and more educated people came from back east, they expected surroundings befitting their status. At more refined drinkeries, aged, high quality whiskey was available, but more often than not, they treated themselves to champagne.

"You should really visit the Cheyenne Club," Harriet Coley, the town's main post office maven advised him a week after his arrival. Whenever he entered, she adopted a flirtatious smile.

"Oh? What is that, might I ask?"

"It's a place for educated, well-to-do gentlemen such as yourself. Cattle magnates, eastern folks, you know." She leaned over the counter provocatively, emphasizing all her physical assets.

"I don't know about the well-to-do part, but I will check them out first chance I get. Good day to you, Miss Coley," he ended, politely tipping his bowler hat. Outside, he shook his head. It certainly wasn't the female attention he wanted. He suddenly wondered what Cora was doing right then.

The Cheyenne Club was definitely not his cup of tea. Pretentious, most of the members appeared to be either snobbish, well-to-do eastern businessmen, or rough-around-the-edges cattle magnates, who, despite their lack of education, felt entitled. All of them seemed to live by the same code: The hell with the little man, we're here to get as rich as we can, at any cost.

He sat with them one evening while they discussed cattle selling, the best 'ladies' for one's every need, and multiple rounds of overflowing champagne glasses.

"I'm telling you, this area is just ripe for the pickin.' Why, since my wife and I have arrived, my cattle business has quadrupled. A powerful country for powerful people, I always say."

"Yes. In very short order, we believe we can take over most of Cheyenne in real estate alone."

Thomas couldn't help himself. "Aren't those lands protected by the U.S. government?"

They all swiveled around toward him, their eyes slit like knife scratches.

"Where have *you* been, mister?" a well-dressed portly man asked.

"Accordin' to the 'sell or starve' rider to the Indian Appropriation Act of 1871, we can take over even more Indian lands than previously agreed upon."

Laughter exploded everywhere as the cattle magnates slapped their knees, easterners nodded vigorously, and 'presentable' waiters stood by, chaffing in their tight uniforms.

The Pinkerton had had enough. Politely excusing himself, he surveyed the crowded room, bowed to the owner, and made a mental note not to return if he could help it. Oh, Mrs. Ana, Cora, Minnie, how real, how comforting you always were.

* *

The next day, his regulation firearm shouldered under his jacket along with his Tower handcuffs, and his Derringer strapped to his right leg, he investigated three local banks. Finding each one's security woefully inadequate, he finally walked into Sutton Bank and asked to speak with the manager.

"What do you mean we don't have enough security here?" the bank manager said. "Perhaps you are too used to Chicago, Agent Garrett. Here in Cheyenne, people are basically good. We don't have any problems."

"Looking around I see open windows, no lock on your cashier drawer or, judging by how quickly your teller had access to it, your safe. I also saw no guards on the premises."

"That's our business, then, isn't it? I think perhaps you are not as needed in Cheyenne as you think you are. Good day, sir."

As Thomas turned away, something caught his eye. Across the room, people were patiently waiting in line to see the single teller. An elderly woman with apple cheeks stood in front of a businessman, opening and closing his billfold. Behind him, a mother was scolding her young child, and behind them a cowboy scratched his stubbled cheek with thick, knotty fingers. At the end of the line stood a roughshod man dressed in black, his gun belt hung low. Too low.

Instinctively, Thomas shifted into surveillance mode, pretending to study a map on the wall and glancing at the man every few seconds. Slowly, carefully, he reached into his jacket to unstrap his holster and free his Model 3 Smith & Wesson.

Suddenly, the front door banged open. A masked man charged in, firing several shots into the air. "G'day, folks! Don't be brave, gist do what we ask 'n no harm'll come to you," he called out to the terrified customers.

The man in black standing in line stepped aside, and drew his gun. "Now, *I* ain't that nice. Don't anyone make a noise, 'cause that'll just get my back up." He grabbed the mother and dragged her two feet away. With his gun pressed against her temple and his free hand tight around her throat, he announced proudly, "See? I ain't so nice!"

While the other bandit shoved the teller and manager into the back room, Thomas made a fast study of the situation, and quietly inched toward the gunman in black. As horrified customers focused on the panicked mother, her son started to whimper, "Mama, Mama."

The gunman twitched. "Shut that boy up!" he growled, tightening his chokehold even more and waving his gun in the air. "If no one stops that little bastard, I'm gonna smack 'im good!"

Slowly, deliberately, Thomas continued his approach.

"Hey! What do you think you're doin'?" the gunman growled.

With both hands slightly raised, the agent said calmly, "I was just trying to help the boy."

"Gist get 'im to stop cryin'!"

"Yes, that's what I aim to do."

"Then *do* it!"

Thomas moved over to the boy and gently pushed him toward the nearby cowboy. Surprised, the cowpoke reached out to the boy and drew him close.

Soon the teller, manager, and other bandit returned, as the boy put up another wail.

"Shut that kid up, or I'll do it for you!" the gunman snarled, his gun pointed at the pleading mother.

The masked outlaw from the back room faced his darkly-clothed accomplice. "What the *hell* is going on out here?" he barked.

"I can't think with all the racket he's makin'," the gunman complained, loosening his hold on the mother.

"Are you *serious*? Forget about the boy! We're here for the money, ain't we?" the masked man shouted at his cantankerous partner, waving his gun around, the 'hostages' momentarily forgotten.

That was all the time Thomas needed. His gun drawn, he took two fast steps and elbowed the distracted, nasty gunman in the chin. Fanning his gun, the Pinkerton pumped a volley of shots into the legs of both robbers. They thudded onto the floor like two sacks of potatoes, and when one of them moved, the Pinkerton kicked his gun away.

The mother and child fell into each other's arms, and the room erupted in cheers.

"Are they dead?" The manager asked.

"No, but they sure are going to be easy to tie up and take to jail," the agent answered, pulling out his handcuffs.

After the sheriff came and carted them off, the manager placed his hand on Thomas's shoulder. "What can I say? Thank you," he said sheepishly.

Word of the incident spread fast—throughout Cheyenne, and as far away as Chicago. By the time Chief Deputy Prather paid a visit with two seasoned agents, he was ready to give Thomas the world.

"I must say, Agent Garrett, your handling of the Sutton Bank robbery is a powerful testament to your fine abilities. I've therefore brought Agents Peterson and Wilheim here so they can easily help you in your administrative duties as you expand your entire operation."

"Thank you, sir."

"It also seems to me that it is about time to commence our plan to send an undercover agent to Omaha soon."

"Really?"

"Yes, agent."

"Might I suggest something here, sir?"

"What is it?"

"I've been thinking..."

Prather crossed his arms. "Out with it, man!"

"Sir, I believe it would perhaps be better not to have an agent go under cover in Omaha, where the outlaws will be looking for anyone deputized. Frankly, sir, they can *smell* a Pinkerton."

"Interesting theory. So where do you suggest we go?"

"I was thinking perhaps a small neighboring town that was separate from, but close to Omaha, would be a better idea. A town like South Benton." Eyeing Prather, he waited.

"South Benton? Never heard of it."

"Exactly. That's why it's so perfect. I've been doing some research. It's only a few miles away from Omaha, and although it's still growing, they have do banks, saloons, and whorehouses. I even found the perfect whorehouse for my undercover operation."

Prather sat still, drumming his fingers on top of Thomas's desk. "Let me think about this, and I will get back to you, all right? You now have two good agents here with you. Either one of them would be perfect for the job. Why a whorehouse, by the way?"

"I figure that's where any riff-raff is going to go."

"Good point," Prather said. "But how will you know which one is the best?"

Thomas cleared his throat. "Actually, I was speaking to someone the other day, who talked about a fine place he had gone to, just a few months ago. It's called Madam Ana's. Biggest one in town, which means lots of visitors. Good reputation."

A few days later, when Thomas got word that an important telegram had come over the wire from the Chicago Pinkerton Agency that morning, he immediately raced over.

"My, aren't we important!" Harriet Coley beamed, handing it over to him and batting her eyes. "I keep telling you, you would be perfect for the Cheyenne Club. I'm a member myself, you know."

But he never even looked up. Focused on the telegram, he was having trouble stopping his heart from exploding out of his chest.

> TO: AGENT GARRETT CHEYENNE OFFICE. STOP. COMMENCE PLAN IMMEDIATELY. STOP. LETTER ALREADY SENT TO DESIGNATED LOCATION IN SOUTH BENTON. STOP. SEND AGENT OF YOUR CHOICE. STOP. SIGNED CHIEF DEPUTY J.PRATHER

"This is good news, then?" She smiled coquettishly.

He thanked her absently and walked out the door, grinning from ear to ear. He knew exactly which agent was going undercover at Madam Ana's.

CHAPTER ELEVEN
Full Circles

"Lord, have mercy," Minnie muttered, as Thomas stepped into the room.

Moving forward with a broad smile, the Pinkerton was certain they could hear his heart banging like a kettledrum.

Eyes wide, hand at her throat, Cora managed a weak "Thomas?" before missing her seat and collapsing onto the floor.

He ran over to her and knelt down. "Cora, Cora," he fussed, stroking her head.

Cora stared up at him, dazed, as if in a trance.

He smiled, assured things would be perfect from this moment on from the way she looked at him. Then her face changed. Her mouth curled downward, and she openly ignored his outstretched hand, taking Minnie's instead.

"Why are you here?" she grumbled.

"Cora. After all this time?" he began.

"Exactly, all this time!" She dusted herself off and moved behind the large desk.

Looking from one sister to the other, he checked their eyes thoroughly before turning business-like. So much for memories, he reflected. "Yes, it's been a long time, ladies. Minnie, Cora."

Minnie broke the awkward silence. "I thought Pinkertons were always clean shaven."

"Interesting statement after all these years," he muttered. "They are usually, but I'm undercover, remember?"

Just then Pete burst in. "My boy! I suppose I can no longer call you that, can I?" he said, outstretching his arms. Reassured, Thomas grinned back, and as the two men gave each other bear hugs, Cora watched, stone-faced.

"There's a lot to do, even if you're not really here as a bookkeeper," she said matter-of-factly.

"But I can do that if need be." He surveyed the room. "I must say you both have done a truly splendid job with his place. Madam Ana would be so proud of you both." But it was Cora he was studying.

"Yes, yes, they certainly have. I'm so happy you're back, dear boy!" With that, Pete tipped his hat and disappeared into the parlor.

Sasha entered again. "Do you still need me, Mrs. Cora?" she asked, smiling coquettishly at the newcomer.

"No, that'll be all," Cora said. "Minnie, please show Thomas the area we've set up for him." Turning to him, she continued. "In the meantime, we can expect you to begin tomorrow, right?"

He nodded slowly, his eyes watchful.

"We can certainly come up with a list of tasks for you, Agent Garrett. In fact that'll be no problem." Not looking at him, she instructed Minnie to go ahead and take him to his new office they had set up for him down the hall.

After a little while, Minnie reappeared. "Life sure is unpredictable."

"Yes, it certainly is," Cora agreed, rubbing the back of her neck.

"Well? Tell me what you're thinking." Minnie came in close.

"I honestly don't *know* what I'm thinking, Minnie. I see him, and it's as if he never went away."

Minnie smiled. "Well, that's good."

"But I also can't stop being furious with him when I see him."

"That's bad." Minnie put her arm around her sister's shoulders. "Just remember, Cora, he's here now. Your true love, and he's …"

"After all these years? After needing him when I was pregnant? After Ellie was born, and during all those years after the war was over? No, the fact is, he deserted me, Minnie. That's all there is to it."

"I don't know. Maybe there were reasons."

"He *deserted* me." Swiveling around, Cora stalked out of their office.

* *

The next morning, the Pinkerton arrived bright and early, well dressed, and declaring he was ready to discuss the premises. Did each window have a lock on it? Was there a separate entrance to the cellar? Was it possible to come in through the roof? How many rooms were upstairs? He went down his list like a well-oiled machine, and when he was formally introduced to the doves as their new bookkeeper, the lingering looks reminded Cora of when Brett had first come in. You'd think these girls had never seen a man before, she inwardly fumed. If he thinks he can just waltz in and get back into her good graces, he's much mistaken.

"Where is your daughter?" he finally asked.

"She's already at school, teaching," Cora replied.

"Thomas, you should see her, she's wonderful," Minnie said, beaming.

"She obviously takes after her mother, not her…" His pause hovered over them like an impending rain cloud.

Without looking at her sister, Minnie cleared her throat. "Yes. Why don't you take Thomas around the house, Cora, so he can see what we need?"

It turned out the house was a total security risk. No locks were on windows, the roof had a ladder down one side of the building, and the cellar door was not only unlocked, it was slightly ajar.

He shook his head. "I hate to tell you, but this place is a train wreck just waiting to happen."

She looked up at him, trying not to stare into those deep pools of blue. "Do you honestly think we're in danger?"

"It's quite possible. Our information indicates that soon a lot of Nebraska won't be safe, and seeing as South Benton is so close to Omaha, it makes sense they'd try here. I must check out the local banks. For your information, my presence was requested by my superior, not by me," he added.

"So it wasn't your choice to come?"

"Oh, Cora, please," he pleaded.

"How did you know?" she said defiantly.

"Know what?"

"About us being in danger."

He shrugged, but his expression indicated otherwise, and when he offered his arm to help her climb up the cellar steps, once again, she brushed off his gesture. Marching forward, she squared her shoulders, his sigh floating behind her.

Back up in their office, he cleared his throat. "How 'bout a short tour of the town now? I really need to check out the local banks and the post office, too."

"Maybe Minnie could go. I should stay here," Cora replied, ignoring her sister's rolled eyes.

"I'd like *you* to come with me, Cora," he said so softly it was almost a whisper.

Minnie practically pushed her out the door with him. Out on the shaded porch that creaked like old times, they seemed like any ordinary couple. Except they aren't, she reminded herself angrily.

Thomas marveled at all the changes; how Madam Ana's now had matching maroon colored awnings and how the little cupola constructed five years ago added a European feel.

Although Cora smiled, she admitted, "Thank you, but honestly, I'm beginning to feel it's too much for me, and for Minnie."

"Oh?"

"Yes, the upkeep is enormous and the customers, they're changing."

"How so?" he asked.

"They've become, unpredictable." She sighed. "Sometimes, I wonder."

"What? What do you wonder? " He leaned in a little closer.

"I wonder if this place is gonna be the death of us."

"Maybe it's a good thing I'm here, then."

He smiled, but didn't take her arm as they approached the nearby bank, South Benton National, a solid brick building with dusty vines climbing up its sides and half-opened windows.

"Disastrous," he kept muttering.

John Corrigan's was next, and when one of the saloon gals leaning against the swinging door offered him a broad wink, Cora stiffened.

"Friendlier town than I remembered," he said.

Her snort sounded like one of Brett's show horses. "Not everyone."

At the post office, Matthew Johnson lit up as soon as he saw Cora. Reaching over the counter for her gloved hand, he ignored the Pinkerton. Instantly, Thomas bristled. Cora coughed, her cheeks dashed with pink.

"Matthew, I believe you've met Mr. Garrett. He's our new accountant."

The postmaster looked at the detective and scowled. "Oh yes, I remember Mr. Garrett very well."

Thomas nodded, his eyes narrowed. "And I, you."

Cora looked from one man to the other.

The postmaster glanced down at her gloved hand, then grinned up at her.

As an afterthought, he turned toward Thomas. "I do hope you're going to help this very special lady out, Mr. Garrett."

"Mr. Johnson, I know how to do my job, thank you very much."

Uncomfortable at the men's exchange, Cora took her old flame's arm and firmly guided him out the door, Mr. Johnson's soft snicker behind them.

"Honestly, Thomas, I don't know why you were so rude to him. After all, we've both known him for a long time."

He drew a deep breath. "I have my reasons."

"Why you even bother getting upset is beyond me. He's a harmless enough man."

"Maybe, but it was because of him that...well, never mind. Let's continue, shall we?"

She put her hand on his arm. "Wait a minute," she said. "What do you have against him?"

He sighed. "Let's just say that because of him, I didn't get to do what I wanted. That's all."

"What do you mean?"

"Cora, let's just move on."

Four blocks away, they passed old Mr. Mahoney's store, where together they had spent many a happy hour begging for candy together. Since he had died, his son had taken over and waved to her from across the street. "Nice day, Mrs. Cora, isn't it?"

He cupped his hand over his eyes and stared at the two of them, prompting Cora to say to Thomas, "I suppose I'll have to introduce you to him soon."

"Yes, just treat me as if I'm one of your employees, not a friend."

"That's true enough, isn't it?" Her sarcasm was meant to hit him full force. It worked. As they moved on, he remained silent, even when she pointed out an old building and chuckled.

"Remember the day that woman flung out her dirty water from the second floor on top of Pete who just happened to be walking by?"

A mischievous grin overtook him. "I surely do. He got *soaked!*"

Still laughing, this time she placed her hand unconsciously onto his arm. "Yes, remember how he tried to quote a famous poem but nothing made any sense? It was all gibberish!"

"I actually remember the poem," he declared.

"You do?"

"Yes, indeed. It was *The Twenty-third Psalm*," he answered, face-to-face with her.

"I suppose the Bible was appropriate to quote in that life-altering situation."

Their laughter was like old times until Cora remembered her pain. Her lips straightened into a tight grimace. Oh, no you don't, Thomas, she thought. It's not that simple.

* *

Turned out Thomas was talented with numbers. By the end of the second day he had their paperwork in impeccable order. Accounts receivable and accounts payable were organized into two separate files. Another file was marked for 'Future Promotional Endeavors,' a third for renovation of their establishment, a fourth for notes Cora had scribbled regarding policies toward the doves.

At three-thirty, when Ellie came home and burst into their office to tell Cora and Minnie about her new plans for a movable town library, she found the Pinkerton. The usually cluttered mahogany desk was neat as a pin, and the file titles clearly legible.

"My goodness, it's so neat in here!" popped out of her mouth first thing.

He looked up and smiled. "Ellie, I presume?"

"You presume right, and you are?"

"Agent Garrett."

"The Pinkerton agent, correct? Oh, no! I'm not supposed to reveal that." She had her hand over her mouth in mock concern.

Chuckling, he stood up and extended his hand. "Pleased to meet you. Please call me Thomas."

Her faced shifted in an instant. "Thomas. *The* Thomas?"

"Yes, I suppose I am." He eyed her carefully. How pretty she was. So similar to the young Cora. Same alabaster skin, same clear, innocent eyes, same sweetness Cora used to have.

"You do realize, my mother is probably going to give you a hard time. She never forgets anything."

He nodded. "Yes, I learned that fact the hard way." Straightening his cravat, he asked, "Well, what about you? You're a teacher. That's wonderful. Helping children is so important."

"Yes, but I'd like to do more than that."

"Such as?"

"Such as starting a movable library. They're doing that in other counties, you know."

Thomas scratched his beard thoughtfully. "Interesting idea."

"Yes, why not educate the entire population, not just the children, I say."

"Excellent. What kind of books did you have in mind? The classics?"

"No, not just the classics. That could be boring to some of these folks. My plan is to engage them, perhaps even some dime novels."

Throwing back his head, the detective roared with laughter. "Dime novels! Now *that* would sure please your mother!"

"That's right, you knew all about that." She joined him in laughter.

He assessed her for a few seconds. "All joking aside, your mother must be so proud of you."

Her "Not sure about that," got him studying her more fully. Then he cleared his throat and look away. Turning back with the hint of a smile he asked, "So, how did this all come about?"

The awkward moment had passed. "I got the idea from a *Chicago Tribune* article. *Ways to improve Westerners*, it was called. And here I am, educating South Benton's children, so why not their parents as well? Of course, I'll have to pass it by the local town committee first, and that may be a problem."

"I have a feeling you'll make a success out of it."

"You do?"

"Yes, I do. I know with determination, you can make anything happen. But once it's in place, it may prove to be a lot of hard work and long hours. Do you have that kind of energy and time?"

Her face pinched as tears formed. "I could use a good distraction right now. Take my mind off other things about to happen." She tilted her head down and eyed the rug.

"Things about to happen?" he asked.

Ellie gulped. "Someone I know is leaving town very soon. But I don't want to think about it."

Thomas looked at her, nodding. "I happen to be an expert on leaving towns." He smiled sadly, then brightened. "Just remember, if you ever need any help, I'm your man. For now, I better go back to the hotel and get some supper. See you tomorrow, I presume?"

Nodding, she watched him begin his exit. "Ah, Thomas?"

"Yes?" He turned around.

"So glad you're here."

He smiled.

"And Thomas? I know you're my uncle."

Stunned, he took two steps toward her. "Cora told you? Are you all right with that?"

She shrugged. "What choice do I have?"

"Ellie, I'm so sorry about my brother."

"I know. Everyone is," she said, sighing. She watched him turn toward the door again and grinned. "Thomas, still glad you're here," she called out.

Later over dinner, just recalling her words gave him hope.

* *

It was as if she were being split into tiny shards of glass. Every five minutes waves of pain rippled through her belly and womb, pain that arched her back and released a series of screams.

"Dis is very bad," Mrs. Ana kept murmuring as the midwife tried to calm her young patient. While thunder clapped ferociously, a horrified Minnie listened to her sister's howls, but every time she tried to approach the bed to hold her sibling's hand, she was shooed away.

"Thomas...where's Thomas?" Cora sobbed between contractions. In bed, her knees drawn, her hand gripping the knotted towel tied to one of the bedpost, she was forever looking at the door, as if he would walk in at any moment.

Cora woke with a start, her nightgown drenched, her half of the bed soaked. Her heartbeat banging inside her chest, she sat up and blinked several times to remember where she was. Next to her, Minnie snorted and wheezed peacefully as she turned over in her sleep, while outside a lone owl *who-whooed* wistfully. Still tingling, she didn't know what to do.

* *

For quite some time, breakfast had been important to the Dolan household—hearty food, business discussions, Minnie's jokes, and whenever Pete was present, a medley of literary quotations, all of which made for lively conversations. That next morning, amidst coffee, warm biscuits, eggs, ham, and Pete's rendition of Wordsworth peppered with Minnie's sexual innuendos, Thomas walked in on a gale of laughter.

The minute he entered, Cora grew silent.

"Cora, for goodness sake," Minnie murmured, shaking her head.

Pete saluted the group with his coffee mug. "All I can say is if Shakespeare were here 'n saw the lot of us, he'd probably say…"

"Something is rotten in the state of Denmark," Ellie called out as Pete chuckled, and Minnie had tears of laughter running down her cheeks.

"You know, Ellie told me yesterday about her grand idea for South Benton," Thomas said, looking over at his niece. "Why don't you tell them all about it?"

The room stilled while she told them about her public library ambitions. Thomas kept pitching secret glances at Cora, touched by her proud face as her daughter regaled them all with her grand plans. Aching to reach out and draw her to him like the old days, he opted for the sidelines. For now.

"Ellie was always a born reader," Cora said. Everyone turned to her. "Remember that, Minnie? We taught her to read by putting up newspaper articles all around her room. Then we'd follow each page as the story continued."

"I remember that, Mama. Sometimes you'd put the pages out of order so I would really have to concentrate on the story to get it right." She looked at her mother and aunt fondly. "You were both wonderful."

Minnie gave her niece a warm hug while Cora dabbed one eye with her finger.

Like old times with the Dolan girls, Thomas thought, his mind floating back even further:

> *"Thomas, Cora! You can stay out on porch for little vhile, but don't be late!" Mrs. Ana said, smiling knowingly before she closed the front door.*

"Let's get our day started, shall we?" Cora turned officious. "Thomas, you did say you could help us with other things?"

"Cora, give the man a chance to settle in." Minnie frowned.

"No, Minnie, it's all right," Thomas said. "I'm at your disposal—as long as I can get my own work done."

"All right then. The attic needs a lot of box moving. I'll show you the way."

Surprisingly hopeful, the Pinkerton followed Cora toward the attic steps, as Ellie went off to school, and Pete and Minnie washed the dishes.

Up in the attic, left to their own devices, Cora and Thomas surveyed the room and sneezed. Dust-covered boxes, cobwebbed rafters, and a few crickets bombarded their senses as the madam handed him a few clean rags.

"So, what would you have me do, ma'am?"

"I'm not sure. We always have so much to do. *Too* much, maybe," she offered. "We need to go through these boxes, one by one, but that will have to be down in our office, step by step. Perhaps today, if you could first dust, then bring down ten of them, that would be a good start."

"At your service," he said hesitantly, then, seeing her smile, grinned full force. "Aren't you going to help me here?" he asked, taking off his jacket and cravat. When she shook her head, he handed her his jacket and rolled up his sleeves.

His easy familiarity irked her. This is not the old days, she fumed. "No, I have business to attend to with the doves. I'll see you downstairs when you're finished." His jacket and tie folded over her arm, she started downstairs, feeling their warmth burn a hole there.

In the end, he brought down around fifteen boxes, some small, some quite large, and by the last trip, he stood in their office, coated in a light, dusty film, and depositing gray droplets of sweat onto his shirt.

"Obviously, I need to wash up. Where can I go?"

"There's a pump well out back. Remember?" Showing him the way, outside she handed him a towel and bit her lip. "Please just return this when you're done."

"Of course. Still bite your lip?" he asked softly.

"I don't know what you mean!" she huffed and strode back into the house, leaving him at the well, his shoulders slumped.

Inside, Cora performed her chores with an angry gusto. Pummeling pillows in lieu of plumping them up, swatting cigar ashes out of pewter bowls with an old, tattered rag, she stifled the urge to scream, *Too late! Too late!* But a couple of minutes in, some sort of magnetic force drew her back toward the window. Leaning against the pane, she sucked in her breath. His shirt lay off to one side, his suspenders dangling, Thomas was pumping the well handle and splashing water onto his face, neck, and torso. His well-developed arm muscles and tight chest made her gulp. Then remember. How good those arms felt around her so long ago. How good they would feel now. She stood there, suspended, shocked at her sudden need to have them enfold her, as she stroked his chest,

"A-*ha!! Caught*-cha!" Minnie snickered from the doorframe.

"Fiddlesticks!" her sister snorted. "The windows needed cleaning, is all."

"Oh, come *on*, Cora. He was a handsome young man before, and he's even more handsome now. You're a full-grown woman. Ain't no crime in wantin' him. The past's over and done with."

"It's not that easy, Minnie. I'm not you."

"You sure ain't. Unlucky you." She left, a loud cackle trailing behind her.

* *

After the third person had mentioned the glory of Buffalo Bill showing the American public all about the West, Ellie had had enough of trying to put Brett out of her mind. Knowing he was to leave in two days' time, she marched over to the tackle room late one evening, where she found him leaning over a table, slowly cleaning various bridle parts.

He jumped. "Ellie! Are you all right?"

"No, Brett, I'm not."

His sigh seemed to last a very long time. "I know, I'm not either. Look, Ellie, this is what I do; what I've always done—move around, and now with the show, I will have to continue doing that more than ever. But I don't wanna leave you."

"Why did you come after me then? Why did you make me fall in love with you? Why?"

"Oh, Ellie," he whispered, his arms around her, his forefinger wiping off each tear. "I'm miserable, too."

The horses suddenly nickered in their stalls as Ellie looked up at him. "So, the day after tomorrow, it is truly good-bye?"

He kissed her, but his lips, so gentle before, this time felt rough, almost angry. He broke and backed away. "I'm so sorry, Ellie, I didn't mean to do that."

"Good-bye, Brett," she choked, and as she staggered off, he watched her go, one finger wiping a tear away.

* *

Thomas was as good as his word. At the end of each day, he made sure to save a few minutes to confer with Ellie on her strategy with the town council. Astute in such political matters, he would sit head to head with her at his desk, discussing the pros and cons of each board member and how to handle even the most unreasonable person.

He soon found himself looking forward to their sessions together. Cora was still emotionally distant, but with Ellie, he could at least feel some of the friendliness and warmth he had experienced with the Dolan girls so long ago.

At first, they were almost Machiavellian in their plans, but soon, levity crept in, ending their sessions with a playful round of verbal one-upmanship and a mutual admiration of each other's dogged determination.

"I wish you had been my father," she said softly one night as he was sorting through her papers.

His head jerked sideways. "What did you say?"

"Nothing important," she sighed. "So tomorrow night?"

"Of course. See you then."

He took a few more minutes to close up his office, but her words didn't leave him for hours. Not until he was in bed, trying to get some sleep. Not until another thought crossed his mind.

Wes, I don't care if you're my kin...wherever you are, you're a sorry son-of-a-bitch!

* *

The week passed slowly for Ellie, each day filled with school activities, brainstorming at night with Thomas and overhearing an unusual amount of merriment in the parlor. As the doves cavorted with customers, told their randy jokes amongst themselves, and called out to her in passing, Ellie could no longer fight her sense of impending doom. She was going to end up like her mother, she could just *feel* it, no matter how many times she told herself that Brett would probably eventually fade and take his place as a lovely memory.

"A penny for your thoughts, darlin'," Minnie said that Saturday night as she and her niece rocked side by side together out on the porch. Her father's timeworn corncob pipe in hand, the madam puffed and exhaled clouds of tobacco, while inside, honky-tonk music played and customers and doves were having a whale of a time.

"Minnie, I'm worried."

"I know, honey, I know about Brett leaving real soon."

"It's not just that."

"What is it then?"

Ellie took a very deep breath. "How do you stop loving someone?"

Looking thoughtful for a few seconds, Minnie put her pipe down on her lap. "If I knew the answer to that, love, I'd be rich. Actually, that's a question you should ask your mama. Something she's currently dealin' with."

"You mean Thomas being here, right?"

"Oh yes, indeedy."

Again they both started rocking. "That's another thing I'm worried about," Ellie added.

"What, love?"

"Being just like Mama. I don't want to grow old and be so mistrustful of men."

Minnie's rocker suddenly stopped, and she reached over to stop Ellie's as well. "Now listen here, young lady. You're not like your mother. Not one little bit. You'll *never* be like she is. Just remember that."

Leaves crackled as a lone man approached, his hat slanted down over his face.

"Brett?" Ellie rose, her hand over her heart.

"Ellie, we need to talk," he answered, taking the steps two at a time, a huge smile slathered across his face.

"That's my cue to exit," Minnie announced, grabbing her pipe and bustling inside.

His arms around Ellie, Brett kissed her this time without any anger or frustration, simply a deep, long-lasting kiss.

"So?" Her heart was pumping.

"I've worked it all out with Annie and Buffalo Bill."

"Worked what out?"

"I will be taking care of any horse they need trained, and the stable's owner, Mr. Hanson, has promised me some clients."

"You mean you're staying?"

"Yes, I'm staying here, Ellie, with you."

"Brett!" Kissing him back, she could feel both their hearts beating in time to each other. He sat down on one of the rockers and pulled her into his lap. "I can't believe you did that for me," she whispered.

"Why, I love you, Ellie. Have ever since that very first day at the stagecoach." He nestled her even closer against his chest. "In fact…" He stopped as she held her breath.

"In fact?"

"I want to marry you."

"Oh, Brett." As they kissed, all thoughts of Cora's disapproval faded fast, but within seconds, they reappeared with a vengeance. "Yes, of course! But promise me, we won't tell Mama right away. Promise?"

He laughed. "Now, that's a first. I thought all mothers wanted their daughters married."

"Typically that's true, but my mama's, well, she's not typical."

"I'd say both mother and daughter are not typical," he replied, chuckling. "Guess that's why I fell in love."

"Am I that untypical?"

"I remember you tearing apart that mail coach for your books. Let's just say that got my attention."

They were both still laughing as Cora peered out of the one of the parlor windows and saw her daughter on the wrangler's lap.

* *

Inside, things had risen to a fevered pitch. Minnie was twirling around, hands and arms in the air, hair flying, a raucous laugh bouncing against the walls.

"Minnie, it's just a new act over at Corrigan's," Cora said. "What's all the fuss?"

"It's not just any act, Cora. It's Lola Montez, for goodness sake! She's coming here, of all places, for a one night only performance. Sure hope she does her famous snake dance."

Cora scoffed. "Lola Montez, really."

"Well, Missy, you have your Buffalo Bill Wild West Show, and I have Lola."

As their argument escalated, the doves abandoned their posts and started to circle around the two sisters. Singing *Tassel on my Boots* at the top of their lungs, the chorus swelled and the room vibrated. By the time Ellie slipped in, the male customers had joined in the festivities, adding a baritone timbre to the deafening female screeches of laughter.

Catching sight of the glowing schoolmarm, the girls didn't miss a beat. They started to dance around her and laughed when she tossed her head back and clapped enthusiastically, then performed a little jig in the middle, one hand lifting up the edge of her skirt.

"Ooooooh la-la! Miss 'Wisdom Bringer' is happy tonight! Wonder why? Tell us, tell us, tell us!" they all cried.

More and more people were calling out, "Tell us, tell us, tell us!" as Cora stood in the doorway, her arms crossed.

In bed that night, Minnie couldn't stop talking. "Tonight I was happier than a lost soul with hell in a flood!"

"Speak for yourself," Cora grunted, then rolled over on her side.

"Cora, Cora, Cora. Stop it. Ellie's allowed to be in love, ya know."

A long silence. "I don't know what you're referring to," Cora finally said.

"If you didn't have your head up your arse, you'd see you could have the same thing, too."

"What in the world are you talking about?" Cora snapped, turning around to face her sister.

"I'm talkin' about the same, good-lookin' man who says good mornin' to you every day, and you don't give him the fly on an elephant's back, that's who I'm talkin' about!"

"If you're referring to Thomas, that's plain ridiculous. I'll have you know, he says it to the both of us."

"Maybe so, but it's *you* he's always looking at when he says it."

With a loud sniff, Cora turned over again, but when the night turned pitch black and the stars sprinkled the sky like jewels scattered across a dark rug, she waited for Minnie to fall asleep, so she could have her own thoughts in peace. In spite of herself, a tiny smile spread across her face.

He must still want me. Still think I'm pretty. Still ...

* *

She watched how happy her daughter was now—peaceful, self-contained. The phrase *tired of feeling angry* did flicker across her mind several times over the coming weeks. Still, she was at a loss of what to do—her patterns were too set.

"You must be so proud of Ellie," Thomas mentioned one day as he handed her the bookkeeping ledger.

"Yes, I am," Cora replied, not even looking up.

"Good. Well, good night then," he said, sighing.

"Good night."

"Thomas." Minnie strolled in. "Been meaning to ask you something."

"Yes?"

"How come you knew we were still here in South Benton?"

Cora's head snapped up. "Yes, Thomas. I've been wondering that same thing, after all these years." Her tone chilled slightly.

"Excuse me, I'll be right back," he said and walked out, leaving them with their eyebrows raised. When he returned, he was carrying a portfolio. Walking over to the desk, he plunked down a photograph, then stepped back.

"Well, I'll be," Minnie laughed. "Where'd you get that?"

"A photographer named Bradford Jones. Says he knows you both."

Cora threw her sister a dirty look. "He sure does. So, in other words, we're not in real trouble?" she asked, bristling.

"Yes, just being near Omaha, you're definitely a target. These outlaws are getting more and more vicious every day. The Soltano gang, for example, they are one of the worst. As a matter of fact, tomorrow, the three of us should sit down and talk about how to protect this place properly while you all watching Miss Lola Montez perform," Thomas said.

"You're coming with us, aren't you?" Minnie asked.

"If you'd like." He stared at Cora.

"Yes, of course we would. Right, Cora?"

Cora took the longest time to nod. "So, you were saying you didn't decide on South Benton, your boss did?"

Thomas sighed. "Let's just say, Cora, I steered him toward South Benton."

"Give the man a rest. Good night, Thomas. Just glad you're here and that you're going with us tomorrow," Minnie said.

"Thank you, Minnie," he muttered, his eyes focused nowhere near the older madam.

Cora stared at the floor for a couple of seconds, sensing he was waiting for her to make some sort of comment. Minnie was glad he was here. Was *she*? A part of her certainly was; the part that remembered his arms around her, the part that hadn't quite completely shelved the memory of that special kiss on Ana's porch so long ago. But what about the other part? What about the numbness she felt—and the words *too late, too late* cropping up over and over again?

* *

The night of Lola's performance, Madam Ana's was locked up tight. For five days straight, Cora had watched Thomas work hard to install extra security everywhere—bolts on the storm windows and shutters, padlocks on the roof, the basement door, and the stable. She had even asked him to place a special latch on Minnie's and her bedroom, which made him laugh.

"Don't worry. I'll make it so secure, not even Allan Pinkerton himself could penetrate this place," he said, chuckling.

Finally, the night of the performance arrived, and with feathered hats, a bright array of satin dresses, woolen shawls, high leather boots, and waves of giggles, the entire Madam Ana's entourage made their way over to Corrigan's Gaming Hall for the celebrity show.

As they all walked along, out of the corner of her eye, Cora could see Thomas starting out beside Minnie, then slowly working his way over toward her, chatting nonchalantly to different doves, and ending up in step with her. In spite of herself, she smiled.

Just outside the swinging doors, Minnie paused. "All right, everyone," she announced proudly. "Let's make a night of it!" and pushing the doors open, led them all inside.

In spite of their good reputation at Madam Ana's, Cora realized that Corrigan's large, wood-paneled establishment was, of late, the talk of the town. Once a single-roomed saloon, now it boasted three interconnecting rooms. The main thoroughfare housed an enormous oak bar, built, Corrigan claimed, by a master craftsman brought in especially from Omaha. Upscale Claret Sangarees and Champagne Flips were served along with rot-gut Cactus Wine and Mule Skinners. At the front of the room stood a smallish stage with a curtain behind it, perfect for the upcoming single performer.

Impressed, as soon as they all entered, Cora noticed off to one side of the main room, was one of the side quarters, where gambling tables had been set up for Faro, Poker, Blackjack and Monte. Corrigan had already informed the Dolans how the Monte shell game pulled in the cowboys, and the card games attracted the higher-end clients. Word had it that his business had expanded tenfold by installing these gaming tables and by luring in different performers, such as the likes of Lola Montez, out of retirement, and hoping for a comeback.

Although Cora had asked Corrigan to reserve an entire section for the Madam Ana contingent, as soon as Ellie spotted Brett, she made a beeline across the room to him.

Cora shook her head.

"Cora, she's a grown woman," Minnie cautioned. "She can sit wherever she wants."

Nodding, Cora said, "Yes, I suppose so."

Thomas, quickly guiding Cora and Minnie over to a seat next to the first gambling room, distracted Cora with comments on how much Corrigan's had changed over the years. Nodding vehemently, Minnie agreed, as drinks appeared and Cora, sipping her first Champagne Flip, began to relax.

"You know, I read an article about Miss Montez. It called her, the very comet of her sex," Thomas said, as one of the doves at the next table almost fell off her chair laughing at some joke.

Minnie smiled. "I heard she kept a couple of bears chained up in her front yard in Grass Valley!"

Cora gaped. "Really? Bears?"

"I also heard she's had different marriages," Pete chimed in. "And they say she's the illegitimate daughter of Lord Byron," he added, reaching for his low-end Mule Skinner. "*There is a pleasure in the pathless woods, There is a rapture on the lonely shore ...*"

A couple of new cowboys at the bar swiveled around toward him to stare, as he continued.

"*There is society where none intrudes, By the deep sea, and music in its roar.*" He added, "Ah, that Byron..."

Just then Marlena let out a huge burp, and everyone exploded with laughter.

At Cora's elbow, Thomas started chuckling, and after two more Champagne Flips, the younger madam couldn't stop grinning. Without thinking, she placed her hand on his arm and gripped it, as she leaned back into his shoulder and arm.

Even under his suit, she could feel how muscular he had become. Slowly, she closed her eyes and let the Champagne Flip work its magic. Her head swirling, she was picturing him, no longer there in a suit supporting her, but drinking water at their well, his shirt off, his suspenders dangling.

"Cora? Are you awake?" he asked.

She noticed his head was cocked at a forty-five degree angle, taking her in—her lavender parfum from Paris, her dangling emerald earrings that matched her dark green velveteen dress, her new green silk hat shipped all the way from the Mademoiselle Costello Paris Millinery. All the finery and scent she had carefully put on earlier, to make sure she looked her best.

"Another Champagne Flip, Cora?" Minnie asked, winking at Thomas.

"I shouldn't, but…"

Newfound co-conspirators, Minnie and Thomas simultaneously raised their right hands to signal a waitress over.

Out of the corner of his eye, the Pinkerton caught a movement at the Faro table. As his body tensed, he ignored the next round of drinks brought to their table, and Cora's warmth against him, and stayed riveted on one of the four card players.

While three of the card players were busy arguing, looking over Cora's head, the detective had a perfect view of the fourth player placing a card on the table. The tip end of a Kepplinger mechanism was peeking out of the man's sleeve, its metallic sheen sparkling under the glowing lights. Recognizing the gambler as Luke Short, Thomas knew what would come next. Sure enough, the card shark exchanged his old card with the new one in a flash, confident no was watching. When it was done, the squat, experienced man drew a quick breath and smiled. Then slowly, casually, he turned and calmly surveyed the main hall.

And Thomas eyeing him.

CHAPTER TWELVE
Temptations

Thomas figured that the infamous gambler Luke Short, already kicked out of Dodge, could sense danger as good as any lawman. One glowering, 'evil eye' from the detective, and the card shark instinctively clutched his stomach, doubled over, and mumbled something to the gentleman sitting next to him, who nodded absently before sliding a hefty pile of 'ivories' across the table into the chip pot.

On his feet, the gambler tipped his hat, and conspicuously avoiding one last look at the detective, made a fast exit just as the lights flickered, and a lone man called out, "Come on out, Lola! Ain't gonna wait no longer!"

A light ripple of chuckles grape-vined throughout the room.

"That's *rude!*" Cora hissed, nestling against Thomas. He was content. With the card shark gone, he could now concentrate on the upcoming show and the closeness of their bodies.

Suddenly, Lola stuck her head out between the curtains to yell back, "I'm a-comin'. Hold yer horses, fellas, I'll git there when I git there!" She disappeared again.

The crowd roared its approval, while the heckler hung his head, and after another round of drinks, the lights lowered for real.

"Here we go, folks," Minnie warbled, leaning back in her chair and hiccupping.

In the half-light, a drumroll rumbled from off stage, then out popped Lola, clad in her famous Lord Byron garb. With her long salt and pepper hair, flashing blue eyes, and bronze skin, it was obvious to all, she had once been quite a beauty.

As the audience whistled, stamped, and applauded, she performed a little curtsey then raised her right hand. Instantly, there was a hush the likes of which the Corrigan establishment had never seen. Every eye was focused on her as she strolled over to a large, handmade Indian basket on stage left. As the drums rumbled a second time, she opened the top, reached in, and pausing just the right amount of time for maximum effect, extracted a long snake, writhing slowly in the air.

The room teemed with gasps that quickly crescendoed into outright screeches and howls when she draped it around her neck and shoulders. Her head high, her eyebrows arching, she began gyrating her hips in syncopated undulations to her snake.

"I heard tell these so-called snakes cost her a small fortune," Minnie whispered to Cora and Thomas.

"You mean they're not real?" Cora asked, swaying slightly across the table toward her sister.

"No, honey, they're made of rubber, cork, and whalebone."

"So she's a fake." Cora sniffed.

"Right. So Buffalo Bill really saved all those people, even at the battle of Little Bighorn?" Minnie retorted.

Thomas laughed. "C'mon ladies. Do your fighting later."

The act was turning serious. As if in a trance, Lola practically moaned an unrecognizable tune. Sad, set in a minor key, the lilting melody captured everyone's attention, even the saloon gals, used to giving all their concentration to drunk customers.

Suddenly, to everyone's horror, the snake snapped in two. Murmurs of disbelief overrode everything until a cowboy in the front called out, "Hey, look! Those snakes are as phony as my cousin, and *he* always lies like a cheap rug!"

Lola stormed off behind the curtain as the crowd began hissing. Soon their hisses became downright boos. "Give us our money back," people yelled, searching for any object to throw at the stage.

As the yells grew, Mr. Corrigan hurried over to the front of the room. "Now, ladies, gents, I understand you're angry, I truly do! I'm sure I'd be as well, don't ya know!" More boos followed. "Look, folks, *folks!*" Sweat was trickling down his face.

More grumbling. "Hey, let's put Corrigan in a blanket and bounce him 'round a bit, like they do in other counties!" barked another cowboy.

Corrigan looked over at the Dolan girls pleadingly. Minnie stood up and swaggered over to the stage, nearly stumbling over a front row patron's outstretched leg. Several hands shot up to save her as she steadied herself and climbed up onto the platform.

"Shush, *shush!* C'mon, there's *no* need to treat Miss Montez or Mr. Corrigan like this. So what if her snakes ain't real. She sure can dance, now can't she?"

"How 'bout *you* dance, Miss Minnie? Or better yet, that pretty sister or niece of yours," rang out from the back of the hall.

Across the room from each other, Brett and Thomas simultaneously rose from their respective seats, their teeth bared.

"What are you doing, Thomas?" Cora asked, pulling on his pant leg and almost falling over.

He looked down at her. "Nobody should talk about you that way."

She stared up into his angry eyes. "That's nice of you, but I can take care of myself." When she hiccupped, he sat down next to her and shook his head.

"I think you've had enough to drink, Cora," he said.

Corrigan quickly took over. "Now, now, now. Ladies and gents, if you want yer money back, I'll give it. Let's forget the whole thing and just enjoy the night out. What do you say?" He paused, then gulped. "Drinks are on the house!"

Wild applause was their response, but as people started lining up to get a refund, suddenly Lola appeared from behind the curtain and defiantly stalked over to the gaming room to play tenpins and smoke a thin cigar. Smiles immediately broke out, the customers drifted away from the money-back line, and ended up surrounding her at her tenpin table instead, begging for autographs.

"After all, she was a legend once," Pete announced, his face so red and bloated, a slight chill settled over Cora's heart.

"See, Cora? People *can* change," Minnie slurred.

Cora shrugged as Thomas murmured, "Time to go home, time to go home."

Tilting and shifting along, the Madam Ana party managed to make it home in one piece. Thomas, realizing getting Cora drunk might have backfired, did his best to prop her up close to him. Pete and Minnie interlocked arms so tight, they became as one, and far behind in the shadows, Brett and Ellie cooed soft words into the night between smooches.

On their porch, Cora looked over at the sweethearts and started to make a comment, but ended up just emitting a simple sigh. "Gotta change clothes," she muttered and disappeared. Minnie took off toward the kitchen for a midnight snack, and Pete collapsed on their settee.

Thomas decided he had better stay a while to make sure Cora was all right, and entered his small office. A report regarding this Luke Short might be needed by the Wyoming office, and now was as good a time as any to do it. His desk light lit, his pen dipped in ink, he started in. Before long, Ellie came by, her face glowing.

"Sleep well, dear Thomas," she said softly. A woman in love entered his mind as he continued writing. When he heard a slight rustle, he looked up.

Cora was in the doorframe, with only a nightgown on and a light shawl loosely wrapped around her. Stumbling a little, she approached the front of the desk and stood there, opposite him. He could tell she was trying hard to act normal, but her eyes were glazed, and when she spoke, her voice held the distinct timbre of alcohol.

"Thank you for being ready to defend my honor," she voiced as clearly as she could.

He stood up and came around to her side. She turned toward him just as the shawl fell onto the floor. Simultaneously, they both stooped over for it and banged their heads together.

"Ow!" she cried, standing up, the outline of her breasts jutting out beneath her gown. He sucked in his breath and gulped. "So sorry," he murmured, not looking at her face at all.

She noticed the direction of his eyes and produced a crooked grin, pleased with her feminine power. "I guess you still find me attractive."

He put one arm tentatively around her waist. "Cora, don't tease me."

She leaned into him for a few seconds, their bodies fitting together like old times. Yet, when she paused and drew back, Thomas could sense a shift.

"I think I'm drunk. I should go to bed," she said.

With a deep sigh, he withdrew his arm, and steadying himself against the desk, listened to her say, "Good night," then watched her straighten up, as if gathering all her dignity, and leave.

* *

Meeting up with the South Benton School Committee the following week was a far cry from Ellie's original encounter with them. Nodding graciously, they all welcomed her heartily, and Judge Endicott even complimented her 'exemplary teaching.' Mrs. Endicott concurred, displaying a rare smile that few ever got to see. Ramrod straight in their seats, they were all expecting the schoolmarm's moxie, but no one had an inkling of what was to follow.

Empowered by love, Ellie was more than ready. "I'd like to propose a project that would be helpful for the entire South Benton community, not just their children," she began.

"And what might that be?" one of the committee members asked.

"A movable library."

"A *what?*" several of them buzzed.

"This is something that other towns have been incorporating into their educational systems. It would entail a covered wagon chock full of books, not only for the children, but for the adults as well."

"What manner of books are you talking about?" Mrs. Endicott's smile had vanished. "And how do you propose garnering extra funds for these books? After all, Miss Dolan, we've already raised quite a tidy sum for school books—at your request, I might add."

"We could do bake sales, raffles, and all manner of things. I could also offer those popular dime novels. Anything to get people to read."

In the silence, a lone cricket sawed.

Mrs. Endicott's face reddened. One loud, determined sniff later, she drew herself up regally. "Perhaps you are used to such influences, given your extraordinary living circumstances, but frankly, we do *not* wish to obtain such low-brow literature. Indeed, I find it surprising that a woman of your intelligence would stoop so low as to even suggest such materials. It makes me wonder."

"Wonder about *what* Mrs. Endicott?" Ellie's stance widened as her jaw set. "Have you not been satisfied with my teaching methods?"

Mrs. Endicott's cheeks flushed pink. "Yes, but…"

"I'm only trying to further the education of all of South Benton. However, I'm also a realist. I understand that not everyone will want to read the classics right off the bat. But I truly believe that once reading is introduced and turned into a habit, no matter the material, people will be more inclined to read higher literature."

Obviously flustered, Mrs. Endicott started shuffling a few papers in front of her as several others cleared their throats.

"Well," she said coldly. "We'll just have to see about that."

All of a sudden, Ellie fully understood what her mother had been fighting her whole life. It was the Mrs. Endicotts of the world, with just a few words or a simple gesture, who could dismiss the likes of the Dolans in an instant.

"Interesting idea, Miss Dolan," Judge Endicott said finally, eyeing his wife. "We shall discuss this privately, and you shall have our answer in due course."

"Thank you, Judge Endicott," Ellie replied, bolstering herself up and trying to remember all Thomas' encouraging words from earlier that morning.

Two weeks later, Ellie, now able to fully concentrate on her students, was in the middle of a lively lesson on Zeus and his nemesis, Hades, when Mrs. Peabody, a member of the school committee, delivered a note from the judge. Smiling broadly, the well-dressed woman with a particularly stylish navy blue hat, handed it over and commented on how much she admired the young teacher, no matter what Mrs. Endicott had said.

A good sign, Ellie thought, hopeful, as she opened up the note. Sure enough, it contained a go-ahead for her project. "Do thank the judge for me," she said, anticipating how excited Thomas and Brett would be when she told them.

Her happiness was short-lived. No sooner did Mrs. Peabody exit when two boy students, pretending to be Zeus and Hades, started a mock argument. That quickly evolved into a physical jousting match, with all the students taking sides, cheering each of them on, and creating a general racket. Thank goodness Mrs. Peabody had left, Ellie chuckled quietly, as she rounded up the happy children for more serious endeavors. Within minutes, they were all sitting dutifully at their desks, concentrating on Greek mythology.

"I *knew* it would happen," Thomas announced proudly when Ellie told him the news.

"What do you mean?"

"Ellie, you are force to be reckoned with. Your intelligence and your dogged determination will get you far." He paused thoughtfully. "In fact, you'd be a wonderful detective."

Ellie burst out laughing. "Oh yes, of course. As if Alan Pinkerton would allow *that*."

"Actually, one of his most successful detectives during the Civil War was a woman by the name of Kate Varne."

"Really?" Ellie's eyes widened. "What kind of duties did she perform? Did she dress up like a man and go riding through the countryside to meet up with dangerous fellows?"

Thomas laughed. "Are you sure you haven't been reading your mother's dime novels? No, Ellie, she would dress up in her most coquettish dresses and attend Washington parties where known Confederate sympathizers would be, in order to overhear any pertinent information regarding military strategies. It worked. Apparently, just by being so charming and gracious, she overheard or was told about vital troop movement and plans that later aided the Union army enormously."

"Me, a detective. Fascinating."

"You never know about life, Ellie. You really don't." He trailed off and stared past her, as if seeing ghosts.

Watching him closely, Ellie wondered which ghost, in particular, was still haunting him.

* *

When Mrs. Endicott and Mrs. Peabody stopped Ellie on the street a week later, Mrs. E's face was cordial, Mrs. P's face, extremely cheerful. Fiercely competitive with each other when it came to fashion, they always made sure each of their outfits would receive many an envious glance from the local townswomen strolling by. Reflecting fine sewing acumen, each dress was made from the latest Parisian silk, with braided trim etched down the bodices, sleeve cuffs, and hems. It all ended in the pinnacle of their bustles. Mrs. Endicott's collar was fur-lined. Mrs. Peabody's was not. Both hats were feathered and tilted at strategic, forty-five degree angles.

"Miss Dolan, we have some good news for you," Mrs. Endicott began.

"Yes?" Ellie couldn't help admiring her braiding and both hats.

"Yes, dear," Mrs. Peabody said, beaming. "We have decided to sponsor a dance at the town hall in two weeks' time, and you shall be our guest of honor, in order to tell the entire community about your movable library. What do you say to that?"

Ellie's eyes grew even larger. "Why, that's lovely. Thank you both so much!"

"Miss Ellie! Miss Ellie!" came two gleeful calls from across the street. Ellie saw Marlena and Rosie and motioned them over, as Mrs. Peabody looked uncomfortable, and Mrs. Endicott positively sputtered.

Enthusiastic before, now standing within inches of the tight-lipped dowagers, the ladies of the night turned edgy.

As the older women's true colors surfaced, Ellie turned mischievous.

"Hello, ladies. I would like to introduce you to Mrs. Peabody and Mrs. Endicott. Mrs. Peabody, Mrs. Endicott, Miss Marlena and Miss Rose."

The two doves curtsied graciously, and the older women dipped their heads ever so slightly.

"Apparently, there is to be a town hall dance in two weeks' time," Ellie said. "Isn't that wonderful? Get out your dancing shoes."

Mrs. Endicott gagged. "Now, wait a moment. I don't think it's a good idea to invite them."

"Yes, I agree," Mrs. Peabody concurred.

Facing the dowagers, Ellie's eyebrow shot up. "Ladies, you did say this dance was for the entire community, did you not?"

The pause seemed endless.

"Yes, I suppose we did." Mrs. Endicott sniffed. "Well, good day to you, Miss Dolan."

When the two women disappeared around a corner, Marlena put her hand on the teacher's sleeve. "Sorry, Miss Ellie."

"Nonsense," Ellie exclaimed. "Utter nonsense." With a quick squeeze to Marlena's shoulder, she headed over to the post office.

* *

The night of the dance, Cora was surprised to see the town hall never looking better. Mr. Corrigan had admitted to her what a tremendous effort it was to get his piano moved in, along with Judge Endicott's 'caller 'n fiddler' hired from a neighboring town. She admired the flowers lovingly placed on tables alongside plenty of whiskey and champagne glasses, and as waves of people arrived with their pies, cakes, barbequed beef, and Sunday-go-to-meetin' clothes, the jamboree chatter rippled through the room like a rain storm blowing in, or, as Minnie remarked, "It's a real goose drowner!"

"There's sure plenty of tonsil varnish here tonight," Pete commented.

"Pete, have a little restraint," Cora said, as she openly searched the room.

"Brett's over there, Ellie, honey," Minnie pointed, then watched her niece scurry over to him. Cora stared at the young couple and sighed.

"Cora, honey, why do you dislike him so much?"

Cora looked thoughtful. "I don't really. Frankly, I'm not sure what I feel, Minnie. I only know she's so young, so trusting."

"Is that what's this is all about? Trust? Just because you haven't had any for years, doesn't mean Ellie can't have some, you know."

"I know." Cora started to bite her lower lip.

"All I can say is, she's got a right to find her own way," Minnie said, gently placing her hand on Cora's arm.

"What is all you have to say?" Thomas asked, his beard freshly clipped, his suit, vest, and cravat elegant.

"My, don't you look handsome!" Minnie exclaimed, elbowing her sister.

Cora presented a half-smile but had trouble meeting the detective's eyes. Damn! He *did* look handsome, she thought. Too handsome.

She turned to see cowboys, wranglers, saloon gals, and doves squeezed in next to farmers, their families, local townspeople, and the expensively-dressed, upper crust of society. Petite napkins and small plates had been provided, and as food was served and eaten, drinks sipped or guzzled, the noise bouncing off the walls reached epic proportions.

"This is really something, isn't it?" Thomas shouted.

"Yes, it is," she answered, feeling his eyes on her. Still, she couldn't quite look at him directly. He was too handsome, too real.

Several glass clinks sounded. When that failed to quiet people, more and more glasses were being clinked, until finally the crowd hushed.

Judge Endicott was holding court. "Ladies and gentlemen," he began. "We are here tonight to first of all, honor the members of the South Benton School Committee."

There was polite applause. A toddler started bawling. Pausing, he cleared his throat and waited until she was snatched up by her mother and escorted outside.

"But we are also here tonight," he continued, "to honor quite a remarkable young lady. A lady, I might add, who at first gave us slight apoplexy." Chuckles broke out.

Clearing his voice, he moved on. "Miss Ellie Dolan has not only proven herself as a truly fine teacher, she is now responsible for instigating a new book program for both children *and* adults in South Benton. It's called the Movable Library. It..."

He never finished. The clapping, stamping, and whistling overtook everything.

Thomas leaned into Cora. "You must be so proud, Cora," he said.

Nodding, she leaned in toward him. "Yes," she replied, slightly teary-eyed.

Across the room, Cora watched as Brett, nestled against Ellie, gave her a quick kiss on the cheek before she stood up to curtsey to the room.

Minnie laughed. "Ain't that cute? They're in love."

Cora nodded, thinking about trust.

"Yes, people *do* fall in love, I'm told," Thomas said, his face inscrutable.

Suddenly, all heads rotated toward the front of the room, as the musicians tuned their instruments.

"The musicians are a'startin' folks," a cowboy in chaps cried.

Sure enough, the fiddler, already settled down onto a chair, was giving the room the proper signal for these kinds of events. *Thwack-thwack-thwack!* went his bow tapping against his fiddle as he grinned, winked, and the excitement tore through the room like the start of a horse race.

Next to him, the caller took a swig of whiskey and clapped his hands together. "My, oh my," he laughed. "Gents, be nice 'n ladies, get your dancin' shoes on and get ready to go!"

As men chuckled, women giggled, and the caller motioned the fiddler to begin, Cora could feel her own heartbeat excelling.

"Grab a partner an' get to the floor..." the caller started, but there was no need. Couples were already up in circles: Marlena and Rosie waiting with two cowboys, Ellie with Brett, farmers and their wives, and a couple of unknown cowhands with scarves wrapped around their necks—the sign that if they wanted to dance and no ladies were available, they could act as one of the gals tonight, no questions asked.

> *Choose yo' partner, form a ring,*
> *Figure eight, an' double L swing.*
> *First swing six, then swing eight,*
> *Swing 'em like swingin on the ol' gate.*

Feet pounded on the floor like a buffalo herd, and Cora noticed the rhythmic clapping grew louder and louder, with even the Endicotts and the Peabodys tapping their toes. Soon, she was tapping hers as well, as the room vibrated with song and dance.

> *Ducks in the river, goin' to the ford,*
> *Coffee in a little rag, sugar in a goard.*

Swing 'em once an' let 'em go.
All hands left and do-si-do.

Sweat dripping from the fiddler's and caller's brows matched the broadening circles of dampness under everyone's armpits. After numerous fluttering fans emerged and hefty women retreated to the sidelines, the caller got the message.

"Folks. Enough movin' round like hornets in a bonnet." He drew a deep breath and patted the fiddler on the shoulder. "Let's slow it down and have a nice waltz."

Many flushed faces nodded, and slowly people drifted together, their palms slippery, their sweaty hair matted and askew, relieved with the new command.

Cora watched the dancers, too keenly aware of Thomas next to her tapping his toe slowly. All at once, Ellie and Brett appeared, holding hands and looking slightly apprehensive.

"Looks like you two are havin' a good time!" Minnie exclaimed.

Nodding, Thomas added, "Yes, you certainly do."

Ellie turned to her mother. "Mama, there's something we want to tell you, and I figure this is as good a time as any."

"Yes?" Cora murmured.

A chest heave, and it floated out. "Brett and I are engaged."

She got no further. Arms encircled her like a tight swaddling cloth as Minnie shrieked with joy and Cora had a frozen smile on her face.

"I knew it, I gist *knew* it! Congratulations, to the both of you," Minnie cried.

As Thomas shook Brett's hand and hugged Ellie, Cora remained quiet.

"Oh, Mama," Ellie whispered, stroking her mother's shoulder. "Can't I be happy?"

"Why, of course!" Cora said, remembering what Minnie said, how Ellie was allowed to trust. And find love.

Without warning, an Irish bodrán drum started thumping. Whoops and hollers were unleased, and all attention swiveled toward the front of the room where the fiddler had started an Irish jig.

Minnie clapped her hands. "Come, girls, it's the Dolans turn to shine!"

Grabbing Cora with one hand, Ellie with the other, she forced them out onto the middle of the floor, and using authentic Irish steps, her hands on her hips, she began dancing. Ellie laughed and chimed in. Cora stayed still, until her sister and daughter were dancing in true Irish style—legs executing intricate patterns, their upper bodies straight as laundry pegs holding steady on a clothes line.

Thinking of her ma, Cora shrugged and joined in, as the dance steps got more complicated and the entire room watched, egging them on with rhythmic applause.

It was as if she were back in that encampment so many years before, dancing in front of strangers in a new land. Only this time, it was in front of her friends, her neighbors, and Thomas. She let herself go.

The music and drumbeats swelling, soon it was over as abruptly as it had begun. People walked by the threesome, slapping them on their shoulders and nodding graciously, as conversation returned to normal and a lilting waltz infiltrated the room.

Thomas turned to Cora, taking in her sparkling eyes, her fly-away hair, her collar opened one button down, and asked in a low voice, "May I have this next dance?"

He held out his large hand.

Exhausted, taken aback, she reacted without thinking. "Sorry, Thomas. I'm quite tired."

Instantly, she regretted her words. When she saw his eyebrows raise, and one of his cheek muscles twitch, she opened up her mouth to explain, to try to soften her remark, but it was too late.

Clearing his throat and straightening his cravat, he turned succinct.

"Excuse me, then. I intend on dancing," he said coldly, and without a backwards glance, walked across the room and stopped in front of a school committee member's oldest daughter, Merribelle. Within seconds, they were twirling around on the dance floor—he talking continuously, she gazing up at him with enamored eyes, hanging onto every word.

"You had your chance, Cora," Minnie snorted, after watching them dance for a while. "He's a handsome devil and if you don't..."

"Just don't, Minnie," she flared. "I'm tired, I don't feel like dancing, and I *don't* need your meddling. Just leave me be!" Still, she couldn't take her eyes off of Thomas' arm around Merribelle's waist.

"Folks, the next dance is Ladies' Choice, so grab the man of your dreams and keep those dancin' shoes goin'!" He hardly got the last words out when the room broke out in a cheer.

Shot full of adrenaline, Cora didn't even hesitate. Charging over to

Thomas and Merribelle, on their way to a second dance, all she could concentrate on was his arm, and how it should be around *her* waist, not someone else's.

"No you don't! Now it's *my* turn, Miss Merribelle," Cora said firmly, gripping Thomas' arm from Merribelle's slim waist and yanking him over to her.

With a slight shrug to the disappointed debutant, Thomas positioned his arm firmly around Cora's waist and brought her onto the dance floor.

"'Bout time!" Minnie called out, then watched them glide effortlessly, with Thomas' Cheshire cat grin growing as large as all of Nebraska.

Pete steadied himself against her and gave out a large burp.

The waltz was extra slow and melodious and to further enhance the romantic setting, Mr. Corrigan had come up with a brilliant plan. Walking around the room, he blew out alternating lamps as the room dimmed in increments, the aaah's grew serious, and the men's arms tightened around their partners' waists.

Ignoring the usual waltz 'space protocol' between partners, Cora's and Thomas' bodies moved together as a single entity as they rotated and swayed, wordless. Pressed up against him like old times, her body tingled. But there was something else. The stirrings she was feeling as his lower body hardened against her, were a sudden reminder of things she had not thought about for years, not since that night on Madam Ana's porch so long ago. At one point, he leaned back slightly and carefully placed several wispy strands behind her ear, and when he stroked her neck with his fingers, she felt it down to her toes.

"Oh Cora," he half groaned, as Cora felt the gooseflesh ripple over her arms. Still waltzing, still floating, they continued on, wordless, as Corrigan kept blowing out more and more lights.

Without realizing it, they had drifted out toward the back door, out where the air felt cool and fresh, and for the first time since forever, she wasn't aware of her brain, only her senses.

"The moon's almost full tonight," she murmured. Biting her lip, she gazed up at him.

"Yes it is," he murmured back, and pulling her close, lifted her face up toward his so they could kiss, for the first time in their lives as grown adults— —slowly, deeply.

Sensations sparked through her like lightning bolts, sensations that made her kiss him back just as fully, as she ran her fingers through his hair. Transported, the screams of laughter and feet stomping inside had become a dim haze, as he stroked her back with his hands, and she melted even further into him.

"Lord!" Minnie exclaimed, coming outside where they stood.

Like two fighting cats being doused with water, the couple jumped apart. Minnie laughed.

"It's about time…"

"Stop it, Minnie!" Cora flared, her chest still heaving unevenly. She glanced at Thomas and said, "I better go in now." Minnie shook her head, while Thomas looked grim.

"Cora, please?" he pleaded.

"No, I need to go. After all, I'm not a young girl anymore. I'm a businesswoman," she answered, fidgeting with her hair before she went back inside.

Thomas turned to Minnie. "I don't understand her, Minnie. I truly don't."

"Thomas, honey, I guess she's lived with a world of hurt, and frankly, she just doesn't want to get hurt again, if you get my meaning," she said, and headed inside.

When Cora saw her, she motioned her sister over.

"Minnie, don't get any ideas about this. My trust will only go so far. It was a one-time kiss." She watched her sister open her mouth. "Don't, just don't."

* *

Cocooned in his arms, she marveled at their strength, musculature, and devotion. Arms that were so familiar and had given her a taste of pubescent love then left her to be broken. But all that was forgotten now because her pleasure centers were on fire. No longer a teenage girl, she was a full grown woman craving his deep, sensuous kisses, his strokes everywhere on her body—her breasts, her neck and most needful of all, her private area that only the doves talked about.

As if in a trance, she began her own response—touching, stroking, exploring, until Thomas' body began morphing into Wes.' Now it was Wes running through the house, a foot behind her, his shoes pounding on the floor boards. Or was that simply her heartbeat exploding deep inside her chest?

His breath, hot and labored on her back, his gulping—or was it her making those half-gasps, half-choking noises? She couldn't tell. It was all tied up together. Until he cornered her in her bedroom, put down his gun on the night side table—the one with the notches he was so proud of—and with a single, back-handed smack, sent her flying.

Mouth tight, eyes like steel, he grabbed her by her hair and flung her onto the bed. On her side, her head pounding, her lip bleeding, the only thing she stared dully at those notches on his gun handle. Then, only blackness.

When Cora sat bolt upright, her hair matted, her nightgown drenched in sweat, Minnie was already sitting up next to her. "What in the world, Cora?" Then she softened. "Bad dream?"

"Just like my old dreams," she whispered. "Strange. After all this time."

"Wes?" Minnie asked softly. There was a long pause. "Honey, maybe you've got too many bad memories locked up tight inside you."

"Well, maybe. Maybe I'm spoiled for any man, even Thomas. Ever think about that, Minnie?" Cora asked, bitterly.

"Oh, Cora, honey …"

* *

In the dark, the fire, crackling and popping, shot tiny embers up into the almost full-mooned sky. Eight gruff, stubbled men rubbed their hands together before splaying them out toward the fire to soak up its warmth.

The Soltano gang had been riding for well over eight hours, and now, tired and hungry, this spot seemed as good as any to bed down for the night.

"So, what were you sayin' before, Clyde?" José asked.

"I was gist sayin' that if you want some money and no problems from Omaha vigilantes, there's another way to go, is all."

José looked over at his brother. This Clyde was good at his job, but as his brother had mentioned privately, something of a *cabrón*. Definitely lower principled than even they were and that said something.

Guillermo cleared his throat, his eyes like nicks. "What's on your mind, then?"

"I was thinkin' that maybe we should try smaller, nearby towns. Towns like Scottsbluff, Brownville, Henderson. Or a town like South Benton."

"What's they got that Omaha ain't got?"

"Well, fer one thing, they don't got the fire power of a big place, like Omaha. Second, I heard tell there's banks that ain't locked up tight but still have some real coin. None of that short bit stuff. It could be enough money to turn a wet mule." He looked around. "That's if yer willin' to try."

"Well, which one, then, since you're always makin' more noise than a jackass in a tin barn?" Juan half snorted.

Clyde kept his eyes steady. "I don't claim to know all them answers. All's I know is I stopped at South Benton a bit ago. Pretty fresh meat there."

"Yeah?" Several of the men licked their lips.

"Easy banks 'n easy gals. What could be better?" Clyde finished, turning his gun over and over again in his hands.

José scratched his head and turned to his brother and Juan. "I ain't sure about this. What do you think, Guillermo? Juan?"

Juan shrugged, but Guillermo leaned back, his arms across his chest. "I'm just wonderin' Clyde," he said, turning to the newcomer, "back in that saloon we all went to in the last town, that old barkeep called out 'Wes' to you when we walked in. What's *that* about? You been lyin' to us?"

Clyde stared at his accuser and blew out a puff of air. "Lyin'? Nah. I figure a man can call himself whatever he's got a hankering fer, right? Gist thought Clyde was as good a name as any, so I took it." He leaned in toward Guillermo. "By the way, how do I know *your* name is really Guillermo?" he smirked.

They all stared at him for a couple of seconds, stunned. Then they bust out laughing.

"This guy's a real card," José said, slapping his thigh.

His brother didn't budge. "Those are some mighty fine notches in your gun handle, *whatever-your-name-is*. They mean something?" he quizzed.

Wes grinned. "They sure do." He snickered, and rubbed his aching leg.

CHAPTER THIRTEEN
When Chickens Come Home To Roost

José Soltano knew better than to enter South Benton full force; too much attention drawn, too easy to attract the local sheriff. So at approximately eight o'clock, under dark cover, just he, his backup man, Frank, plus his lifelong friend, Juan, and Wes slow-gaited their horses into town. Guillermo and the others would join them later.

Weary, expressionless, riding in a slightly triangular formation, all four of them transitioned from a jog to a walk as their bodies shifted back and forth in their saddles and their right hands loosely held their split-reins. Slowly, they surveyed the wooden buildings around them—the locked up stores and churches, the still open saloons and hotels.

In front of the Wayward Hotel, they pulled their horses up short, tied their reins to the large wooden hitching post, and headed for the lobby, their boots stomping on the weathered boardwalk hard enough to make it creak and groan.

"Got two rooms for the four of us?" José asked, half smirking at the nervous hotel clerk, Tobias.

Thin, bespectacled, the young man gulped. For all their attempt at cordiality, there was something about these strangers that didn't quite sit right. He thought of ringing for Mr. Belmont, then remembered his boss had taken the night off to go to Madam Ana's for Miss Ellie's engagement party. So he cleared his throat, straightened his tie, and nodded twice.

"Would you please all sign the register?" Tobias asked, stepping back a pace as José stepped forward, his Colt six-shooter glistening in the desk lamp's glow.

Guns. All of them had one—actually one man came with two—and from the looks of it, they might very well use all of them, Tobias reasoned, suddenly noticing that one of them hesitated before registering his name. Not a good sign. Beads of sweat started polka-dotting the young man's brow as he handed two keys over to José, who tipped his hat, looked at the keys' room numbers and headed upstairs, the other three in tow.

Tobias wiped his brow and wished with all his soul that Mr. Belmont were there and he had gone to that engagement party.

* *

Ellie never looked lovelier. Flushed cheeks the color of budding pink roses, her hair rinsed in lilac water, now reflecting off the chandelier's glitter and producing an almost iridescent sheen. Newly imported from France, her rich, forest green dress, bought at a local dressmaker's shop, was of the finest silk. Although she had scoffed at its expense and her mother's insistence on buying it, when she saw Brett's eyes light up and his hands instinctively reach out to encircle her waist, she glowed. Perhaps it was worth it after all. She smiled, gave her mother a fast wink, and leaned into her fiancée.

Just then Thomas entered, dressed in his Sunday best. Paying no attention to the various doves' side-glances at him, or Marlena reaching out to stroke his shoulder, he headed straight for the Dolan inner circle.

"Ellie, you look beautiful tonight!" he said.

They all turned toward him as he added, "As does your mother."

"Thomas, you know how to spoil a girl. Doesn't he, Cora?" Minnie said loudly, elbowing her sister in the ribs and tossing out a roaring laugh.

Blushing, Cora cleared her throat, clanked on her glass with a spoon several times and announced loudly to the guests, "Everyone, dinner is served!"

In the dining room, five long tables had been set up with assorted donated-for-the-occasion chairs, table cloths that didn't match, an odd mix of china and tableware, and fresh flowers picked by Rosie and Marlena earlier that day. Since all the invitees were mostly friends of the household, as food was eaten, and whiskey and champagne sipped or guzzled, a half-hour in, the din had grown exponentially.

Brett and Ellie were next to each other, of course, with Thomas alongside the horse wrangler, and Cora beside her daughter. Pete and Minnie were across the table as were Marlena and Rosie, now known, after the Wild West show lottery, as the 'special' doves.

As Ellie and Brett talked, laughed, and slyly touched each other, Cora studied them carefully. Perhaps Minnie was right. Perhaps trust for Ellie was possible, because Brett had never caused a reason not to trust him. Then she looked over at Thomas. He was here now, but why not for all those years?

After Pete's second glass of whiskey, he couldn't help himself. "Ellie, you are a treasure to us all." He looked around to make sure everyone was listening. "As Shakespeare would say:

Shall I compare thee to a summer's day?
Thou art more lovely and more temperate;
Rough winds do shake the darling buds of May,
And...and..."

He paused, his eyes rolling upwards as if searching his brain.
Brett stepped in to help. *"And summer's lease hath all too short a date..."*
Pete's eyes were saucer-sized. "How 'bout a little Percy Shelley, hmm?"

Hail to thee, blithe spirit!
Bird thou never wert,
That from heaven, or near it,
Pourest thy full heart
In profuse strains of unpremeditated art.
Higher still and higher
From the earth thou springest,
Like a cloud of fire:
The blue deep...the blue deep..."

He paused again, his brow furrowed in concentration.
The blue deep thou wingest, And singing still dost soar, and soaring ever singest, Brett continued.

"My boy, what a superb specimen you are," Pete roared. "How do you know the poets so well?"

"His ma read it to him all the time," Ellie explained, her face flushed with pride.

Minnie laughed. "A-hah, a real dash-fire! Now who can resist a handsome horse wrangler with a brain."

Embarrassed, Brett looked down until Ellie announced, "You are a wonderful combination, my soon-to-be husband."

"How about Brett being such a good man?" Ellie offered next. "As Wordsworth said, *The best portion of a good man's life, His little, nameless, unremembered acts, Of kindness and of love.*"

Applause came loud and fast, particularly from the doves. Marlena, standing up and holding onto Rosie's shoulder for support, giggled. "Now, Miss Ellie, if you ever get tired of your Mr. Brett, you just send him over to us!" When she plopped down in her seat again, the doves cackled loudly.

Thomas patted Brett on the shoulder. "You'll have to get used to this, I'm afraid."

Brett produced a lop-sided grin. "I suppose I can handle it." He leaned back slightly. "How do you know the Dolan sisters, by the way?"

Sighing, Thomas said, "It a long story that goes way back."

"Oh?"

"I knew Cora and Minnie before the war, but I had to go fight."

There was a slight pause before Brett spoke. "My father fought in the war. For the South."

"I fought for the North, but none of that matters now, does it?"

"No, I guess not." Brett paused. "Killing is killing."

"It sure is." Thomas' voice sounded as if he were far away at another place and time.

"You know, I was a real good shot growing up," Brett admitted. "My pa taught me how to do that along with how to treat horses. Why, I could take out a rabbit at a hundred yards. But the first time I saw someone killed, it wasn't so pretty. My pa was killed in the war," he finished.

"Sorry to hear that. No, killing sure isn't pretty. In fact, it's enough to make you gun-shy."

The two men fell silent as the chatter around them climbed up another rung.

Without warning, Pete rose, his glass high above his head. "Here's to Ellie, for bringing literature to our fair town," he sputtered.

"Here, here!" the crowd cheered.

"Miss Ellie, may your life be as full as your..." Marlena began.

"Marlena!" Rosie cried, slapping her hand over her friend's mouth. "Don't even say it!"

"May your little boys have fame and fortune. And your girls..." another dove started.

Everyone waited.

"…have big titties!"

"Dear lord!" Ellie muttered, looking up at her fiancée shaking his head, his mouth definitely curling upward. "Welcome to my family," she ended, laughing.

Minnie stood up. "Seriously, folks, before we get too budgy, let's bend an elbow and make a toast to the happy couple. To Ellie and Brett." She clapped three times. "Hip-hip hurray! Hip-hip hurray!"

After the cheering subsided, Brett also stood up, his glass in the air, half empty. "Ladies and gents, Ellie and I would like to make an announcement of our own."

All eyes drew a bead on him as Ellie stood up beside him, buoyant.

"We decided not to calf around. So we're gettin' married real soon."

"How soon?" Mr. Belmont, the Wayward Hotel manager, called out. Chuckles followed.

"Two weeks' time. Come Saturday the twentieth, we'll be man and wife. You're all invited, of course!"

Cora, Minnie, and Pete stared at each other, their eyes popping.

"What the…" Cora started as Ellie leaned down to kiss her.

"Sorry it's so last minute, Mama. We just decided this morning. I hope we still have your blessing," she ended, searching her mother's face.

"Yes, you do, Ellie, of course."

By the time they returned home, Brett got an extra-long goodnight kiss, and just shy of the house, Thomas pulled Cora into the shadows.

"Cora," he murmured, wrapping his arms around her. He could feel her body soften as his heartbeat quickened. Then, as if a candle had been snuffed out, she stiffened and stepped back.

"Oh, Cora, please," he pleaded.

"Trust, Thomas. That is what's stopping me."

He heard her exhale; saw her features soften. Hopeful, he tried putting his arm around her waist again.

"No!" she said, pushing him away. "How can I ever trust you again?"

Sighing, he shook his head. "Cora, I swear, sometimes I think you're gonna be the death of me."

"I'm gonna be the death of *you*? Now, *that's* rich!"

He pulled back, his jaw clenched hard.

"Enough is enough," he said.

As she watched him walk off, she noted there were no backward glances, no last minute turning around. So he missed it. He missed her sitting down on the porch swing, missed her one hand covering her mouth, missed her eyes beginning to glisten.

* *

While the entire Dolan household was sleeping in the next morning, Wes was up bright and early, itching to go.

"I'm checkin' out one of them saloons today," he mentioned to José over breakfast in the hotel's dining room.

José's eyes grew steely. "Whoah, how's about you checkin' out the bank situation first, seein' as you was the one who ribbed us up to come here to this nothin' town. 'This is where we could get some coin,' you said. Remember?"

"Yeah, that's what I meant. After visitin' the bank," Wes said, trying to look indifferent as he fingered the notches on his gun handle.

In order to do some home-brand reconnaissance, the Soltano foursome split up that morning. As two of them checked out the Holten Bank, José and Wes sauntered over to The South Benton, where Wes put on the appearance of 'being all ears' to José's dictates.

"Now, you pretend you wanna open an account to see how the cashier operates in this here bank, and I'll check out the other employees and the safe. Let's get a feel fer the place."

The morning stretched into the afternoon with both banks given the once over and the townspeople assessed. By evening, Wes was informed that the bank robbery would happen in two days' time and laying low was of the utmost importance, or as José expressed it, "No knockin' about, no jarrin.' Fights bring in the law. Gist save part of your breath for breathin'."

He turned to Wes. "And Wes, no cattin' around, if you git my meanin'," José emphasized, his eyes scoping out his renegade bandit.

"Sure thing, boss," Wes replied, flipping out a one-fingered salute from the side of his head as he exited the door to a saloon he had passed by earlier that day.

* *

Corrigan had been smart. Recently, he had posted a discreet little sign next to the bar saying, "Friendly drinks served upstairs," and his clientele had doubled. He hated to compete with Cora and Minnie, but business was business, and a little side step into their territory wouldn't hurt anyone, now would it?

He even thought of mentioning it to them at Miss Ellie's engagement party, but a jolly good time and free likker got in the way, and now, seeing someone like Wes walk in, order a drink from the barkeep, and slowly point to the sign made him smile. Another customer willing to pay extra.

After an exchange of coins and a visual sweep of the gals, Wes pointed to a young, dark-haired beauty named Evelyn. The barkeep shook his head by way of protest, but Wes stood firm. Fingering his mustache and swatting her bottom once, he slowly guided her upstairs.

At the top of the stairs, Evelyn swiveled around, and with a frantic, pleading gesture, grabbed the top post and looked down at her employer—her eyes the size of saucers, the post gripped so tightly, even from far away, Corrigan could see the white spreading across her knuckles.

With a short little yank, Wes took her elbow and maneuvered her down the second floor corridor, out of sight.

"It'll be all right, it will," Corrigan tried to reassure the two saloon waitresses standing nearby. But his voice was shaky, and it was pitched higher than usual.

Upstairs, Evelyn had trouble lighting the lamp, her hands were trembling so hard. When Wes chuckled and struck a match next to her, she jumped a good foot.

"Hey, little gal, what's the matter, huh? Ol' Wes will give you a good time. Just relax."

She stepped back two paces, turned, and charged for the door, half-crying. "This is a mistake, Mister. I ain't up to it."

He grabbed her arm and shoved her against the door. "Nobody tells me what I can or can't do, you hear me?"

Her breaths were coming in choppy waves, but strangely enough, instead of pursuing his prey, he stopped, leaned back, and belched.

"Hmm. Maybe it ain't your time yet, honey. Besides, I got bigger plans," he added, releasing her. He watched her yank open the door and scurry down the hall. Within seconds, he could hear her boots thumping downstairs and recognizing the rhythmic pause of her taking two steps at a time, he threw back his head and let out a huge belly laugh.

Exiting Corrigan's, Wes banged the double-hung swinging doors outward and stood for a moment on the sidewalk, tipsy and determined, serenaded by a short round of applause from inside.

The hell with them, he thought, as he made his way over to the destination he had dreamt about visiting for many years.

* *

Across town at the Cattle Saloon, Brett and Thomas were getting to know one another. Embroiled in numerous topics, after three rounds of whiskey, they were still discussing law and order, horse wrangling, the surge of outlaws coming out of Wyoming, and the Dolan ladies.

"They sure are a unique little clan," Thomas said, holding up his third whiskey glass, eyeing its golden hue for several seconds before downing it in a brisk gulp.

Brett followed suit. "I knew the minute I met Ellie that not only was she the most beautiful woman I had ever seen, she was a force to be reckoned with."

As he proceeded to recount her stubbornness and determination regarding the books she had ordered, Thomas listened, a slight smile etched across his face. Suddenly, the detective paused, drew a deep breath, and shook his head.

"Wish Cora was as receptive as Ellie," he half-muttered.

Brett hesitated. "I didn't want to say anything but yes, I've wondered why she's always giving you such a hard time. I mean, there's no doubt she cares about you."

Thomas looked up, genuinely surprised. "You really think so?"

"Of course, Thomas. It's as plain as day. Ellie and I've even discussed it. In fact, we…" Brett's mouth clamped shut with a little plop. "All I can say is some things are worth fightin' for, Thomas," he finished softly.

"And some aren't!" Thomas snapped. As more and more people sauntered in, they both rose, paid their bill, and together, exited to head back to the Dolans.

* *

Although Thomas had been careful to secure Madam Ana's, a recent downpour on top of dry rot was enough to weaken the lock hold on the cellar door, so when Wes tried to wriggle the door free, he was surprised at the ease with which it opened.

"Must be my lucky night," he snickered, then shivered with excitement, remembering the last time he was there. He pushed the door inward slowly and tried hard not to let the squeaks and groans of the old door make too much noise. The dark murkiness instantly brought beads of sweat and, wiping off his brow with his hand, he quickly smeared the moisture on his pants.

Had to keep his trigger hand dry 'n ready, he chuckled, imagining how the night was going to play out. And the look on Minnie's face when he aimed his gun directly at her head. Let's see her try 'n run him out this time. He felt his way through the basement toward the stairs he had once trudged up so long ago with Thomas, Cora, and Minnie, after getting some of Madam Ana's famous preserves out of her special cellar larder.

Driven, he snaked up the steps, listening to some female chatter, most probably coming from the saloon. He licked his lips, fingered his gun handle, and slowly opened the hall door an inch or two. With no one nearby, he inched it open even further. The piano was clunking out a jolly tune, and the soft clink of glasses was unmistakable.

He pictured Cora and Minnie's bedroom and wondered if they still might be sharing the same bed. Flattened against the wall, he slid his way in the opposite direction from the festivities and smiled. Like ol' times, he mused, remembering Madam Ana's office and chasing Cora from her bedroom into the kitchen, her face, so scared, so young, so vulnerable.

The back of the house seemed silent, almost calm. Gist waitin' for 'ol Wes to lay in wait for Minnie. His Adam's apple rose and fell in high anticipation. Peering around the doorframe, the bedroom hadn't changed all that much from so long ago: one bed, two sets of pillows, matching dressers, lace curtains tied back with slim cords, an old rickety looking rocker—was that also there back then?—and a small mahogany desk off in one corner next to the window.

He walked over to one of the dressers, picked up a petite tintype photo of some woman and scowled. Cora? Minnie? Don't look that familiar, he thought, with a quick shrug and a single eyebrow lifted. He put it down again.

The tiny rustle of a dress coming in from the hall had him slipping quickly behind the bedroom door, to create a full on surprise attack. Suddenly he had to control an urge to laugh—who would it be? Minnie? Cora? He sure hoped it was Minnie. Although reuniting with Cora wouldn't be so bad at that.

From the sound of the light humming, it was obvious a female had entered the room. It must be Cora, because of the gentle sound. He smiled. Minnie's hum would definitely come out tough, masculine. He fought off another snicker as whoever-she-was opened one of the dresser drawers then closed it with a clunk, her humming never stopping for a moment.

Closing the door behind him, he turned to face his victim. But she didn't look familiar at all. Beautiful, but definitely not either Cora or Minnie.

"Who are you?" Ellie cried, her hand up at her throat.

"Who the hell are *you?*" Wes replied, grinning, licking his lips in sudden high anticipation. Maybe this was gonna be even better than he had thought.

One step toward her, and she let out a shriek. Still, he took a hold of her shoulders, and with a fast tug, held her against his chest. His breath reeking of tobacco and whiskey, his body clammy with the foul sweat of the unbathed, she struggled against him, and as she raised her fist to strike him, he laughed. Grunting, he smacked her on the side of her head, spinning her across the room into a wall. After she sank down onto the floor, he charged over to her, yanked her up onto the bed and watched her wriggle over to the other side of the bed. Flashes of Cora raced through his mind, and he smacked her again, relishing her falling backwards, almost unconscious.

Like a pent-up bull, he snorted and started unbuckling his belt, his pupils dilated, his face red. He hadn't felt this excited since forever. A beautiful dove for the taking, he thought, bending over her and gulping hard. He hovered over his victim, savoring every detail of her body—her tiny waist, her pert bosom, her full, luscious lips. Not believing his good luck, he began to slowly pull down his pants.

"You touch her, and I'll blow a hole in you a mile wide," Cora growled from the doorway, a Winchester rifle tucked squarely under her chin, aimed directly at Wes.

Startled, he straightened up. "Cora! Hell, gal, good to see you!"

She cocked the hammer and stepped forward.

"Hey now, you know damn well you ain't gonna fire at ol' Wes."

He turned back to Ellie who was half coming to. "Look how pretty she is. She…"

The Winchester pitched a bullet that whizzed a half inch from Wes' ear and left a deep hole in the wall.

Cora cocked it again. "Get the hell away from her, you son–of–a…"

"Bitch!" Minnie finished for her, her eyes slit in hatred as she fired her Colt Single Action and carved out another hole in the ceiling.

Outside, a half block away, upon hearing the double shots, Brett and Thomas started sprinting. At Madam Ana's, they both took the front steps two at a time and lunged inside.

"They're in in Minnie's and Cora's room!" the doves screamed as the two men barreled back toward the Dolan's bedroom, Thomas commanding, "Get the sheriff!"

Once inside the room, he charged over to Wes, knocking him to the floor and holding his stepbrother down until he could pull his own belt out of his pants and tie the bandit's hands behind his back.

"Well, well, well, Thomas," Wes started, his face pressed against the floorboards from his stepbrother's boot.

Thomas yanked him up to a standing position. "Shut up! Just *shut* up! You're coming with me now," he snarled, glancing over at Cora to see how she was doing. She was white as a sheet and trembling.

On the bed, Brett had Ellie encased in his arms as Minnie came up front and center to land a wallop across Wes' face.

"You sorry sonabitch! I've half a mind to string you up right now. We got an old oak gist outside."

Wes cast a large 'hell-with-you' wad of spit onto the floor. "Minnie, you ain't nothin' but a man-hatin' bitch."

"Enough!" Thomas barked, jerking his childhood nemesis down the hall, past applauding doves, and out onto the porch where the sheriff and his deputy had just arrived to take the prisoner to jail.

As soon as they left, Thomas pivoted around and hurried back toward the bedroom. Brett was still holding a shaken Ellie, and Minnie was fisting her gun tightly and sputtering. Cora was off to one side, alone, rifle down, still shivering. When she spotted Thomas, she blinked back tears.

Slipping his arm around her shoulders, he guided her into the office. Just inside the door, she clung to him, her chest heaving, limp and in shock, until Minnie handed her a large shot glass of whiskey. She shook her head.

"Cora, honey, if you don't take this, I'm gonna shoot you myself!" Minnie hissed.

"She's got a point there, Cora," Thomas said, settling her into the large desk chair. "Take the whiskey, you need it. Hell, we all need it," he added, signaling Minnie to pour him one as well.

THE DOLAN GIRLS

* *

"Guess what I gist saw?" Frank asked José.

"Don't play games with me. Get it out, man."

"Well, gist a while ago, I saw our pal Wes goin' off to the local jail with the town sheriff and what looked to be his deputy."

"Hell, *now* what's he gone and done?" José grunted.

"I *knew* somethin' 'bout him weren't right," Juan declared, gloating. "What are we gonna do about it, José? Do you think they know we're here?" he added.

Their leader seemed lost in thought for a couple of seconds. "One thing's sure, I think this ain't the town fer us right now. But I don't wanna leave him in jail in case he talks."

"How we gonna git him out of there, then?" Frank quizzed.

José grew pensive. "Juan, you ain't got a price on your head yet. So you go in there, say you got a complaint about gettin' yer wallet stolen, somethin' on that order. Take a look 'n check it out. We still have plenty of dynamite, you know." He tilted his head and scratched his chin. "If they don't have nothin' but one man there at night, maybe we can corner him and make him let ol' Clyde, I mean, Wes, out."

The next night it was all set. Juan walked into the jail at ten o'clock, feigning just the right amount of distress. "I gotta problem!" he blurted out, taking in the deputy's legs lazily hitched up and crossed on top of a giant mahogany desk.

"Don't we all." The lawman chuckled.

Maybe this was gonna be easier than we thought, Juan mused. "I got my wallet stolen," he continued.

"You know who did it?" was asked in the midst of a yawn.

"Nah. You pick up anyone recently? Maybe it was him."

The deputy sighed, annoyed at having to make any effort. "We do got someone in the cell right now. You kin take a look if you've a mind to."

Juan's eyebrows shot up. "Sure thing," he answered and followed the deputy into the next room.

There was Wes, lying on a cot, picking food out of his whiskers. When he spotted Juan, he immediately sat up, his body on high alert. But his fellow Soltano gang member flashed a subtle 'don't recognize me' hand signal, and he lay back down again.

"Nope, don't recognize him," Juan muttered, eyeing the room set up and the deputy's weapon.

Back in the main room, the deputy pulled out a form from inside the desk's top drawer. "Fill this out, gist for your name is all, and I'll give it to the sheriff."

"Is the sheriff usually here at night? I wanna speak to him."

"Nah, he'll come in only if need be. Otherwise…" he smiled conspiratorially.

"Otherwise?"

"He's at home with the missus and them four brats."

Both men laughed as Juan carefully wrote down a fictitious name. *José's gonna love this*, he thought.

Sure enough, it was a piece of cake. When Juan returned with Frank and José, the deputy gave in so easily, it made Juan snicker. Leading the armed visitors over to the cell, the lawman's hand shook as he opened the lock. And when Wes called out, "You sure took your time, fellas!" José let the prisoner out and shoved the deputy into the cell. Within seconds, the gunmen were gone, leaving the deputy with his face in his hands.

Just outside the back of the jail, José handed Wes his gun and the reins to his horse, and, mounting their rides, they all galloped out of town toward the far hills. Halfway there, Juan suddenly held up his hand and reined in his horse.

"What you stoppin' fer?" Wes asked.

"This is the end of the road for us."

Wes' eyes widened "What the hell does *that* mean?"

"It means we don't want you with us no more!" Juan sneered, his Colt already out and aimed at Wes' head.

"I ain't askin' you, *cabrón*," Wes sneered, "I'm askin' José."

The head man also had his six shooter out, aimed at Wes' head. Cocking it, he was cold as ice. "Gist like he said, we don't want you with us no more. Clear enough for you now, *cabrón?*"

Wes gulped. "Well, I'll be. Once a 'greaser,' always a 'greaser,' huh?" With a quick click, he reined his horse in another direction. "*Adiós, amigos!*" drifted back over his shoulders as the Soltano trio themselves turned and headed east toward Guillermo and Omaha.

* *

"Sheriff, no! It *can't* be!" Cora cried.

The sheriff glowered at his red-faced deputy. This had been the hardest news to tell anyone, and as the lawmen stood there, helpless, they could feel the full wrath of the entire household raining down on them.

"What do you intend on doing, sheriff?" Thomas finally barked. "A search party, of course, right?"

Brett stepped forward. "I'm in. *No one's* gonna treat my future wife like that 'n get away with it!"

Thomas placed a hand on his new friend's shoulder. "I agree. My stepbrother's a menace, and we need to track him down as fast as possible. Sheriff, you can deputize a group of us for a posse, can't you?"

Nodding the sheriff muttered, "I'll put a guard here at Madam Ana's. Meanwhile, come with me, fellas," and as he led both men out, the doves stood by silently watching them leave. Running toward the front, Marlena called out, "Go get 'im, boys! God bless you."

Within the hour, a newly deputized posse had been formed, and when each man loaded his Colt and Winchester, filled his saddlebags full of bullets and food, and mounted his horse, they all understood it could very well end up being a long night. A few long days, for that matter.

Several of the men were holding torches, and as they grimly rode out of town, Rosie, hanging out of a second story window, exclaimed, "Look, girls! Look at their faces. So grim."

She thought a moment. "I gist pray they get that son-of-a-bitch."

Next to her, Isabel, new at Madam Ana's, concurred. "Ain't seen nothin' like this before. Why, in other places, the sheriffs take their sweet time. This posse's got together real quick."

"That's 'cause Ellie is loved in this town," Minnie said from the doorway, her ample chest heaving. "Ain't *nobody* gonna treat her…or *any* of us gals that-a-way."

* *

Two miles out, the sheriff pulled his reins up short, and held up his hand. "All right, fellas, I think we better split up here, so we can track better and cover more territory."

He was met with numerous nods and murmurs of "good idea."

With one quick spit, the sheriff started giving directives. "You two go there, in that direction; you two take the eastern route. You two…"

Before he could finish, Thomas spoke up. "I'd like to go with Brett off toward the southwest, if you've a mind to it."

Nodding absently, the lawman made a go-ahead nod.

Brett and Thomas had been riding a mile or two when the wrangler suddenly asked, "Thomas, why southwest?"

"There's a place where Wes and I used to go when we were younger. A place where the trails are hidden by heavy brush and woods. From there we could go to neighboring towns without my stepfather finding out. I figure Wes might well have headed there. Besides, I just wanted you and me to get first crack at capturing him and sending him back to jail, you know? We deserve that."

Brett drew a deep sigh. "Yeah, I don't want anyone but us to take him down."

Thomas stared into his companion's intense eyes and nodded slowly. "So you're thinkin' what I'm thinkin'?" When Brett nodded, he added, "So much for us both hating guns."

"Yeah," came out low and firm. Clicking to his horse, Brett suddenly started up, and Thomas, a second behind him, headed further southwest.

Unlike the devil's walking stick or the hawthorne trees so prevalent in the low-lying, sunny areas, the two men were now entering a different terrain. Here, the black alder, sweet gum, and dogwood had merged together into a dense wooded area, perfect for much needed shady respites. And perfect for hiding.

A few hundred feet shy of Thomas and Wes' childhood play spot, they could hear in the distance a brook gurgling its soft, rhythmic babble. An owl hooted and a couple of wolves throated lonely, eerie cries.

Dismounting, the men tied their horses around the first available tree trunk and cautiously proceeded into the dense shrubbery, their guns cocked, ready to fire.

Behind them, far off toward the north, the posse's torches flickered and glowed like fireflies, as the men stretched out into a line. The brook's babbling was growing louder, the wolf howls more distinct, as the two men closed their eyes and tilted their ears toward the heart of the forest to listen to all the sounds Thomas had grown up with. Sounds that now, if it weren't for their mission, would certainly bring them peace.

Suddenly, another sound surfaced, an unmistakable, manmade noise.

CHAPTER FOURTEEN
Tightening Up the Reins

The whistle—loud, resonant, slightly off key—was accompanied by a *step-slide-step-slide* against the soft ground.

"It's him," Thomas whispered, motioning his partner to follow his lead.

They flat-footed their way carefully like Indians, silent, alert, meticulous, until the sounds stopped. Much like statues, Brett and Thomas remained suspended as they eavesdropped on Wes' unique traits. Suddenly, they heard his voice.

"Damn this leg!" he cried out to the dense woods, as the two men continued their approach.

Within minutes, the outlaw had started up again, this time accompanied by a more restrained whistle. The closer the men got to him, the more discernible and pronounced the outlaw's odd-gaited hitch became as he kept on whistling and foraging, seemingly oblivious to them and their position.

Until Brett stepped on a fallen branch.

"Who's there?" Wes shouted. There was a two-second pause. "Now, I ain't gonna ask you twice!"

The owl repeated its hoo-hooing, the torches still flickered off in the distance, and Thomas stepped forward to face his childhood adversary.

"It's me, you sorry son-of-a-bitch." He squared his gun on Wes' head.

"Well, if it ain't my little sap of a brother. Come after me, did ya? All heeled up with guns, huh? Think you're gonna turn me in?" He started snickering.

"Yeah, that's *exactly* what I aim to do," Thomas answered, eye-signaling Brett to outflank the bandit.

The horse wrangler didn't get far.

"Whoah, cowboy! Don't come any closer." Wes waved his gun at the wrangler. "Back off or I'll shoot."

Brett stalled as Wes continued. "Besides, Thomas, you ain't got the guts to shoot me. Don't matter you beat me that one time, wrasslin'. Don't matter."

"More than one time, Wes. More than one time," Thomas answered slowly, anticipating any sudden movement.

Wes aimed his gun directly at his stepbrother's head. "You know, I always knew it might come to this. Also knew you'd have a problem pullin' that trigger," he snarled, firing at Thomas, and purposely missing him by only inches.

"I got no problem pullin' it!" Brett barked, shooting Wes' right leg out from under him.

On the ground, Wes winced in pain. "Now, *this* gets me riled up. Got your pal here doin' your dirty work, huh, Thomas? You sorry excuse for a man."

The two men watched him hold his bloody leg, trying to stop the bleeding.

"You always thought you were better than me. So high-falutin' and all," he grunted. "Well, I'm glad I went to town with Cora all those years back and taught her what a real man was, and I'm glad I had a go at that perty dove back there. Glad I…"

Thomas aimed and shot at Wes' other leg. When his brother screamed, he pulled back on the hammer and aimed again.

"You ain't fit to live, you piece of vermin, you …" he growled.

When the Colt Peacemaker behind them popped a fast *one-two-three-four-five-six* times, they watched Wes' body twitch and spasm as each bullet hit him—his chest, his shoulder, his arm, his stomach, his neck, and finally, his head.

Instantly swiveling around, both men faced a grim Cora.

"Cora!" Thomas cried.

"How did you find us?" Brett finally asked.

Her eyes gritty, her mouth in a downward curl, she looked straight at Thomas and hissed. "You don't get to kill him. Only me."

When she started to tremble, Thomas pulled her in close. "How did you know where to find us?" he asked gently as he stroked her hair.

"You took me here once, remember? I..." She tried to say more, but her body's shaking had taken over.

Thomas looked down at his stepbrother. "Shoulda done that years ago."

The owl was no longer hoo-hooing, the torches were long gone, and the body before them lay as still as a slab of mutilated beef lying on a butcher's table.

All business, Brett sniffed once. "Gotta bring him back to town."

"Yeah. Remember, this was self-defense, in case anyone's asking," Thomas added, always the detective.

* *

As soon as the threesome returned to South Benton—Brett and Cora riding their horses, Thomas on foot, holding his mare's bit with Wes' body dangling across her saddle—the twenty-four hour pall that had taken over the town instantly lifted.

Exhausted, Cora could barely see in front of her, Brett looked fierce, and Thomas called out to the small, gathering crowd, "Someone get the sheriff."

Sheriff Whitman soon appeared. Back from a long night of scouring the plains, he met the threesome with a grin.

"Bless you," he said simply, and took Thomas' horse and its cargo away.

When Madam Ana's household heard the good news, and who made it happen, Minnie, her arm around her sister, turned to her niece and announced gleefully, "Ellie, honey, here's your mother's first wedding present!"

"Amen to *that!*" the doves hurrahed, clapping heartily as Cora slowly sank down on the settee, her only thought: to crawl into bed, pull up the covers, and sleep for days.

Minnie sat down beside her. "You did good tonight, Cora."

Close to tears, Cora nodded. Still, in spite of feeling spent, she managed, "Brett and Thomas deserve some of the credit, too."

Minnie smiled. "Glad to hear you say that, Sis." Then she stood up. "Drinks on the house, everyone!"

The household exploded with cheers, Ellie stayed planted in Brett's arms, and the Pinkerton quickly bypassed all the hugs and shoulder pats to get to Cora.

As he sat down next to her, she looked up into his face and murmured, "My, oh my. That was something, wasn't it?"

His voice turned husky. "Yes, it sure was." He stroked the side of her face. "You were magnificent, Cora."

Suddenly, the doves and customers were whooping it up as whisky was being freely poured and making the rounds. Pete tried several times to recite a poem, but no one was listening.

"Cora, I need to talk to you," Thomas continued softly, his words swallowed up by the din.

"What?" she asked, dazed, only half hearing him.

"I need to talk to you. Now."

Nodding, she motioned him toward the front porch, where once outside, they made their way over to the two rockers.

"This all right?" she asked.

"Minnie's smokin' chairs. You bet," he replied, smiling for a second before turning earnest.

Inside, the festivities were going great guns. "Any excuse for a party," Cora commented, shaking her head. She waited for Thomas to say more, but he was silent, looking pensive.

"A penny for your thoughts," she said, rubbing the back of her neck.

His sigh was deep and shaky. "Cora, God knows you've been hurt. I know how much you've been hurt." He trailed off. Gulping once, he continued. "Honest to God, Cora, you must know I love you—have always loved you."

She began to chew on her lip. "I guess," she replied.

The sound of a glass breaking and screams of laughter filtered out around them.

"What I'm trying to say is, I want to marry you, Cora. I've always wanted that."

She swiveled toward him, her eyes saucer sized. Always wanted that? Then why didn't he come back to her?

"I have to return to Cheyenne right after Ellie's wedding, and I want you..." He swallowed hard. "I want you to come with me."

Numb, she tried to comprehend what he was saying, but her brain couldn't quite take it in.

"Cora? What do you think?"

"*Cheyenne!* What would I do there? And what about Minnie? Ellie, and now Brett?" The tiniest spot of blood had surfaced on her lip from her intense biting.

"Why, Cheyenne's an up and comin' town, with a definite need for another Madam Ana's, if that's what you want. But remember that first day I came, and we explored the town? Remember you told me how the business was too much for you and Minnie? How it might be the death of you? Remember that? This could be your chance to get out from under it."

"Wait, wait. This is all too much for me. How could I leave Ellie and Minnie?"

"Minnie could do anything she wanted, with us, of course. And Ellie? Why, good teachers are always golden—anywhere. The same with Brett. He could make a sizable living over there, training horses, doing what he does best."

"And Pete?" she asked, her eyes dark with worry.

"Of course Pete!" His voice lowered. "What do you say?"

There was a long, long pause. "Thomas, you hurt me so much."

"I know you've said that, but I don't understand."

She turned toward him, her face tense. "How do I know you won't hurt me again? I can't give you an answer right now. I just can't," she blurted out, rising to head for the front door.

As she strode by, he grabbed her hand and pulled her close. "Do you love me?" He looked up, searching her eyes. "I need to know."

She stared down at him, softening.

Hopeful, he repeated himself more slowly. "Do you love me, Cora?"

Her receptive mood suddenly gone, she looked away. "Right now, I'm too tired to think about it. I'll tell you my answer before you go. For now, that's all I have to give." Inching her hand out from under his grasp, she slipped into the house.

Later, lying in bed, she could hear the festivities in the parlor still going strong, but that wasn't what kept her awake. Trust Thomas? Uproot her entire life, everything she had built for herself and Minnie, for someone she wasn't sure she could really believe in again?

She closed her eyes, trying to remember their good times together, and the way she felt in his arms. But try as she might to block out all bad thoughts, her mind kept reciting a single word: *trust*.

* *

Since much of the town had been invited, it had been decided that the only venue large enough to accommodate Ellie and Brett's wedding was the town hall. Mrs. Endicott tried to create a special committee for the occasion, even venturing forth to Madam Ana's herself one morning when the doves were sleeping it off. Disdainful, huffing and puffing up their front porch and into their vestibule with her fine feathered hat and ample bodice, she was determined to get things done 'properly.' But Minnie and Cora would have none of it.

"Thank you kindly, Mrs. Endicott, but she is my daughter, after all," was Cora's polite, slightly chilled response.

It galled her to think that these women, these entitled grande-dames, felt they could take total control anytime they wished.

She could hear Minnie's indignant mutter, "And *my* niece," as she looked the matron squarely in the eyes.

"Once again, thank you for coming today, Mrs. Endicott. We shall let you know exactly what we need in good time. Do have a pleasant afternoon."

As she closed the front door, they could hear Mrs. Endicott's more than audible "harrumph!" floating out toward the street, but being the gracious person she was, Cora held up a one-finger warning to Minnie. They both waited until the town's matron disappeared around the corner before Minnie exploded with laughter.

"Now, that'll teach her," Cora commented as Minnie hugged her.

"Love you, little sister. Just love you to bits."

"Back to work," Cora answered, extricating herself gently.

Minnie stepped back and shook her head. "Now, ain't it time to think about yourself, Cora?"

"I'm sure I don't know what you mean."

"Cora, this is your sister talkin'. What were you and Thomas discussin' out on the porch the other night?"

"Nothing gets past you, does it, Minnie?"

"It sure don't. So, tell me."

Cora's chest heaved a swift up and down. "He asked me to marry him, is all."

"Is *all*? Why, that's grand!"

"Is it?" Cora's eyes moistened.

"Honey, why are you still not sure of his love?"

Cora plopped down on the settee. "I can't explain it. All I know is I'm angry, and I don't completely trust him. But in the end, it may just be I've packed ice around my heart for too long."

"You can carry that ice around with you forever, you know. Even die with it. Is that what you really want? To go to your grave, never being with your one true love? Bein' with someone like that ain't even in the cards for most people."

"I know, I know."

Minnie stood over her sister, tapping her right thigh with her hand, thinking.

Cora stiffened. Here comes another lecture, she thought, waiting.

But it didn't happen. "Time to get a move-on, Sis," Minnie remarked, clapping her hands twice. "We have a wedding to prepare for." Turning, she almost bounded out the door toward the kitchen. "Comin', Cora?" she called out over the shoulder.

* *

Before the special day, Ellie sought out Thomas at his hotel. "What has Brett been up to these last couple of days? He hasn't been in the stables, and when I ask him why, he just tells me he has some things to do. Do you know what these things are, Thomas?"

Thomas shrugged, but his mysterious smile suggested otherwise.

"You two have become thick as thieves, and I'm not sure that's such a good thing," she laughed. Her next question was more pointed. "As a matter of fact, why haven't you been around us lately? Everything all right with you?"

"Ask your mama," was his short reply.

In no time at all, there was only one day left. One day of making sure the town hall had been decorated up to the gills, a job the Dolans had been more than happy to delegate to the town's overly zealous matrons. And what a job they had accomplished. Saturday, Cora happened by, and ignoring Mrs. Endicott's chilly demeanor, stood in the doorjamb, flabbergasted by what she saw as she surveyed the room.

A brightly colored muslin bunting banner was suspended from the balcony in repeated, swooping loops, tables had already been set up in the middle and the back of the room, with fine linen tablecloths, neatly folded and ready to put into place on the special day. Silverware and plates, donated for the occasion, had been put into baskets, to be returned to their rightful owners later on.

Corrigan's 'piana' had been brought over and moved into a corner.

"Thank you *so* much, Mrs. Endicott. You are a true inspiration," Cora exclaimed when she saw the room.

A smile crossed the matron's face.

Meanwhile, on the home front, the food preparation was nearing its close: roast turkey, roast pig, boiled ham, boiled mutton, stewed liver, poultry, and cutlets for the main course. Hot bread, croquets, and vegetables, puddings, custards, stewed fruit, and of course, a three-tiered wedding cake, courtesy of Marlena.

"Where did you learn how to do this, Marlena?" Cora had asked.

The dove gave a fast wink. "I once worked in a certain gentleman's household. He was a restaurant owner and taught me how to bake, among other things." She giggled.

Clothes were also discussed in some detail. Informing her sister that she had gotten a proper dress made for the occasion, Cora asked, "So, I assume you've had a dress made up for yourself, right, Minnie?"

"No thanks, Miss High 'n Mighty. I just got me some lace trim and put it on one of my own dresses, thank you very much. Besides, it's not me you should be thinkin' about. What about the fact that the doves want to help Ellie paint her face, hm?"

Cora turned to her daughter. "Is this true?"

Sheepish, Ellie nodded.

"Oh no, you don't. That's fine for the girls, but not for you. I really don't think Brett would appreciate that, either."

Ellie sighed. "Actually, he's already told me he doesn't think I need it."

"Smart man," Cora muttered.

When time came for Ellie's final fitting, her wedding dress turned out to be breathtaking. Fashioned after a picture in one of Cora's imported fashion magazines, Madam Laforte, the town's best seamstress, had cut and sewed morning, noon, and night until the poor French woman's fingers were numb and blistered.

Two different fabrics had been used as befitted the newest fashion: an ivory satin for the skirt and bodice, trimmed with lace and held together by shell buttons. And for the three quarter sleeves and the flowing train, a beautiful brocade material had been attached as a 'compliment subtile.'

"Isn't it beautiful, Mama and Auntie?" Ellie cried, stepping out from the seamstress' back room.

Cora gasped. How could she have produced such a beautiful daughter? So much grace, such big bright eyes, and top it all off, a girl with an intelligent mind that soared.

"Cora, are you listening to me? I said doesn't she look grand?" Minnie asked.

Cora smiled. "She certainly does."

Picking up the edges of her dress, Ellie flew over to hug her mother. "Oh, Mama," she murmured. She turned to her aunt.

Minnie couldn't help herself. "Well now, Missy, are you plannin' on having petticoats underneath your dress…or maybe your ridin' bloomers?"

Madam Laforte was not amused.

* *

Finally the wedding day, on Sunday—something Cora had insisted on—had arrived.

"Why Sunday, Mama?" Ellie had wanted to know earlier.

"It has to be on a Sunday. That way we'll know that people have taken their Saturday night baths!"

Bright and early, as was custom, Brett was retrieved from his stable lodgings by various townspeople. Mr. Corrigan led the pack made up of locals, most of the doves, the blacksmith, Bradford Jones, in town for the occasion, and several of Buffalo Bill's entourage who had shown up at the last minute. Jokes about marriage—and the wedding night—multiplied as the noisy crowd surrounded the groom who kept fiddling with his stiff collar.

Just outside the town hall, Minnie was the welcoming committee. "Brett, all's I can say is you're walkin' just like a man with a new suit of underwear," she cried, triggering a round of explosive laughter.

Inside, the buzz of excitement was quickly mounting. Chairs had been set up for the people closest to the bride, plus dignified visitors—Mrs. Endicott and her crowd, and a beaming Annie Oakley.

Brett, armed with the rings in his pocket he had secretly commissioned the blacksmith to make, walked up toward the front to join the local clergyman and Thomas, who snatched a glimpse or two of Cora sitting in the front row when she wasn't looking.

Suddenly, the younger madam gave a quick hand signal to the piano player to start up with a slow march. In came Ellie on the arm of a surprisingly sober Pete, so beautiful she brought tears to Brett's eyes. And as soon as their Biblical vows ended, the minister pronounced them man and wife, and Brett kissed his new bride tenderly, the crowd almost brought down the roof with their whistling and clapping.

During the meal, the head table housed the family, Pete, and Thomas. The Pinkerton had stayed clear of Cora, but at one point, when their eyes locked, he watched her rubbing the back of her neck as he felt the sweat gathering beneath his suit.

Toasts were in order, including a very sweet one from Annie, welcoming Ellie to the Buffalo Bill Wild West family. People, caught up in a cheery mood, applauded when Thomas stood up and raised his glass.

"It has been my great privilege to not only get to know Ellie Dolan—excuse me, Mrs. Brett Parker..." He waited for the titters to cease. "...Mrs. Brett Parker, but also her first rate husband, Brett. No two finer people could be getting married today. So here's to a long life filled with good health and happiness. Congratulations, you both deserve it. Here, here!"

Glasses were lifted, clinked, and "here-here's" echoed across the floor.

Cora's toast was short and sweet. "Here's to the newlyweds. May you always be healthy and happy." Raising her glass, she smiled at the couple. Then, facing the guests, she announced, "Folks, now it's time to dance!"

All eyes turned toward the musicians. A waltz started up, and the bride and groom took center stage. Instantly, a wide-berthed circle of invitees surrounded them, spilling over with encouraging "aahs," and "Look how beautiful they are," as the newlyweds twirled around together, in front of everyone.

Cora watched her daughter and her new husband happily floating on the dance floor, with other couples soon joining in. When Bradford Jones approached, she heard Minnie giggle.

"Hey, gal, ready for a spin?" he asked, looking his playmate up and down.

Much like a schoolgirl, Minnie blushed, causing Cora to laugh out loud and say, "Minnie, come on! At your age?"

"One of us has to get some," she quipped, and grabbing the photographer's hand, left her sister standing next to a now inebriated Pete.

From across the room, Cora could see Thomas talking to a few of the more genteel ladies. Annoyed, she was about to turn to Pete when she noticed him bringing Mrs. Endicott's niece out onto the dance floor.

"Food. I should see to the food," she said so abruptly to Pete, he spilled his drink.

"Cora, what the hell?" he asked, as she scurried over to the dessert table.

"Mr. Garrett, you haven't heard a word I've been saying, have you?" the plain-faced niece complained, encircled in the detective's arms and seeing her partner glance over toward one of the food tables.

"Sorry," he muttered, taking one last peek at Cora. "What were you saying?"

"I was saying that you must come over to dinner some night. Alone, without the Dolans, if you don't mind," she sniffed. "Mr. Garrett?"

"I won't be here much longer," he answered when the dance ended. He gently, but firmly brought her back to the sidelines.

"Thanks for the dance, Miss Rebecca." Nodding, he made his way over toward the desserts.

Cora's eyes widened. Seeing him approach, she hurried back to Pete, leaving Thomas midway across the floor, open-mouthed.

Toward the end of the night, Ellie, Brett, and Minnie drifted over to Cora and Pete.

Minnie, sweating profusely, pushed back her wispy hair and turned to the newlyweds. "Gotta go protect you newlyweds from the Chivarees."

Pete laughed. "Ah, that time-honored custom of harassing the bride and groom on their wedding night. Reminds me of when my wife and I were married. We were thrice interrupted in our, shall we say, loving expressions."

"What happened, Pete?" Ellie asked, twisting her hands together back and forth.

"They kept on coming to the hotel where we were staying and banging on our door. Third time, they grabbed me and would have kidnapped me, if it hadn't been for the hotel manager."

Cora glanced over at Ellie's stricken face. "Pete, I don't think this is the time to…"

"Ellie, don't pay no mind to this ol' coote!" Minnie said. "That ain't gonna happen to you two. Now, go on. Go to your new husband." She gave her niece a little push toward Brett standing on the other side of the room.

Noticing Thomas walking by, Minnie called out, "Hey, Thomas, how you doin'?"

Thomas stopped and came over. "All right. Just wanted you all to know I'm leaving in two days' time, if anyone's interested," he said, scoping out Cora's face.

"Good to know, good to know. Ain't it, Cora?" Minnie side-commented.

Cora avoided Thomas' eyes. "I know about it, already," she said, and looked off toward the newlyweds across the hall.

There, a small band of cowboys and doves had surrounded Ellie and

Brett, patting them on their backs and holding up their glasses for another toast.

"Time to go, all," Minnie urged, and quickly charged over to the newlyweds.

Ten minutes later, in front of the hotel, she used a wide stance in front of the doors, shotgun pitched against her shoulder. "You two go on upstairs to your room now. I'll stand guard. *Nobody's* gonna bother you tonight, I can promise you that!"

Ellie gave Minnie a big hug. "Thank you, Auntie. Thank you so much."

Upstairs on the second floor, their wedding suite had been carefully prepared. Champagne was chilling in a silver bucket; bread, cheese, and fresh fruit lay on a small platter.

Down below, they could hear the noisy cowboys whooping it up, and as they cocked their ears toward the window, they could hear Minnie expressing something strong, because soon, the crowd had disappeared.

"Well, that's a relief," Ellie said, fidgeting with her hair. "Those rings sure were beautiful. By the way, the blacksmith confessed." She smiled. "So that's where you disappeared to for two days. Thank you."

"Yup, special rings for my special lady." Brett chuckled. Walking over to the champagne, he withdrew the cold bottle and turned toward his new wife. "Want some? I bet it's good."

Ellie gulped, then looked up, her hand stroking her throat.

His eyes turned insightful. "Sweetheart, I know you're nervous."

"I never, you know." She studied her hands.

Placing the bottle back in the bucket, he went across the room to her.

"Ellie, I know you're scared. But I'd never hurt you. Don't you know that?" he asked, reaching for her hand.

She placed her hand in his, and let him guide her gently over to a large chair with him.

"Let's just talk," he said simply, sitting down and drawing her onto his lap. He could feel her trembling. "Talk to me," he said. "Tell me what's wrong."

"Well..."

"What, sweetheart? Please tell me."

"Marlena told me the first time it would hurt," she admitted, as he stroked her hair so gently with one of his hands. She drew a breath and tried to smile.

"Oh, sweetheart, I can wait. Whenever you're ready, I promise, I'll be so gentle." He paused. "Do you believe me?"

She nodded slowly. "I want to believe you, I swear I do!"

"This is me, Ellie, not someone like Wes." He could feel her body relaxing more and more as she leaned forward to give him a quick kiss. He didn't move a muscle. Then she continued, her kisses lasting longer. Still, he kept his arms gentle around her and let her take the lead.

Her pupils were beginning to dilate, and as her response deepened, he groaned slightly, particularly when she began stroking his neck, chest, and shoulders. In between her increasingly sensuous kisses, her breath had become almost ragged, and it took all his willpower not to undress her until she was ready. All his instincts were screaming that he must take her now, on the bed; still, he held back.

Until she started undoing his shirt, almost ripping out the buttons. Then he moved quickly, opening up the little shell buttons on her dress, pulling the bodice and skirt over her head, and finally, gaping at her in her chemise.

"Oh, Ellie. You are so beautiful."

She gazed up at him, her eyes half closed, her mouth parted open just like the first time they had really kissed. He couldn't help himself. Picking her up and carrying her over to the bed, although it flitted through his mind for a second or two this might be too much too soon, there was an urgency now for both of them, so he tossed out all caution and began his own touching, his own exploring.

Within minutes, it wouldn't have mattered if the entire town were gathered at the foot of their bed, bellowing and laughing, as the newlyweds made passionate love that night, consummating their marriage.

Three times.

* *

Back on their porch in the pre-morning hours, Minnie, Cora, and Pete sat back, inhaling the fresh, Nebraskan night air.

"Thank you for not drinking before the wedding ceremony, Pete. That showed much will power and..." Cora reached out to stroke his hand.

"Respect?" he interrupted. "Because that's what I was aiming for, dear girl."

Minnie took several puffs on her pipe. "Yep. Our gal now belongs to another." She turned to Cora. "He's a good one."

"Yes, I do believe he is."

Minnie chuckled. "Glad you can at least see *him* right." She rested her pipe against the chair arm.

"Don't start with me, Minnie. Not now."

Pete, his eyelids closing slowly suddenly popped them open. "Don't start what, Minnie?"

"The fact that Cora's been asked to marry Thomas, and she'll have none of it."

"Are you out of your mind?" Pete exclaimed, sitting ramrod straight, his rocker stalled.

"Minnie," Cora said, her voice strident. "You talk so much about trust. Trust for Ellie, but what about me? How can I trust Thomas after what he did?"

Puzzled, Pete shook his head. "What Thomas did? I thought it was *Wes* who hurt you. What are you talking about?"

Cora stopped her rocker short. "Really, Pete? The fact that Thomas didn't come back to be with me after Wes violated me, how he just disappeared. That's what I'm talking about."

"My dear girl. Did I not tell you? Didn't Minnie ever tell you?"

Cora was surprised to see tears welling up in the old man's eyes. She choked. "Tell me what?"

"That Thomas was determined to get back to you as soon as he heard what had happened. But I stopped him. Told him not to come back. At least not for a long time."

A tiny wheezing noise squeaked out of Cora's throat. "Why would you do that? I needed him so much."

"It was an ugly time, Cora. Folks were ready to lynch Wes and anyone connected to him." He paused. "I—we—just wanted to save his skin. Wouldn't you have wanted that?"

Minnie sat suspended. "Oh, my Lord. I never told you, Cora, because I just figured Pete had already done so."

"And I thought...well, I don't know what to say," Pete added.

"Finally, you have no quote ready for us?" Cora snapped.

Minnie reached over to cover her sister's hand. "Cora, that's not fair."

"Fair?" As Cora rose and took her first step down toward the street, she suddenly swiveled around. "All this time wasted and now, it's too late!"

* *

In her fury, she almost forgot Thomas' room number at his hotel. Charging through the halls, she woke up at least two people before someone pointed out another door down the hall.

A tipsy Thomas opened up. "Cora! Are you all right?" he began.

"Why didn't you ever come back for me?" she cried, her red face blotchy from crying.

He grabbed her and drew her close.

"Why? Why?" she moaned, her fists beating on his chest. "I waited for you for *so* long."

He broke away, and sank down on his bed. "First of all, I nearly died in the war. Did you know that? Those Texas Rangers almost did me in. I ended up in the hospital for a long, long time. Then, when I was finally released from there, William from our town, remember him?"

She gave a slightly annoyed nod.

"Anyway, he said he was going back to visit his folks in South Benton and would look you up before returning. Told me he would let me know how things were before I either started my new job with the Pinkerton outfit, or do what I was hoping to do—come back to you."

"So? What does any of that have to do with William?"

"It has *everything* to do with him. When he came back, he told me that he had spoken with Matthew Johnson at a dance. Claimed Matthew said he was going to ask you that night for your hand in marriage, and he was completely confident you would say yes."

"Matthew? *Marriage?* That's ridiculous!"

"William told me you were there with him at the dance, pretty chummy 'n all."

"He was always just a friend to me, nothing more."

His sigh was very long and measured. "It seems we've been at cross purposes," he said sadly. Standing up, he took a step toward her. "But we have a chance to begin again, don't we?"

"Oh, Thomas, I don't know if I can change. I've been this way for so long," she added, close to a whisper, as she moved to the door.

"Think about it, Cora, please?" he called out. Two minutes after she had left, the smell of her lavender water was still lingering in the room.

* *

The next morning, when a knock on Thomas' hotel room door came out of nowhere, the detective jumped. Slowly, as if drunk, he got off the unkempt bed and looked around him. Dirty shirts were tossed on the chair, breeches lay carelessly on the floor, and his two half-filled bags stood in his path. Stumbling over them, he cursed as he instinctively picked up his gun.

Praying it was Cora, his heart pumped furiously as he flung the door open. Minnie stared back at him and tried to smile.

"Oh…" he sighed, and motioned her inside.

"Like the way you're keepin' house," she muttered, then stopped when he shot a warning finger up in the air. "You all right, Thomas?"

"No, I am not. I am most certainly not," he said, placing his gun back on the dresser.

"Can we talk about Cora? I know about you askin' her and all."

He gazed absently at her for a second. "So you're here to tell me it's over, right? Even though I tried to explain everything to her last night."

"Honey, I don't really know. Cora ain't talkin' except to say she's comin' over tonight to tell you her decision."

"It's useless…so useless." He sank back on the bed, his shoulders hunched over like an old man's.

Minnie cleared her throat, flung a couple of his shirts off of the bed and sat down next to him. "I've been thinking. I suddenly remembered something important about Cora." She watched for a reaction, got none, and continued. "I've been remembering what Cora did when she was really happy. More than that, it was when she trusted someone completely. She did it with our mama and our papa.

He raised his head to listen.

"It was just a little thing. She did it with you."

"She used to place her hand over her heart. I do remember," he said. "She doesn't do that anymore with me."

"Or anyone else, for that matter."

He stared at her.

"So all's I'm sayin' is when she comes over tonight, before she even speaks, if she does that same thing, you know she really trusts you. If she bits her lip or…"

"Rubs her neck."

"Yes, rubs her neck, why then you're in trouble. So just remember, hand over heart, if she's open to you, biting her lip or rubbing her neck if she ain't." She reached out for his hand. "Just thought it might be easier for you to prepare yourself before she spoils anything by talkin'."

She got up and holding out her arms, gave him a warm hug. "God bless, Thomas. Hope it works out. Even if it don't, Cora loves you, whether she'll admit it or not."

His smile was closer to a grimace, but he managed to lead her out into the hall and gently kiss her cheek. "Good bye, Minnie, and thanks."

* *

By quarter to eight he could feel his pulse picking up. By eight-thirty, he reached for one of the hotel's courtesy glasses and poured himself a stiff one. Here goes nothin' was his last thought before the familiar burn went down his gullet and the double knock echoed in the emptied out room.

His pulse raced, as he stumbled to the door, leaned his head against the wood, and tried to gather some courage. He had never noticed a slight creak in the door hinges before, but he sure did now as he opened up to his future.

It was her. Smartly dressed, her hair shiny, her face—was it guarded? He couldn't tell. He drew a very deep breath and prayed.

Suddenly, she placed her hand over her heart and smiled.

Instantly, he jerked her into his arms, the intensity of her kiss matching his own. A tangle of arms, hands, necks, hair, they stripped off each other's clothing and fell hard against the desk together, still kissing, still yanking off her petticoat, his pants, her undergarments, his long-johns so they could explore each other's naked body. All the while, the room felt as if it were swirling around them, their breaths more like gasps and moans as they shifted over toward the bed. No longer teenagers, their mature needs were different––hers, urgent, almost aggressive; his, needing to savor every inch of her. She no longer thought of the phrases the doves had told Ellie so long ago, because she had desires of her own as they completed the lovemaking they had missed all these years.

When it was over, cuddled silently against each other, their chests still heaving, each one satiated, she finally spoke.

"So, it's on to Cheyenne?"

"Yes. On to Cheyenne." Thomas paused. "What made you finally change your mind, sweetheart?"

"Sweetheart. I like that," she said, with a tiny, high-pitched giggle.

"Well?"

"Of course, once I knew you didn't really desert me that made all the difference. And I knew Minnie and Ellie would support me, no matter where I went. But in the end, it was something else."

He wrapped both of his arms around her and nuzzled her neck.

"What was it?" His words came out like a low-pitched hum.

"Trust. I watched Ellie have it so easily with Brett, and it even came for Minnie, whenever Bradford Jones was around. So I began to think, why not just give it a try?"

Sitting up, he looked down at her, with her hair loose around her shoulders, the rose in her cheeks like old times behind the barn.

One of his eyebrows arched. "As simple as that?"

She smiled. "Yes, as simple as that." Chuckling, she pulled him back onto her.

THE END

THANK YOU

Thank you so much for taking the time to read *The Dolan Girls*. I hope you enjoyed it; I had a blast researching that time period! If you did enjoy reading it, I would certainly appreciate a short review of it up on Amazon. Alas, we authors count on those.

I would love to hear from you directly as well. Please visit my website at www.srmallery.com. Also, you might enjoy my history boards on Pinterest at www.pinterest.com/sarahmallery1.

ABOUT THE AUTHOR

Now, please understand I have always scoffed at astrology pickup lines such as, "What sign are you, baby?" and I would *never* base my entire future on astrology, but recently, I was flabbergasted to read the following list of astrological traits which explained so much of whom I am.

According to this list, Gemini's are socially outgoing, adjustable, restless, creative, sometimes unable to pay attention to details, good with their hands, easily distracted, anxious, humorous, and love to share. Suggested careers for this sign include writer, teacher, inventor, and craftsperson. Now, go check out my bio.

Wildly eclectic, I've worn a myriad of hats in my life. I started out as a classical/pop singer/composer. Next, I moved on to the professional world of production art and calligraphy. After that, came a long career as an award winning quilt artist/teacher and an ESL/Reading instructor. By the time I started writing my first story, I was a middle-aged English teacher, in a twenty-year marriage, with two teenage children. I couldn't be stopped. Before I had my first book published, my flash fiction short stories had already been published in *descant 2008, Snowy Egret, Transcendent Visions, The Storyteller,* and *Down In the Dirt.* Most of these can now be found in my short story collection, *Tales To Count On.* When I was a professional quilter, I had several non-fiction quilt articles published through *Traditional Quiltworks* and *Quilt World.*

Made in the USA
Columbia, SC
04 December 2023

27729385R00126